CELG

Pecan Pie and Deadly Lies

Center Point
Large Print

Also by Nancy Naigle and available from
Center Point Large Print:

The Adams Grove Novels

Sweet Tea and Secrets
Out of Focus
Wedding Cake and Big Mistakes

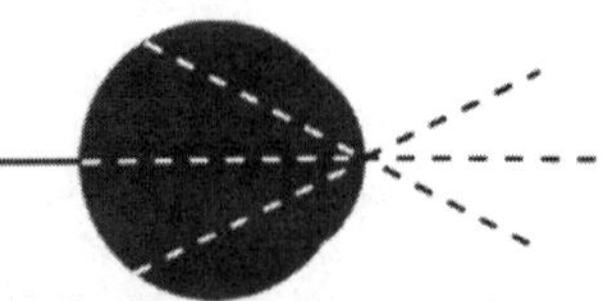

This Large Print Book carries the
Seal of Approval of N.A.V.H.

Pecan Pie and Deadly Lies

An Adams Grove Novel

NANCY NAIGLE

CENTER POINT LARGE PRINT
THORNDIKE, MAINE

This Center Point Large Print edition
is published in the year 2016 by arrangement with
Amazon Publishing, www.apub.com.

Originally published in the United States
by Amazon Publishing, 2013.

The text of this Large Print edition is unabridged.
In other aspects, this book may vary
from the original edition.
Printed in the United States of America
on permanent paper.
Set in 16-point Times New Roman type.

ISBN: 978-1-62899-972-3

Library of Congress Cataloging-in-Publication Data

Names: Naigle, Nancy, author.
Title: Pecan pie and deadly lies : an Adams Grove novel / Nancy Naigle.
Description: Center Point Large Print edition. | Thorndike, Maine :
Center Point Large Print, 2016. | ©2013
Identifiers: LCCN 2016008251 | ISBN 9781628999723
(hardcover : alk. paper)
Subjects: LCSH: Singers—Fiction. | Large type books. | GSAFD: Love
stories. | Mystery fiction.
Classification: LCC PS3614.A545 P43 2016 | DDC 813/.6—dc23
LC record available at http://lccn.loc.gov/2016008251

To my husband, Mike,
who gives me the leeway to chase my dreams,
and who still, even after all these years, sends
my heart on a race every time our eyes meet

❖ Chapter One ❖

A convoy of antique tractors sputtered down Main Street in Adams Grove, a tradition for the last day of the kids' summer vacation. Kasey Phillips focused her camera on the bright green equipment and took a picture, then lifted her hair from her neck. The air was sticky, not uncommon for late August in southern Virginia, but she didn't mind standing out here in the heat in exchange for the joy she saw on Jake's face. Her son bounced at her side like a jack-in-the-box. She captured another shot of the parents and children who lined the parade route catching up on the local goings-on between squeals of excitement.

Riley leaned in toward Kasey. "Who knew a parade could be this much fun as an adult? I'm so glad you talked me into coming up for it. I totally get why you love this town." Riley's glance swept the crowd, then settled back on Kasey. "But I miss you like crazy."

"I miss y'all too. If I could just talk you and Von into moving up here it would be perfect."

"Von's already been looking. If they switch up the Oceana flight patterns like they've been threatening to, those Navy jets will go right over our house. If that happens, we'll be outta there so fast." Riley snapped her fingers. "We may not even pack."

"I hate to hope for that, but I'd be lying if I said I wasn't—just a little. I guess that's the great thing about Von being a private investigator—he can work just about anywhere."

"Look, Mom!" Jake shouted. "That tractor is just like Daddy's."

Kasey stooped next to him and followed his line of sight. She doubted anyone else would notice the light that seemed to shine behind those eyes when he spoke of Nick, but she saw it and it tore at her heart every time.

The old putt-putt tractor chugging down the street was just like the John Deere Model B that Nick had restored.

"You're right," she said and gave him a squeeze. Jake had been only two years old that winter before Nick died—that kid didn't forget a thing. Nick was still so alive in Jake's mind. She wished her memories were as vivid, but she felt Nick's absence every single day. A big void that nothing seemed to fill.

"I can't believe Jake is starting school," Riley said. "It seems like it wasn't that long ago when you were pregnant with him."

Kasey glanced down at Jake. His face beamed as the homemade floats celebrating the end of summer break passed by. In Jake's case, that meant his first day of kindergarten would be

Monday and he hadn't stopped talking about it since she took him to register.

"I'm not as excited as he is." Putting Jake's abduction behind her hadn't been easy. Even leaving him in Sunday school class had been so hard that she nearly always slipped back down the hall to peek in the window and check on him.

Even now, over a year later, the fear that something might happen to Jake again ran strong.

Kasey reached for Jake's tiny hand.

Riley gave her a nod of encouragement. "It'll be okay."

"It'll have to be." Kasey wrestled with the worry and tried to garner strength from the smiling locals who filled the sidewalk two and three deep as far as she could see. She was thankful she'd landed here in this little town—a place she'd never even heard of a year and a half ago. Nick's death had left her hurt and empty, but this town had tugged her into a hug that helped her get through the tragedy. She was finally finding a new routine, a new home—finally in focus.

Jake tipped his face to hers and grinned. No matter how bad things had seemed, Jake was the light that led her through every day.

You're the best thing I ever did in my life, sweet boy.

Nick would have loved this parade. For a moment she drifted away in the memory of his warm touch. How it would feel with him standing here next to her. One arm around her and hugging her close.

Who am I kidding? He wouldn't have been by my side. He'd have been in *the parade.*

That made her smile, and her heart lift. *You'll always fill my heart, Nick.*

Jake let go of her and threw his hands in the air, then darted into a group of bobbing school-aged kids, nearly disappearing from her view.

Kasey's heart lurched. She pushed away the desperate feeling that invaded her sensibilities more often than she liked to admit. Fighting the urge, she folded her arms to keep herself from grabbing Jake and holding him close.

Although Riley didn't say anything, Kasey felt her friend watching her reaction. *I know you're worried about me. I wish I could tell you I'm okay.*

High school football players in full gear walked the edge of the crowd handing out candy.

Jake swerved to the outside of the clump of kids at the sidewalk's edge, then ran back toward her with his treat. He opened his hand to show her the surprise.

"Our favorite," she said as she eyed the red licorice candy.

"It's like he knew!" He dropped the bounty into the plastic Piggly Wiggly bag she held for him. "This is the best parade ever!" He turned toward Riley. "I can get you one too!" He darted into the crowd, then came back to deposit something else in the bag.

"Thanks, Jake." Riley raised her hand and Jake high-fived her then dropped his hands to his hips. "This is fun work."

Riley nudged Kasey. "Wouldn't it be awesome to be that young and naive again?"

The Adams Grove Fire Department truck rumbled by with the volunteers hanging precariously from it. Right behind that, Scott Calvin cruised by in his sheriff's car with his blue lights flashing and a whoop of the siren.

"It's Mr. Scott." Jake waved frantically. "Look, Mom. Look!"

"I see." She waved at Scott. He looked like a movie star version of a cop with his deep tan and mirrored sunglasses.

He slid off his glasses and winked as he waved.

She felt the heads turning in her direction. *Great. Now the whole town will be talking again.* It had taken months for people in Adams Grove to finally quit trying to make more out of her friendship with Scott after he'd talked her into partnering with him for the chili cook-off. All she'd done was stir, but folks around here seemed to think their relationship had more fire than the chili—and that simply wasn't true. He'd brought her joy she didn't think she'd ever feel again, but she wasn't ready to explore that kind of relationship with him.

Kasey ran her fingers through Jake's sandy blond hair as a shiny burgundy antique woody towed a small flatbed trailer for the local veterinarian. Four vet technicians in blue scrubs wore Elizabethan collars around their necks as they marched alongside with dogs from the local shelter on leashes.

"Are they wearing those cones that keep dogs from scratching?" Riley asked. "I bet those dogs think it's karma day. Hilarious!"

Click-click. "You can't make this stuff up."

The thump, thump, thump-thump of the street beat filled the air. The high school band marched toward them in perfect step, lifting and lowering their instruments in unison. As they passed by, the school mascot cartwheeled and spun holding a sign that read THE END.

The crowd started peeling away as the band continued down the street and the music began to fade.

A line was already snaking out from Mac's Bakery as they walked by.

"Mom, can we get cupcakes for your birthday?"

"Sure," Kasey said.

Riley shook her head. "I'm going to pick you up Friday, and we're going to make your mom a birthday cake and bring it back with us on Saturday."

Jake clapped his hands. "I love your cakes. You're the best cook ever."

"And I thought all little boys loved their mom's cooking best," Kasey said.

"Well, I am one heckuva cook," Riley said.

They walked hand in hand back to the car in the primo parking spot Scott had saved for them behind the sheriff's office.

Kasey unlocked the car with a click of her fancy new key fob, and Jake whipped open the door to climb into the backseat and buckle himself into his booster. She'd finally parked Daddy's old Porsche and bought the new car. Being alone, she couldn't risk the unpredictable nature of that car, and Jake's safety in the two-seater worried her too. So now she was a four-door-driving single mom. Who would have ever thought?

"I got lots of stuff." Jake dug through the bag of treats. "School things too."

"Are you excited about starting school?" Riley asked.

"Yeah! It's going to be so cool. I'm going to put all this stuff in my lunch box."

Kasey slid into the driver's seat. "Where will you put your lunch?" She glanced at him in the rearview mirror.

"I'll put this in the backpack Aunt Riley gave me. Then I can have lunch in my lunch box." His head bobbed as he planned. "That'll be good."

Sometimes he looked so serious that it was hard to believe he was just five. A tap on the driver-side window glass startled Kasey. It was Scott.

She pressed the button to lower the window. "Great parade. You're a good waver."

"Thanks. They give us a lesson on proper parade waving. I got an A." He winked at Jake.

"I waved to you!"

"I saw you, buddy." Scott nodded to Riley, and patted Kasey on the arm.

"Mr. Scott." Jake lifted his bag. "The parade was so fun. Look at all this stuff."

Scott leaned his forearms on the window opening. "Adams Grove has the best parades in the world."

"We all enjoyed it. I got some really good pictures too," Kasey said.

Scott glanced down at his watch. "Can I talk you into letting me come over and cook you lovely ladies burgers on your grill tomorrow for lunch?"

He hadn't bothered to put her in the position of cooking a meal for him since that bad Crock-Pot incident.

Jake yelled from the backseat. "Cheeseburgers!"

"Of course," Scott said. "Is there any other kind?"

You know Jake's "like" buttons.

"Yes! Yes! Yes!" Jake chanted.

"Sounds like a yes to me," Scott said.

"Not for me. I'll be heading back to Virginia Beach, but thanks for the offer," Riley said.

"So, the three of us? Tomorrow?" Scott looked hopeful.

Kasey was reluctant, but Jake was already

excited and it would be the day before his first day of school. “How can I say no?”

“You can’t. I’ll see you later.” He gave a thumbs-up to Jake, then hesitated and for a second Kasey got the feeling he might lean in and kiss her. She held her breath and leaned back in her seat.

Scott stepped back from her car. “Have a safe drive home, Riley.”

“I will.” Riley waved as Kasey started the car and backed out of the parking spot.

“I thought he was going to—”

Kasey stopped Riley midsentence. “I thought so too. Sometimes he tries to sneak that stuff in out of the blue.”

“Out of the blue for you, maybe. He’s nice, and he really likes you. What’s wrong with that?”

Kasey motioned toward the backseat. “Little parrots,” she said in a singsongy voice.

Riley nodded. “Got it. Later.”

Jake hummed as he dug around in his bag of goodies.

This was the most traffic she’d ever encountered in Adams Grove. Usually it only took a few minutes to get back out onto the main road, but today it took two cycles of the stoplight. Once Kasey turned onto Route 58 it was back to smooth sailing the rest of the way to her turn onto Nickel Creek Road.

The corn was so high on either side of the

road that it was like driving through a tunnel to the house. The tassels on the large ears were browning, a sign they were beginning to dry out and would be harvested soon. Last year, she and Jake had sat outside on the front porch swing and watched the local farmers harvest late into the night as they tried to get the crop in before the rain. Hopefully, they'd have more cooperative weather this year. Besides, she wouldn't be able to let Jake stay up that late now that he'd be going to school, and pulling him away from the sight of tractors and combines in action was nearly impossible.

As soon as she pulled the car into the driveway Shutterbug, their yellow Lab, bounced up and down on the other side of the fence, and welcomed them with her high-pitched hello bark. The little butterball of a puppy Scott had given Jake last year was now nearly eighty pounds of lean and lanky muscle.

"That dog is in perpetual motion," Riley said.

"Compared to Von's basset hound, I bet Shutterbug looks twice as crazy to you, but that's fine with me. At least she can keep up with Jake. I swear that child has more energy than a hummingbird on sweet tea."

"I can't believe you just said that."

"I know. I think Scott's mom is rubbing off on me with all those Southernisms. Sometimes living here feels like another planet."

"Your prim and proper Grandma Emily would die if she heard you talk like that."

"Grem practically dies every time I talk to her anymore. I never realized she was such a fussbudget until the last few years. If I'm still in the will it'll be a shock."

"I remember her giving me a lecture about not going out without my toenails painted when we were in your backyard at the pool one summer. Scarred me for life. I still can't stand to have my toes naked anymore. Her voice haunts me." Riley pressed her lips together in a tight line. "You know she loves you in her own special way."

"You mean her own special old crabby way." Kasey turned and looked over the seat. "Need help with all your stuff?"

"No, ma'am." He unlatched the seat belt and waited just like she'd taught him for the okay to open the car door. "I'm ready."

She took her keys from the ignition. "Let's go."

Still clutching his Piggly Wiggly bag, he jumped out of the car and slammed the door behind him. "Can I go play with Shutterbug, Mom?"

"Sure. I'll get us something to drink and meet you out back."

"Okay." Jake ran full speed to the back gate. Shutterbug jumped in the air and then the two of them ran through the yard toward the swing.

Kasey's thoughts drifted to Libby Braddock

and her role in Jake's abduction. Thank goodness his captor had been good to Jake. In fact, Jake still talked about Miss Libby whenever Kasey pushed him on the swing. Other than the loss of his dad, which they were both still healing from, Jake didn't seem any worse for wear.

Her own recovery wasn't as complete. She wondered if it ever would be.

Chapter Two

Just like on a hundred other nights, Cody Tuggle tossed his guitar to the roadie stage-left then made a dash for the makeshift dressing room. Nearly seventeen years ago this bar had felt like the big time. The funny thing was that after playing outdoor arenas in front of forty thousand screaming fans, he'd take this three hundred–seat joint any day of the week.

As soon as Cody was offstage the lights dimmed, and the noise from the crowd grew.

In the dressing room Cody tugged off his sweaty bandanna and turned the blow-dryer on his hair for some quick relief. With his free hand he tugged the snaps on his black Western short-sleeve shirt, peeled it off, and tossed it on the table. The cool setting felt good against his hot skin. He had the routine down to a science after all the touring he'd done. He guzzled a small bottle of water and tossed it into the recycling bin across the room.

He toweled off, combed his fingers through his hair, and put on a black T-shirt. The rest of the band came off and grabbed towels.

Cody dug into his duffel bag, only the bandanna he'd planned to wear wasn't where he'd put it earlier. He hated it when fans helped themselves to his stuff. He picked up the black Stetson he'd planned to wear after the show and put it on instead.

The crowd cheered, chanting for more so loudly that it sent a vibration through the whole space. In the dressing room, no one spoke. Everyone stayed in the zone, feeling the building excitement of their fans and getting ready to reenergize them one last time.

Pete, the lead guitarist, walked up to Cody. "Did you see your little Georgia Peach out there?"

Cody gave Pete an I-told-ya-so look. "Yeah. I told you she'd be back around as soon as we got close to Virginia."

"Guess I owe you that twenty bucks. I thought she'd have moved on since she got married last year."

"If she ever stops showing up, then something's wrong." Cody couldn't recall her real name, although he'd known it once. They'd called her Georgia Peach for at least ten years running. That gal had been to every concert of theirs within a day-trip drive of her home in Georgia since the year he cut his first number one song, "It's a Tragedy." When he released "A Mother's Love" last year and it went straight to number one, everyone knew he'd written that song about Kasey and Jake, but Georgia Peach had sent him a note saying the words must have been from God to him just for her. Some said his Georgia Peach was crazy, but he knew she was just a superfan having a good time. For some reason his music connected with her in a special way. Fans came in all shapes and sizes and all attitudes, and even after all these years he still appreciated every single one of them. His security took care of the downright crazy ones.

If there was one thing Momma had taught him well, it was that if he ever got the chance to make a living as a musician it would be because of something more than just talent. God had a plan and he'd been fortunate enough to be given a gift he loved, that he felt duty bound to share. Music was his vehicle, but the fans were his fuel.

The homegrown rhythm of hands and feet stomped out a mantra for more. They had to know he'd be back for an encore. After all, he hadn't sung his signature song yet. He wished he'd kept count of how many times he'd sung "It's a Tragedy" over the years. That song never got old.

The band was packed in the small backstage area like shoppers waiting to get in on Black Friday. Some of his peers wouldn't dream of playing in a small joint like this, but it wasn't about the money or the ego, it was about the people—sharing the music and making memories.

Pete led the band members back on stage and hit those few well-known chords.

Cody stood just offstage as the crowd grew louder in response to it, then gave the nod. The lights hit the stage at exactly the same moment he did. Sometimes the way that cheering swirled louder, it felt like they'd lift him right off his feet.

He pushed past the lump in his throat to sing. The fans knew every word and when he pushed the microphone toward them, they filled in the blanks.

"Come on, y'all." He clapped his hands over his head and watched the audience turn into a human kaleidoscope as he sang. "That's right, Maryland." He sang, "Call it a legacy." Then shouted, "Sing it with me."

He waved the microphone toward the crowd and they finished the verse.

"You can call it heredity. But to the child caught in the middle . . . *it's a tragedy*."

A woman to the far left of the crowd caught his eye. From a distance it looked like Lou, or maybe it was just the way she was standing. He stepped back as Pete moved to the spotlight for the guitar solo, but when Cody glanced over where the woman had been standing, she was gone. *Probably my imagination. Not likely she'd be in Maryland anyway.* Unlike some of the fans, Lou was more of a two-hour max kind of concert-goer, unless he flew her in.

Georgia Peach swayed to the music with her arms overhead, offbeat from the rest of the folks and wearing a grin that said she didn't really care.

The song came to an end and she and the rest of the crowd exploded into applause.

"Y'all keep that love in your heart. Thanks for coming out." Cody jogged backstage, then straight to his bus.

He knocked twice and the door opened. "You got company," the driver said with a nod toward the living area.

Cody stepped up and saw Arty Max sitting on his couch holding a Scotch.

Unexpected. "Hey, man." Cody shook Arty's hand and dropped onto the other end of the couch. "Didn't know you were going to be here tonight. Did you catch the show?" He took off his hat and set it aside.

"Most of it. Sounded good."

"What's up?"

"I wanted to talk to you about coming up to the house for the party. You didn't give me an answer."

"Yeah, I did. I told you I've got plans."

"Okay, so you didn't give me the answer I wanted to hear."

Nothing new there. "That's why you're here?"

"Yeah, I'm harder to say no to in person."

Not for me. "Can't do it. I've been on the road for twenty-one straight days. As soon as I get through this week I'm taking a few days for all of us to recharge before we head to Texas to shoot the commercial. Then it's back to the house to finish up the new release."

"You wouldn't have worked twenty-one straight days if you hadn't tucked all these little podunk gigs in between the real concerts." Arty hated it when Cody took it upon himself to add these small gigs between the scheduled arena dates, but that was a pill he'd just have to swallow as part of the ride. Small price for the payoff he'd earned from being Cody's agent for the last seventeen years.

"Don't start." Cody raised a hand. "Doesn't matter. I can't make it."

"Come on, man. If you're at the party it'll bring in more press."

"You know I don't like that stuff." Cody poured a glass of water and gulped about half of it.

"No, but Dustin Barnes could use the extra attention that having you there would bring."

"So, that's what this is about. Your new kid on the block." *Of course there was more to it. Always was with Arty, but then that's why Arty had done so well for himself over the years.*

"Making an appearance wouldn't kill you. You'll like Dustin. He reminds me a lot of you when you were just getting started."

Now they were getting to the crux of the matter. Arty wanted him to boost the new solo act he'd just signed. Next he'd be asking Cody to let Dustin open for him. "Sorry, man. Send Dustin my best. I'll make it up to him some other time."

"You're killin' me." Arty leaned forward. "Don't you remember when you cut your first record?"

"I haven't forgotten that. Can't do it this time though."

The bus door opened and this time Annette walked in. She'd been on the payroll for more than five years now and Cody wasn't sure how he'd get along without her handling all the PR and media stuff. She could do damage control better than anyone he'd ever met, and she'd learned pretty quickly to ignore Arty, which was something he'd never seen anyone else get away with.

She looked surprised when she saw Arty sitting there. "Hey, Arty. You should have told me you were coming. I'd have made sure you got the royal treatment you love so much."

"I don't think they serve that here," Arty said.

She shook her dark hair back over her shoulders and rolled her eyes.

Cody gave Arty a warning nod. “Don’t underestimate her. That girl’s magic. She can make anything happen anywhere. She’s never let me down.” She popped in and out as needed whenever there were interviews to do, and when he needed damage control, there was no one better to have on his side. The dark-haired beauty knew her business. He owed Arty big-time for bringing her onto the team.

“Thanks, Cody. It’s nice to be appreciated by someone.” She glared at Arty.

“You might be assigned to work for Cody, but I’m the one cutting the checks that pay your salary, Annette. Don’t push your luck with me.” Arty steadied a don’t-screw-with-me look on her until she rolled her eyes again and walked away, then he turned back to Cody. “What are you doing that’s so damn important you can’t give me two hours for the party?” He waved his wiry arms around as he spoke. “Don’t tell me you’re tired. I don’t want to hear it because these gigs weren’t in the plan when we set up the tour—the profitable part of your schedule. These little shows are barely worth the gas in the two buses to get here.”

“You get your cut no matter what, so don’t worry about it.”

Arty pushed his hand through his hair. “Yeah, but I’ll never understand why you do it. Look, what’s one more day? Just come and make a short appearance; hell, even just an hour, that’s all I ask.

Besides, the publisher for your coffee-table book is going to be at the party and it wouldn't hurt for you to give them an update on that barbecue book project you've got on the back burner with them."

"You're way better at that kind of talk than I am. That's why you get paid the big bucks." Cody stood up and poured another glass of water from the pitcher in the refrigerator. "Look. I've got meet and greets to do. Is that all you came for?"

Arty shrugged. "Yeah. Waste of good time."

"Hey, I could've saved you the trip with a phone call."

"Fine. So where are y'all going to be after the Virginia Beach show?"

Cody wasn't about to get into this with him. "I made plans to drop in on an old friend."

"Anyone I know?"

He turned his back on Arty. "We're not having that conversation. It's personal and you never like who I like anyway."

Arty laughed. "That's because you have a lousy track record. They're either gold diggers or . . ."

"They dump me. You can say it. They dump me because I work too much or whatever, but that's my problem to deal with. Not yours. Besides, I already know this one."

"You're going to look up someone who already didn't work out. That's just stupid."

"People change. *I've* changed, and I'm not getting any younger." Truth was he'd looked up his first serious gal, Lou, a while back. Although recently he'd put off getting back together with her for so long he wasn't sure if it was even a good idea anymore, but that wasn't the point.

"It's a mistake. Don't do it." Arty shook his head. "You never listen though."

"Don't worry. I'm not as tenderhearted as I was back then."

"You say that now. You know if this mystery someone came looking for you, she wants something."

"Thanks for the vote of confidence there, buddy. But that's where you're wrong. This time I went looking for her." Cody stood at the door of the bus and nodded toward Annette. "Found her, too, with a little help from my friends."

"You did this?" Arty glared at Annette. He looked like he was going to pop a vein. "You've heard the stories about Cody when his heart's broken."

"It was a long time ago, Arty." She ripped a sheet of paper from her padfolio and handed it to Cody. "Here are the rest of the details you need for the week." Then she handed him a stack of glossy photographs. "These are for the meet and greet."

"Thanks, Annette." Cody hugged her and she turned to leave.

"Annette, give me a call tomorrow. I need to talk to you." Arty slung back the rest of his drink and muttered as she walked off the bus. "She really ought to mind her own business."

"I asked her to help me, Arty. Don't give her any shit. It's going to be fine. It might not even go anywhere."

"Damn right it won't. You need to leave the past in the past."

"Couldn't agree with you more. She and I haven't even talked about the past, and I'm fine if we never do. But we have been talking and I think we're going to give this another shot now that things aren't so crazy like they were when I first got into the business."

"Which one is it? Let me guess. The brunette from Florida. What was her name?"

"I'm not telling you."

"No. No. I know. That girl Jackie with the horse farm. She lived up near DC, didn't she? Up near Pete's folks."

"You never give up."

"Fine. Don't tell me, but I'll go on record. Don't do it, Cody—you know it's never wise to go backward. You could have any woman in the world."

"That's a total line of BS and you know it."

"Why are you barking up an old tree? If you want to settle down, find someone new. Find someone who is on your level."

"My level? You know I don't think that way."

"Well, you should. Let me set you up with someone. I know lots of nice gals in the business."

Cody laughed aloud at that comment. "You don't know any nice girls."

"I know people who know nice girls."

"That's more like it, but no thanks. I think I can handle this on my own."

"Well, fine, but don't come crying to me when it blows up on you and expect me to forgo the pleasure of a good told-you-so. But then again, you *have* written some of your best hits after breakups. On second thought, this could just work to both our benefits."

"It's not going to be like last time."

"Oh really? What makes you so sure?"

"I'm older now. I'm in a different place."

"Haven't you heard the saying that you can't go back home?"

"This is different."

Pete pounded on the door as he stepped up into the bus. "You ready, Cody?"

"Sure, yeah," Cody said. "Look, I've got to run. Good to see you."

"Well, if you change your mind, head on up to the estate. It's going to be a helluva party and Johnny G. will be there. You know he's been talking about doing a remake of that movie. It could be your part. Come up and make it happen."

"Tempting, but I'm ready for some downtime. Besides, I've got that album to get out before spring and I can't possibly put something else on my plate right now."

"Never thought I'd hear you pass up an opportunity like this."

"Maybe my priorities are shifting."

"I don't think I like the sound of that."

"You'll be fine." Cody walked to the back of the bus to change shirts, then grabbed a handful of permanent ink markers, black and silver, and tucked them in his back pocket. He cuffed Arty's shoulder as he headed down the stairs. Cameras flashed as Cody exited the bus, and Arty slipped out behind him.

For an hour Cody shook hands and posed for pictures with fans and street team members. By the time he'd said good-bye to the last person, the guys had everything packed up and ready to go. Cody was barely settled in the front lounge area of the bus when the wheels started to spin.

Pete gave a nod to Cody as he strummed his guitar. He was tinkering with a melody they'd been working on the last couple of weeks off and on. "I think I got it figured out." He played the chords.

Cody bobbed his head to the beat and then smiled wide. "Yeah. That's it. Perfect." He grabbed his guitar and they played it again together until it was just right. Then they hunkered down over the table and reworked the lyrics for about the hundredth time.

Pete laid down his guitar. "Want something to eat?" He opened the door of the full-size Sub-Zero fridge and took out a tray of deli meats. "I'm going to make a sandwich."

"No thanks. I'm going to hit the shower." Cody went back to his room, finally able to slow down a little now that the adrenaline of meeting all those people had worn off. He pressed the button that closed the door behind him. This bus was his home for over half of the year. Even when he flew in, he chose to sleep here on his own bus rather than the hotel rooms they were given. Some people might think that was hard, but it wasn't so bad. He had the best of the best amenities on this bus. More than most musicians ever had the chance to enjoy, much less own like he did. Besides, he liked being on the road, and that had always been more than enough, until lately. Lately, he'd found himself a little restless. Yearning for something else. Not really for more, just something different.

He reached inside the oversize shower to turn on the steam. He had more showerheads and jets in his bus shower than he did at home. Cody let the steam fill the glass enclosure as he stripped down. He stepped inside and turned on the rain shower and closed his eyes for a second. He lathered up and scrubbed the sticky sweat from his body, thinking about what it would be like if he wasn't on the road over half of the year. It was nearly impossible to imagine. He loved every minute, every venue, big or small, and even his worst days were pretty damn good. *It would be even better if I had someone to share it with.* But it wasn't an easy life, and not one that just anyone could handle.

He dried off and threw his towel over the shower stall to dry, then changed into a pair of sweatpants and a T-shirt.

Pete rapped twice on the door. "Hey, man. Just wanted to let you know we're stopping at the next exit to refuel and get some stuff at Walmart."

"Okay."

"We've got a couple tagalongs."

"Thanks for the heads-up." Cody opened the door, then lay across the bed. It wasn't all that unusual to have carloads of women follow the bus after a concert. Less likely at the small events, and they usually gave up after a few miles as they sobered up, but there'd been some who had followed them for a whole twelve-hour drive.

He felt the bus slow to a stop just as his phone vibrated on the nightstand. He thumbed through the messages. There was one from Lou from earlier in the day saying she'd seen the schedule update that they'd be in West Virginia.

He rolled over and typed a response. ON THE ROAD NOW. WE WON'T BE TOO FAR FROM YOU. YOU SHOULD COME.

The phone beeped. He glanced at his watch. It was nearly four in the morning. Her response read, IT'S BEEN A WHILE.

WHAT ARE YOU DOING AWAKE?

She texted back that she couldn't sleep, and she wished she could make the show but she had to work.

It *had* been a while since they'd gotten together. No fault of hers. He'd invited her out to a few shows and it had been fun to talk about the old days although they'd tiptoed around the fact that she'd dumped him all those years ago. His relationship with Lou, short for "Bettie Lou," had been hot and heavy at one time. In fact, he'd always figured she'd be the one he married, but when his career got going, the relationship sank, and she hadn't even given him the chance to choose—instead she'd dumped him. Too big for his own almost-a-star britches at the time, he hadn't even tried to get her back.

Now that his career was in a much different place, he had the time and flexibility to have more in his life, but the two times he'd sent her tickets to shows, the sparks just hadn't rekindled like he'd hoped.

I'LL CHECK IN WHILE WE'RE IN YOUR NECK OF THE WOODS, he typed. Only he didn't know if he should even bother. If she was interested she'd have found a way to work in the trip to West Virginia.

His thoughts turned to Kasey Phillips. He hadn't been able to get her off his mind since, well, hell, since the day he first laid eyes on her at the photo shoot at Arty's estate. His celebrity hadn't seemed to impress her at all, and that impressed him a lot. She was crazy about her husband and kid and that had been nice to hear too. Maybe that's why he'd felt inclined to stay in touch with her after her husband's death. *Why can't I meet someone like her?*

He used to love the attention from all the women, but the lies got old. Women were always talking down their husbands in front of him. If he went by what they said, there wasn't a happy marriage left. But he knew better. These women just wanted to play in his VIP world for a little while, but that made it too damn easy to not even bother getting to know their names. The fun in that had died a long time ago.

Cody pulled a pillow under his head, flipped on the television, and clicked from the sports station to his second favorite, the Weather Channel.

It looked like a big storm was heading right up the coast. It was that time of the year when hurricanes favored the Eastern Seaboard.

Life on the road. Never a dull moment.

❖ Chapter Three ❖

The next morning Riley gathered her things to get on the road early.

"I wish you could stick around," Kasey said as she put away the coffee.

Riley shifted her overnight bag to her shoulder. "I know, but I'll be back on Friday."

"Don't remind me. I'm not ready for another birthday." Kasey pulled the skin taut by her eyes. "I'm almost at the Botox-away-the-crow's-feet age."

"Stop it." Riley tugged Kasey's hands from her face. "You're beautiful, and when we get that old you can just airbrush us pretty in all the pictures."

"I can totally do that. I've done some real magic on lots of celebrities over the years. But I still hate birthdays."

"Too bad. If I have to have them, so do you."

Kasey walked Riley to the front door. "Speaking of airbrushing celebrities, I still don't know how I'm going to juggle photo shoots and Jake in school. I've got to figure out something soon."

"Until then you know Von and I will watch Jake anytime for you."

Thank God for them. She still couldn't leave him with anyone else without a complete meltdown. "I know, and I appreciate all you've done for me, but that's not a forever solution. We both know that."

"Are you going to tell me what's going on with you and Scott? There was that little sparky moment where he almost kissed you yesterday. Were you hoping I forgot about that?"

Kasey tipped her head back. "No." She sighed.

"I love our friendship. He's super. It's just not that kind of a relationship."

"Does he know that?"

"I've tried to be so careful about not encouraging him, but he seems to have selective hearing."

"Men can be like that. So, no fireworks, huh?"

"Not a thing. Lord knows I've tried. Not a spark. Heck, not even a lightning bug flash. He's more like a brother—no, not even that. A cousin. I already had my one true love. I just wish Scott could get it through his head, because I'm starting to feel bad."

"He's a nice guy. He loves Jake. He's sure not bad to look at. Maybe it's good enough."

"Enough? Maybe I've already had enough. More than most, and no one will ever be able to fill Nick's shoes."

"That's a tall order. Maybe he fills *different* shoes."

"I can't see it." She shook her head. "No. I can take care of myself. Nick and I worked because we could take care of ourselves. We didn't *need* each other. What we had was more. We were more with each other."

"What you had with Nick was special."

"The best." Kasey closed her eyes. "I still get goose bumps when I think about seeing him standing in the field. He made my heart race every time I looked at him. It was more than special. It was uncontrollable. It was real." She opened her eyes. "I could never settle for less than that."

Riley took Kasey's hand in her own. "Maybe someday you'll feel that again."

"I'll just be thankful that I had it while I did." She sniffed back the emotion that threatened, and smiled. "Plus I've got Jake, and he's the best kid in the world, and I don't need more friends. I've already got the best friend in the world. You."

"Well, yeah!" Riley gave Kasey a hug.

"Thanks again for offering to take Jake next Friday night so I can go to that thing up at Arty Max's place. It's a good way for me to keep my name circulating until I figure out what I'm going to do for work."

"Yeah, it's a great networking opportunity for you. Besides, Jake's such an angel. He's no trouble at all. You better keep your fingers crossed that Von and I are blessed with a little angel like that, because I'll be calling in the babysitting paybacks someday."

"Oh honey, it's going to happen. I just know it. Of course, me keeping you from Von on a regular basis isn't going to help you get pregnant, but maybe he'll have missed you so much that there'll be magic tonight."

"I like the sound of that," Riley said.

"Then go. You can have phone foreplay all the way home. I'll be the one back here trying to figure out how I'm going to make a living now that Jake is in school. I can't be on the road doing photo shoots. That's not fair to him."

"What about that orange building that's for sale on Main Street?"

"I'll take a look, but I have no idea what kind of business could survive in this small town that they don't already have." She'd been trying to come up with alternatives all summer but commercial photography was her thing, and nothing else she knew how to do seemed suitable for a small town.

"It would make an adorable tearoom."

Kasey put her hands on her hips. "Do I need to remind you that the cooking thing might be a problem for me?"

"I know. Too bad. If you could at least heat stuff up you could use locals to provide the noshes, but I'm afraid you'd catch the place on fire the first week. No offense, but I'm not sure I'd even trust you boiling water for the tea. Maybe that's more my dream than yours."

"Definitely more yours than mine. I couldn't see myself being cooped up serving tea all day."

"Maybe . . ."—Riley got that look. The one she did when she was getting ready to be a smart aleck—"you could open up a place that does cooking lessons. You could be your own best customer."

"Now that is pitiful. I'll figure out something. I just hope a good alternative comes to me soon."

"Seriously. Don't sweat it. You'll figure something out. You always do." Riley hugged Kasey. "I'll be back to pick up Jake on Friday, and Von and I'll bring him back on Saturday afternoon to celebrate your birthday. We've got a plan, right?"

Kasey watched Riley pull out of the driveway. *What am I going to be when I grow up?* She wasn't in a bind for money yet; Nick had left her pretty financially stable and she had her own savings too, but that wasn't going to last forever. Even if it did, she needed something to do with herself or she'd go crazy.

After going through some bills, she grabbed a juice box out of the fridge, poured a glass of sweet tea for herself, and went outside wishing she hadn't agreed to the cookout with Scott. She had too much on her mind, but then that's probably why he'd offered to come over. He'd know she was feeling apprehensive; he was thoughtful like that, and coming over to barbecue for them would be his way of trying to help.

Kasey balanced the juice box in the crook of her arm so she could carry her laptop out with her too and work on the parade pictures while Jake and Shutterbug played. Jake sat in the swing, throwing a tennis ball for Shutterbug, who was more than happy to bring it back and do it again and again.

She cropped and tweaked the pictures, and picked a couple to send over to the *County Gazette*. There was no big hurry since the paper only came out twice a month. Everything ran a bit slower here in Adams Grove and she was falling into its rhythm . . . finally.

A horn honked twice and her mood instantly dipped a little. Jake came running toward her with Shutterbug on his heels. "That's Mr. Scott."

"It sure is."

Even Jake had picked up on Scott's habit of honking when he arrived. She figured it was Scott's way of not popping in unannounced since he never called before he showed up.

Jake ran to the side gate and came back with Scott in tow.

"Hope you're hungry," he said, placing the grocery bag on the table. "I'm starved."

"Me too," Jake said. "I can help."

Scott made himself at home in the outdoor kitchen and started the grill. He took a pack of beef patties from Spratt's Market and a package of individually wrapped cheese slices out of the bag.

"I'll get the chips and some plates. I'll be right back," Kasey said.

By the time Kasey walked back outside Jake had his head tilted back with a piece of cheese laid over his face. Shutterbug licked at the edges of the cheese while Jake laughed.

"What are you doing, silly boy?"

Jake jolted straight up. "We were playing cheese tricks." He laid four pieces of cheese on one of the plates and then jumped from the chair. “Come on, Shutterbug. Let’s show Mom and Mr. Scott how smart you are.”

Shutterbug let out a woof.

“Sit.”

Shutterbug sat.

“Stay.” Jake held his hand straight out. Once Shutterbug had obeyed the command, Jake rolled a piece of cheese into a tube and placed it on the patio about ten feet from Shutterbug. She looked anxious but she didn’t move.

Jake walked away and went and sat down at the table while Shutterbug stayed right where he’d told her to. Then Jake yelled, “Get it!”

Shutterbug took one flying leap to the cheese and gobbled it up, looking pretty pleased with herself.

“She’s really smart,” Scott said.

“Mom and I have been practicing getting up at school time so we’ve been teaching Shutterbug tricks, but tomorrow I go to school and Shutterbug will have to wait to have her classes when I get home. I’ll teach her everything I learn. Right, Shutterbug?”

Shutterbug woofed and Jake took off running across the yard with her at his heels.

“He’s excited about going to school,” Scott said.

Kasey sucked in a deep breath. “We’re both pretty anxious. Me in not such a good way.”

Scott closed the lid on the grill and took the

chair next to her. “You’ve toured the school and met the teachers. It’s going to be fine.”

“My head knows it, but my body is in a panic. If anything ever happened to him again . . .”

“I know.” He put his hand on her arm. “I’d like to say it won’t. I believe it won’t, but I can’t promise that. What I can promise is that if anything happens, you know we’ll get through it together.”

“Thanks, Scott.” There wasn’t anything he could say that would make her feel better, but it was nice that he wanted to try.

When the burgers were ready, Jake and Scott talked about school while they ate.

“It’s only a half day for kindergarten,” Jake explained. “I don’t even get to ride the bus yet.”

“There’s a . . .” But Scott stopped midsentence.

She gave him the eye. She knew full well there was a bus for the kindergarteners but that wasn’t something she was ready to deal with.

“It’ll only be a few days this week and then next week is cut short with Labor Day,” Scott said.

Kasey dabbed at a glob of ketchup on Jake’s cheek. “We’re thinking about visiting Grem for the Labor Day weekend.”

“Since I can’t make it for the get-together with y’all on Saturday to celebrate your birthday I was hoping the three of us could take the boat out Sunday and then I’d take you out for a nice dinner. Mom said she’d watch Jake.”

The bite of burger stuck in her throat. Riley had been the only one she'd been able to leave Jake with since the incident. Scott took it personally that she wouldn't let his mother watch him, and she loved his mother, but she just couldn't do it.

"That's sweet, but I don't even want to celebrate my birthday. Riley's the one all excited about a party. Besides, we haven't been down to see Grem in a few weeks. I need to get over to see her."

Scott looked disappointed. He'd been like that a lot lately, like he expected her to always be available. She enjoyed the time they spent together, but she didn't like being on anyone else's schedule. *Better to just change the subject.* "Do you know anything about that building for sale on Main Street?"

Scott dipped a chip into the onion dip. "You must mean Mac's building."

"He's selling the bakery? No, I was talking about the orange one on the next block."

"He owns that one too. It's the one he'd been renovating for his girlfriend, before she turned out to be a murderer."

"The yoga lady. Yeah, I guess murder has a way of leaving a bad taste in a guy's mouth."

"It's a nice space though. Big, and pretty much ready to go. Why? You know someone who's interested?"

"I don't know. Me. Maybe. Riley fell in love

with it. We've been trying to brainstorm ideas."

"I'm done, Mom." Jake put his napkin on his plate.

"Take your plate inside and put it on the counter."

He hopped down from his chair and then slid the last piece of burger from his plate to Shutterbug.

"Come here, you," she said to Jake, and he ran into her arms. She hugged him tight. "I just needed some sugar from my boy."

Jake ran inside.

Scott pushed his plate to the side and leaned on the table. "Are you going to survive him going to school?"

She shrugged. "I'll have to."

"Why don't you let me pick you up in the morning and we'll take him together?"

"No, no." It would be worse with him there. He'd be telling her what not to feel. "It'll be fine. I can do this."

He leaned back in his chair. "You know there's nothing wrong with asking for help once in a while."

"I know, but I'll be fine. Really. Besides we have to go early on the first day."

"I could stay over."

She was getting tired of having that discussion. He must have read the look on her face because he backed off immediately.

"Okay, okay, don't say anything. Forget I even

said it. I know the answer. But it's been a year. I want to move things to the next level. You're really never going to let me in, are you?"

And there it was. At least he'd said it. "It's not you, Scott." *Oh Lord, that's the oldest empty breakup line in the book and that's not how this is.* "I love spending time with you. Your friendship means the world to me, but I don't see me ever being in another relationship. I'm sorry." She lifted her hands to her eyes and then pushed them through her hair. "I had my one true love with Nick. You deserve that kind of relationship. I really don't want to hurt you."

"But?"

"No buts."

"But I want you," he said.

She'd known this was something they were going to have to discuss, but she'd dodged it for so long she wasn't even sure how she felt about it anymore. "I don't feel like there's a place for that in my heart. No one will ever fill that spot that Nick carved out."

He looked away.

You don't understand. I can see it in your eyes. I'm so sorry. Missing Nick was still part of every day, and she didn't feel any urgency to try to start something new either. In the beginning there'd been days that, had it not been for Jake, she'd have rather died. There were days when she was so mad at Nick for having died that she blamed him for breaking the forever promise he'd made. But more often there were days filled with good memories and she wasn't ready to push those aside.

"Well, promise me you'll call if you need me."

He'd gotten up, and she hadn't even noticed. "I will." But she knew she wouldn't.

❖ Chapter Four ❖

The alarm clock buzzed, and Kasey reached over to turn it off with a groan. She'd been awake for a while, but her heart still raced from the bad dream. It had been a while since the bad ones had bumped the good ones out of the lineup, but whenever the going got tough, the sad memories she'd tried to keep tucked safely away snuck up on her. She pushed the image of Nick's truck down in the river out of her mind. She could still feel the steel guardrail against her hands the day he died as she leaned over screaming for him, for Jake, and wondering how the heck she'd ever get through it all.

But I did get through it.

She closed her eyes and tried to picture better days. New memories with Jake here in Adams Grove. Shutterbug. Riley at the parade. Then she said a little prayer and climbed out of bed.

It only took a few minutes to change out of her pajamas and into a pair of jeans and a shirt. She swept her hair back in a ponytail, and then knocked on Jake's door on her way to the kitchen. "Rise and shine. It's time to get ready."

Before she could get two steps down the hall he raced through the half-open door, but it wasn't her little sleepyheaded boy who walked out. Instead, Jake was dressed in the outfit they'd laid out last night for his first day of school and even had his backpack on. He'd slicked his hair into a severe side part. "I'm ready!"

"My goodness. I see." She tried not to laugh, but he was so darn adorable with that hairdo and his shoelaces tied in big loopy bows it was hard. "We've still got lots of time. Come on, let's eat some breakfast."

He followed her into the kitchen with his thumbs under the straps of the backpack. He climbed up into one of the kitchen chairs. The awkward backpack made him lurch forward.

I guess it won't kill me to let him slump one morning. She wished now that she'd planned a special breakfast for him, but then stressing her kid out with the smoke alarm the first day of school wouldn't be the best start. She grabbed the box of cereal from the cabinet and placed it on the table in front of him.

"Can I use the Redskins bowl?"

"Sure, baby." She slid Nick's favorite bowl in front of him, and he poured the cereal to cover the bottom. She topped it off with milk, then poured herself a cup of coffee and Jake a small glass of juice.

He chomped on his cereal and stared at the side of the box. "I can read almost all of this."

"I know. You're going to learn lots of new stuff in school too."

"What if I don't?" He looked worried for the first time.

"You will. It'll be fun."

He took another bite and then looked up at the clock. "When do we have to leave?"

"We have plenty of time. You take your time eating. I'm going to go get ready." She left Jake eating to put on a little makeup in case she bumped into any of the teachers or parents. Then she went into her office and picked up her camera case. She glanced at the family portrait of them that sat on her desk. *I wish you were here this morning, Nick.*

When she walked back into the kitchen Jake had just finished his cereal and Shutterbug was lapping up the leftover milk from the bowl.

"I think Shutterbug is going to miss me a lot when I'm in school."

Not nearly as much as me, little man. "I'm sure she will, but she'll be so excited and ready to play every day when you get home."

"You're a good girl," he said to the dog and looked back at Kasey. "Are you taking our picture?"

"Of course."

Jake put his arm around Shutterbug and posed. *What have I done to my child? I guess it's the occupational hazard of children of photographers that they know how to strike a pose.* She snapped a few pictures of them together. "Grab your lunch box and let's take a couple out front."

Jake raced to the counter to grab his Spider-Man lunch box.

Kasey put Shutterbug out back, grabbed her keys and purse, and locked up the house.

"Can you take all your pictures here so no one sees you taking them at school, Mom?"

Her heart dropped. It was the first time he'd ever said something like that. Her little man was growing up. "Deal."

Just as they got to the end of Nickel Creek Road, they pulled up behind a school bus. Kasey hoped Jake didn't realize he could be on that bus. If he did, he didn't mention it, but they followed the bus all the way to school.

She parked the car in the visitor parking lot. "I'm going to walk you in today. Is that okay?"

"Yep."

They got out of the car and walked hand in hand up the sidewalk to the school. The crossing guard stopped and said hello and explained there were always "helpers" with blue tags on in the bus lanes to be sure the children got to their rooms safely and on time. *That makes me feel better.*

Jake hadn't said a word. Although he'd been excited, she could tell he was a little nervous too. Or maybe he was just nervous because she was.

Kasey walked Jake to Miss Roane's kindergarten class. Bright colors decorated the bulletin boards and rosy-cheeked faces already filled over half of the desks in the room. Other parents and their children lined the hallway.

"I can go by myself, Mom."

Miss Roane met them at the door and gave Kasey a wink.

Kasey bent down to whisper to Jake. "I'll meet you out front at the end of the day."

"Okay." He turned to walk away and she thought she might collapse right there. He looked so grown up.

Then he stopped, turned, and came back to the door. He motioned for her to stoop down again. "I love you, Mom."

"I love you too," she whispered into his ear, and then gave him a secret kiss in his hand. He still held it balled in a fist as she watched Miss Roane settle him into a desk.

She stepped out of the way of other parents going through the same routine. It was easy to tell which were sending their first children to school—they looked like she felt. *Like we're hanging on to our last thread of sanity.* She hugged her arms around herself and tried not to totally lose it in the hallway. Morning kindergarten was only eight thirty to eleven forty but she had a feeling the next few hours were going to be the longest she'd survived in a long, long time.

As she drove, even the radio couldn't snap her out of the crying jag. There was a storm heading their way. She'd hated hurricanes ever since Hurricane Ernesto swept in the day after Nick's accident. She'd never felt as helpless as when that storm had forced them to stop searching for Jake. Her palms felt sweaty on the steering wheel just thinking about it.

When she turned into the driveway, it wasn't even nine o'clock. She puttered around the kitchen, unsure of what to do and not having the focus to do anything anyway. She nuked a cup of coffee and sat on the couch staring at the photo of Nick and Jake over the fireplace.

When the phone rang, it startled her, causing her to spill the coffee she'd yet to sip. She swept at the droplets on her jeans as she glanced at the screen on her phone. Cody Tuggle? "Hey, there. What a nice surprise."

"Are you okay?" he asked.

"Yeah, sure. Great."

"Sounds like you've been crying."

Of course, you can tell. Cody had come into her life in the most unexpected way, but at the perfect time. He'd been there through the many tears over some of the worst moments of her life—right after that accident took Nick from her. She could probably fool anyone except for him. "I'm sorry you know me so well that you can tell that."

"Don't be. I'm glad I was there for you."

"You were my anchor in the storm. If it hadn't been for you . . . for that tour . . ."

"It was good for me too. I got great photographs and a hit song out of it."

She started to say she was fine, but something about him made her open up. "Jake started kindergarten today. I'm a little emotional."

"Oh. I've heard that's hard for moms . . . the first day of school, I mean."

"It is, but then I'm still having trouble leaving him at all after everything."

"Kasey, you should talk to someone about that. People just aren't meant to have to deal with things like what you went through without help."

"No. It's fine. I know in my head that we're safe here. Adams Grove is a wonderful community. I'll be okay."

"Of course you will. You're one of the toughest gals I've met. How's Jake?"

"You should have seen him this morning. He looked so cute with his little lunch box for his snack, and his backpack on. He was so excited."

"But?"

"But . . . I'm a mess. I've been sitting here crying and staring at the clock, and he hasn't even been gone an hour. Plus, I didn't tell him there was a bus. I let him believe it was for the big kids, so I could take him. I'm going to turn him into a neurotic wreck or a momma's boy."

"No you won't. Besides, he's only five. We're all momma's boys at five."

"I sure hope you're right."

His laughter filled the air in a comforting way.

"I think I might still be one," Cody said.

She could picture his smile, and that slight dimple on his left cheek. "I somehow find that hard to believe, but I appreciate the laugh."

"Hell, I'm the last person who should be giving advice about kids. I don't have any, but then I've been accused of still being one. That should count for something, right?"

"For sure." Kasey pulled her knees up onto the chair. "And I know firsthand that you're still a boy at heart."

"Well, it'll turn out fine. Trusting things are going to go the way you want them to without intervening is hard as hell though. I've never been good at that, so I know how you feel."

"It's torture. But let's talk about something fun. How's the tour going?"

"Great. We've sold out in almost every city. Really good shows. All work and all play. Just the way I like it."

"I know." She remembered how much fun they'd had on the road. When she photographed the tour it had been a whirlwind. It was so fast-paced, she didn't even have time to be exhausted, but as hard as they worked, they did have a good time. It was like spending every day at a family reunion. "Are you playing tonight?"

"We're playing West Virginia tonight, then down to Virginia Beach."

"I know. By the time I tried to buy a ticket it was sold out."

"Don't you ever buy a ticket to one of my shows. I'll put your name on the list."

"Don't be silly. You don't have to do that."

"I'd love to see you. If you'll make the drive down it's the least I can do, but I still want you to come see me backstage. I'll leave a backstage pass for you at the will-call window."

"Thanks. It'll be good to see you. Sounds like you're busy as heck."

"It's all good. Once we're on a roll it all feels good. The pace won't hit us until we slow down. Honestly, all those little breaks they try to work in sometimes make the tour harder."

"I understand. I'm the same way when I'm on a shoot. If I keep going I can work for hours, but when I have those clients who need a ton of breaks, it's just exhausting."

"Yeah. Just like that," he said. "By the way, I was just watching the Weather Channel—"

"Of course you were. It's your favorite channel. You got me hooked on it last year."

"Oh, sorry about that, but this storm, it looks like it could be an issue down there."

"Not here, but on the coast, yes. I'm pretty far inland. We shouldn't get much of anything but some rain out this way."

"That's good. Hey, you can say no, but since we'd be coming through that way . . . well . . . would you mind if we stopped by after the concert? Is there somewhere nearby we could park it a couple days before we head down to Texas?"

"Here? In Adams Grove?"

"Yes. It's right there where we pick up I-95."

Without a second of hesitation she answered. "Yes. I know the perfect place."

"Cool. Where?"

"Right here. I can be your rest stop."

"You wouldn't mind?"

"Are you kidding? It would be great to see everyone. I'd love it. Wait until you see Shutterbug . . . she's huge. And Jake. He's growing like a weed."

Cody paused. "Kasey. It would be really good to see you."

"I know." She sucked in a breath. "It would be good to see you too. I can't wait."

She hung up the phone and pulled her hands to her face. She'd been looking forward to the concert, but him coming here had left her feeling as anxious as a high school girl vying for prom queen. Cody Tuggle didn't call often, but somehow he had a knack for calling just when she needed it the most.

❖ Chapter Five ❖

Cody had slept hard after the concert in West Virginia, but this morning was already busy with new challenges. He walked up to the front of the bus and sat down next to Pete.

Pete looked up from the book he was reading. "What's up?"

"I got a message that we have to reschedule the Virginia Beach show." Cody drummed his fingers on the table as he looked out the window of the bus. The sky was a perfect blue here, but the coast was getting one pile driver of a storm. That wasn't all bad though. It meant they could chill out an extra day in Adams Grove. It had been good hearing Kasey's voice.

Cody turned toward Pete. "I'd told Kasey we might stop in Adams Grove after the concert for a couple days. I know you wanted to head up to see your folks. I thought it would be a good central point."

"Yeah, it would." Pete snickered.

"What?"

"You. That's what. You've got a silly-ass grin on your face just talking about her."

"I do not." Cody moved from the table to the couch. "Quit looking at me like that." He picked up one of the pillows and hurled it across the space.

“Whatever, man.” Pete leaned to the side to dodge the airborne pillow. “How long have I known you? I know that look.”

“Don’t get started.” Cody got up and walked toward the back of the bus.

“Where you going?”

“To call Kasey.”

Pete shrugged and held his hands up.

“Shut up.”

“I’m not saying anything,” Pete said, then mumbled, “but you can’t call her from in here? Just sayin’.”

“I heard that.” Cody closed the door behind him and dialed Kasey. *Why do I feel so anxious about calling her?* Just as he got ready to hang up, she answered.

“Me again,” he said.

“Hey there. What’s up?”

She sounded happy to hear from him, but then she always sounded like that. “So, looks like we’re going to have a little more time between our last show and when we have to be in Dallas.”

“I bet you’re rescheduling the Virginia Beach dates. I was just talking to Riley and she said it’s a mess down there.”

“We’re just a little over an hour north of you. Still up for some company?”

“Absolutely. There’s plenty of room.”

“Jake settling into his routines at school?”

“We’ve got three days under our belts and we’ve

both survived," Kasey said with a soft giggle. "Thanks for asking."

"Awesome. Then I guess we're heading your way."

"Hey? Cody?"

"Yeah?"

"You're not doing this because I sounded like I was losing it on the phone before, are you?"

Maybe a little, but the act of God helped with a good excuse. "Of course not, and I promise we'll stay out of your hair."

"I'd love you to be in my hair . . . around. You know what I mean. It'll be nice to see you, and if you're going to be stranded, you may as well be with friends. It'll be more fun that way."

It would be way more fun stranded with you alone, and I sure wouldn't want my band around if that were the case.

He hung up the phone then yelled out to Pete. "We're on for Adams Grove."

"Great. I'll let my parents know I'll be there sooner than I'd planned."

Cody stretched up to check his look in the mirror across the room. *No silly-ass grin for Pete to make fun of. But damn if I don't feel like I'm wearing one.*

He walked back out to the living area and grabbed his guitar. When Pete got off the phone with his parents he updated the driver and then called back to the second bus to give them the update on the itinerary change.

"All set," Pete said.

When the tour bus turned down Nickel Creek Road, Cody got up and stood next to the driver.

"Not sure how much room you'll have to turn into the driveway," Cody said.

The driver laughed. "Now you're worried? Trust me, it can't be as tight as some of the parking lots of those joints the past couple of weeks. It'll be fine."

He was right. The driver swung wide and pulled into the paved driveway with room to spare. The crew bus followed his lead with the trailer in tow. The two forty-five-foot buses and the equipment trailer filled the better part of the length of the driveway.

Jake and Kasey came out of the house as the bus door opened and Cody stepped out.

Kasey was carrying her camera. *I'm not sure I've ever seen her without that in her hand. I wonder if she sleeps with it too.*

She met him halfway and gave him a hug. "It's so good to see you again."

He gave her a friendly kiss on the cheek. "You too. You look beautiful." And that didn't begin to describe it. "Y'all really didn't get much weather up this way, did you?"

"Just a little rain."

Jake tugged at the hem of his mom's shirt. "Did you really ride around on that big bus?"

"Hey, sport," Cody said. "Not this bus, but one just like it."

Kasey gave him a funny look.

"It's a new bus," Cody explained.

"I thought the other one was brand-new."

"It was a couple years old. We put a lot of miles on them in a year. I trade them up every couple of years."

"That's so cool, Mom."

"It was fun," Kasey said.

Cody added, "She's been on my plane too."

"The same airplane I was on with you?"

"The very same one."

"I love that airplane," Jake said, then turned to his mom. "Can we get an airplane someday?"

"Maybe when you're all grown up you can buy one." Kasey lifted her camera.

"Pose," Jake said, putting on his biggest grin. Cody smiled that celebrity smile that he was known for.

She lowered the camera. "That's not the good smile, Cody."

"What?"

Jake said, "You have to think about the happiest thing in your whole life. Then it looks like a real smile."

Cody laughed and swept Jake into his arms. Kasey snapped the picture.

"Now that's a smile!" she said.

Cody put Jake down and they fist-bumped. "Does your mom take pictures all the time?"

"That's my mom," he said. "Always clickin'."

"I'm beginning to remember that." *And a few other things about her.*

"Why don't you tell the guys to come on inside and spread out. I got enough pizza for everyone."

"You shouldn't have gone to the trouble," Cody said. "I could have sent someone out for stuff."

"It wasn't any trouble. I just made a phone call and picked them up."

"We'll do the dishes," he said.

"Deal. I might have to get a picture of that," Kasey said, knowing there'd be none since she'd gotten paper plates, but at least it would appease him.

"Fine by me." Cody jogged back to the bus and pounded on the side and then walked back to the other one and leaned inside. The guys started filing out of the buses. The bus that pulled the trailer of merchandise and equipment slept twelve, and his trailer had a suite for him and three bunks. One for the driver, one for Pete, and a junk bunk.

By the time Cody walked back to Kasey's side the guys were saying their hellos and hugging her. It felt like a family reunion and a few of the guys even offered up the latest pictures of their little ones at home. Cody had a sneaking feeling this was what the reception line at a wedding would feel like as he stood holding Jake's hand next to Kasey. Surprisingly, it felt kind of nice too. He watched her interact with the guys. *She can dish it out. I remember some of those zingers we tossed back and forth.* Funny how he really hadn't thought about that until just now. Maybe he'd pushed those memories back in his mind since she was off-limits back then.

He wasn't the type to take advantage of a situation like her recent widowhood, although he sure had been tempted. That attraction was at the "wrong place, wrong time" back then, but Jake was home safe and sound, and it had been over a year since her husband had died. Maybe this year would be different.

He stood at ease for the first time in a long time as he focused on her interactions with the band. Sincere and warm welcomes intertwined. Not planned. Just the real deal. It was a refreshing change from the fake and manipulative world of music.

That restless feeling he'd been saddled with lately ebbed. Maybe it was Kasey. She'd come to him out of the blue and they'd shared an almost immediate bond on that photo shoot. His momma swore she'd been praying for a long-lasting and loving relationship. Momma did have a way with the man upstairs. She'd once told him that she'd prayed a hedge of protection around him, and he was darn certain that's why his path to success had been unchallenged and free of some of the dark things that happened to others who tried to earn a living in this business.

As the last guy said his hellos and meandered inside, Cody placed his hand on the small of Kasey's back and guided her toward the house too.

The smell of pizza hit them as soon as they walked in. She had a tub of iced Coronas and Miller Lites, and two pitchers of sweet tea on the counter. Pizzas were stacked five high in three flavors.

"You remembered what's on the rider?" Cody said.

"I was paying attention."

Pete walked over to Cody with a slice of pizza in one hand and a beer dangling between his forefinger and thumb. "Look over there, man."

In a glass shadow box, a fancy one like someone might display a prized football helmet in, there sat the red-licorice-rope cowboy hat Mark, the drummer, had made for Kasey last Christmas. "She kept it."

Cody tipped his head back and laughed. "No way. Hey, Mark. Come look at this, man."

"Can't believe you kept that thing," Pete said.

"Hey, it was the perfect gift," Kasey defended Mark. "I loved it. It was way too cool to eat."

Pete nudged Cody. "After Mark had those

licorice whips in his grubby drummer-boy hands for four days making it, I wouldn't have eaten it either."

"Can't say that I'd blame her," Cody said.

Mark punched Cody in the arm. "Shut up. It was the thought that counts."

"Just sayin'." Cody rubbed his arm. The pain wasn't from the punch but a little pang of jealousy that Kasey had kept the hat Mark had given her from the tour. It was stupid. He knew that. It really was a cool gift. Mark was crafty like that. He was always making stuff out of nothing.

Mark and Pete went back for more pizza. "Need another piece?" Pete asked.

"No. I'm good," Cody said, trying to remember what he'd given her for Christmas. He couldn't even remember, but he did remember what she'd given him. A picture collage from the shows they'd played. It was propped up on the second shelf behind his desk.

"I have quite a few souvenirs from the tour," Kasey admitted. "Speaking of stuff from the tour, have you and Lou spent any more time together?"

Cody shook his head. "Not alone time really. I flew her out to a couple of shows, but I've been busy. She's been busy. It was . . ." He shrugged. "I don't know. Fun, I guess."

"But?"

"There isn't the spark I expected there to be. It's good, but not great."

"What exactly were you expecting?"

He felt stupid and all of a sudden very awkward. "I'm not sure I want to tell you."

"Try me."

"I expected to feel like I couldn't focus on anything but her. Like the rest of the world slid away when I was talking to her." *Like it is right now as I'm talking to you.* "You think I'm silly, don't you?"

"No. Not at all. That's exactly how it was with Nick and me." Her voice got quiet, and she shook her head. "So, no. I'm not going to call you silly, but y'all already know each other. That changes things a little, I think."

"You don't think I'm expecting too much?"

"No. I really don't, but it's probably not fair to judge a quick get-together at a concert. I mean, that's your normal turf, but not most folks'."

"True. I guess I hadn't really thought about it that way. I'd been thinking about making a run down to Raleigh to visit her."

Her eyes brightened. "You totally should. You can use my car."

"I've got my bike in the trailer. I'm prepared." Cody held up his fingers. "Like a Boy Scout."

"I don't know about that whole Boy Scoutt thing, but I do know that you're a good man, and she'd be lucky to have you."

"Don't let that get around, because the bad boy in me makes a helluva living with that reputation."

"Your secrets are always safe with me." She turned and motioned for him to follow her. "Come here. Let me show you something."

Cody followed her to her office in the back of the house. Light streamed into the space through the windows that lined the back wall. From here you could see the backyard, and out to the vast pastures. He could picture Kasey working while watching Jake play out back from right here. Long work spaces spanned two walls with storage underneath. Rows of neatly stacked colored mat board filled cubbyholes like a rainbow.

"See." She pointed to the wall.

She'd matted the CD he'd given her with pictures from last year's tour, one of them together and the picture they'd posted of Jake holding his Bubba Bear. The dark walnut frame accented the jewel-tone mat. "That looks nicer than the one I got for it going platinum," he said, only half joking.

"Yep. You get to learn how to do it yourself when you take as many pictures as I do."

"Nice work. I'll have to get you to mat and frame my stuff from now on. I pay a fortune for framing and it never looks this good." He stepped closer, smiling at the memories. "That was a good tour." She'd been a big factor.

"There's not a day goes by that I don't reflect on this time in my life and thank God that he led you into my life when he did. You helped me keep my faith through it all. It would have been so much easier to just give up like everybody kept telling me to. But you didn't. You believed in me, and you gave me strength when I needed it most."

Cody opened his arms. She leaned into his chest and he tightened his arms around her, holding her . . . maybe a little too long. He didn't want to let her go. When she leaned back, he looked into her chocolate brown eyes. Tears threatened to spill. He dropped a kiss on her nose. "You're okay."

"You've got a lot of love to give, Cody Tuggle."

"You think?"

"I know." She nodded, then tugged away and lightened up. "You need to surprise Lou. Go to her. Make the effort. She'll appreciate it. Spend time with her on her turf. It'll be different. Trust me."

Where did that come from? I was thinking about you. Me and you. Not Lou.

"What are you waiting for?"

I'd rather be with you. He longed to reach out. Touch the curve of her cheek. Run his thumb along her lip. *I'd promise you anything.* He dragged in a breath. Obviously that wasn't where her head was. "Fine. I'll give it another shot on her turf. Maybe you're right."

"You won't know if you don't try."

"I guess we'll just have to see, then." *And*

if it isn't right, will you give me a chance?

"Good. Let's go back out there and see what kind of trouble Jake and Shutterbug are causing with your boys."

There wasn't much left but some random scraps of crust and Shutterbug looked like she'd probably had more than her share.

Kasey stacked the empty boxes.

Cody reached for them. "Here, I'll take those out to the trash. And let me at least pay you for the pizza."

"Nope. We can barter though."

"You want to take it out in trade? Please tell me you don't mean with photographs." He looked to the heavens. "Please let this be my lucky day."

"No." She swatted at him. "I was thinking more along the lines that y'all could play me a song or two."

"That's not exactly the same thing I was thinking, but yeah, that's doable." Cody grabbed a couple of the guys and asked them to get guitars from the bus.

"We're on it." Pete threw a stack of plates in the trash. Jake was right on his heels, like a little shadow. "Jake, you wait here."

Jake looked disappointed. "Where are they going, Mom? Do they have to leave already?"

"No, honey. They're going to play some music."

"We love music," he said.

Cody nodded. "My kind of guy."

The guys came back in with a couple of guitars, a set of maracas, and a small drum.

"Cool," the drummer said. "I was eyeing that fancy hat box on the shelf, but that'll work even better."

Jake ran from the kitchen. When he returned Kasey hitched a breath.

Cody looked up and saw Jake with a guitar.

Kasey's jaw went slack, but she didn't say a word about him carrying his father's guitar.

"You okay? I can go get another guitar for him to play with. We have a trailer full of equipment out there."

"No, no. It's okay. It's fine. Nick would love it." Her brows knit together a little. "I'm okay."

"You sure?"

"Yeah. It's fine." Kasey sat down on one of the bar stools and put on a strained smile.

"Come here, Jake." Cody lifted Jake up on his knee and helped him with the position of the guitar. "Do you know how to do the chords?"

"I don't know."

"Here. I'll help you." Cody held the guitar in front of them and placed his own fingertips on the chords, then guided Jake through the strumming motion. "Good job. Now kind of do it in time with the song." Jake watched Pete and tried to mimic his strums. "You're a natural."

Cody couldn't stop smiling at the serious

look on this little boy's face. You'd think he was cracking the code to cancer or something.

"Sing for us, Pete," Cody said. "We'll do one of your favorites."

"You're the singer."

"Don't go all modest on us." Cody put his hand on top of Jake's and helped pick through the beginning of Dylan's "Knockin' on Heaven's Door." "Your favorite. Come on, man." Cody leaned in toward Kasey. "He's a good singer. You'll love this."

Pete closed his eyes through the first few chords, then started singing. Everyone else joined in, some playing, some singing along.

Cody nudged Kasey to get her attention, then nodded toward the front door. "You've got company."

Kasey jumped up and went to the door to greet Scott. One of the roadies must have heard him at the door and let him in.

Cody watched her. He recognized that look on Scott's face from last year. He'd kind of hoped he'd fallen out of the picture by now, but if he was still around, then it was likely something more was going on between the two of them.

Scott followed Kasey into the room, then walked over and extended his hand to Cody.

"Been a while," Scott said.

"Yeah, it has." *Could have been longer and I'd have been okay with it.*

"Didn't know you were going to be in town. Good to see you."

Bullshit. "Concert's flooded out."

"We're playing music." Jake strummed the guitar with enthusiasm.

"I see that." Scott edged closer to Kasey, but she stepped out of Scott's zone. "That's what Kasey was just saying. It's a mess down there."

Cody felt a little joy rush through his veins when she dashed off to the kitchen. Scott's little claim-stake move didn't work.

"Nice that you had somewhere to stop as you passed through."

"Couldn't have worked out better," Cody said.

Kasey came back in the room carrying a bottle of water. She leaned on the edge of the sofa a safe distance from either of them.

Scott said, "Yeah, I stopped in the diner and they mentioned Kasey'd just picked up fifteen large pizzas. I figured something was up."

You sure as heck knew what was going on by the time you drove up and saw my name plastered all over the side of one of those buses.

"How long y'all going to be around?" Scott asked.

Longer than you'd like, I'll bet. "Couple days."

Scott's radio sounded and a staticky message, that probably no one but Scott understood, interrupted the greeting. "Duty calls. Good to see ya."

Cody was thankful something took him out of

the picture just then. It looked to him like Sheriff Scott Calvin had signed up to be next in line for Kasey's affections, and that shouldn't even bother him. Scott was a nice enough guy, but right now Cody had to admit that he felt like the guy was just in the way.

Kasey closed the door behind Scott and came back to the couch. Cody grabbed her hand as she walked by.

The guys transitioned from the song they were playing to Cody's very first number one song, "It's a Tragedy."

Jake belted out the words. Cody liked the thought of Kasey playing his music enough that her son knew all the words to his songs.

"You're a good singer, Jake," Cody said.

"Me and Mom sing in the car all the time."

Kasey blushed and stood up. "Come on, Jake. It's time to call it a night, buddy."

"Mom?"

"Sorry, sport. You need your sleep. Give everyone a high five, then run get in your jammies and brush your teeth."

Jake raised his hand in the air and then zoomed around the room, slapping everyone's hand in the process and then flinging himself into Cody's arms. "G'night!"

"Sorry," Kasey said, reaching out for him.

"Come back when you're changed and I'll come tuck you in," Kasey said to Jake.

"I want you to tuck me in," Jake said to Cody.

"Me?" He looked to Kasey to see if she was okay with it.

"You don't have to."

"No. No . . . it's fine. I want to." Cody stood, lifting Jake as he did. "We're good. Come on, little man." Cody spun Jake from his hip to his back and then galloped back to his bedroom. He waited in the hall as the little boy changed into his pajamas and then ran to the bathroom to brush his teeth.

Jake came out and smiled a toothy grin. "All clean!"

"Good work," Cody said, then stooped to let Jake climb onto his back again. "You ready for a crash landing?"

Jake laughed and bobbed his head. "Yes!"

Cody galloped around the corner to Jake's room, then let go of Jake's legs and let him fall back onto the bed.

"Good night, bud."

"Prayers first," Jake said.

"Right."

Jake scrambled to the floor and knelt beside the bed with his hands folded on the comforter. Cody followed his lead. Jake peeked up at Cody and whispered, "You have to close your eyes."

"They were closed. I was checking to see if you were checking."

"Okay," Jake said. "Dear God, it's me, Jake.

Thank you, God, for helping me to do the things we should, to be to others kind and good; in all we do, in work and play, to grow more loving every day."

"A—" Cody started but Jake continued on.

"God bless Daddy in heaven, and Mommy, and Grem, and Aunt Riley and Uncle Von, and Mr. Scott, and Shutterbug is sorry for chewing the rug on the back porch, and God bless the parade tractors and all of the band and the songs and Cody for bringing me home before and coming here again tonight. He makes us happy."

"Me too, buddy." Cody hugged Jake.

"Amen." Jake unclasped his hands and nudged Cody. "Now you say it."

"Amen." Cody said and then Jake scrambled underneath the covers and squeezed his eyes tight as Cody tucked them in and around his little frame.

❖ Chapter Six ❖

Kasey watched from the hallway as Cody tucked Jake into bed. She hoped it hadn't made Cody uncomfortable. Her heart hammered and she suddenly felt hyperaware of the emotions that had been buried since the day she lost Nick. She hadn't felt like this in a long time. *Since you, Nick.*

Cody looked surprised to see her standing there as he walked out. "He's the coolest kid."

She smiled extra wide, hoping he wouldn't notice the tremble of her lip. "Yeah, he is. Best thing in my life. He thinks you're pretty cool too."

"I am." Cody slipped his arm around her waist.

"And modest." She loved how he kept things light. He made it easy to be around him. If she didn't know firsthand just how big a star he was, she'd never believe it. He was more down-to-earth than just about anyone she knew. Too bad they didn't make Cody Tuggle in a regular working-guy-dad model.

"Come walk with me. I have a little something for you," he said.

"For me?"

"Yeah. You. I don't see anyone else standing next to me," he teased. "Am I wrong or is your birthday Saturday?"

"It is." She was surprised at the thrill him remembering it stirred. "I can't believe you remembered."

"I didn't exactly. I saw your calendar in the kitchen. I knew it was the first week of September, but couldn't remember which day. I do have a gift on the bus for you though. I'd planned to mail it this week, but since we're here . . ." He pulled his arm from around her like he knew she'd be uncomfortable in front of everyone like that.

"We're gonna step out for a second. Pete, you got Jake?"

"I'll listen for him," Pete said.

She lowered her voice. "Where are we going?"

"Just to the bus." He led her to the front door and held it for her.

What are you up to? What are the guys going to think? She hesitated but only for a moment, then she stepped outside and he closed the door behind them.

The wind was kicking up but the air was as sticky as a midsummer night. The cloud cover made it extra dark. She let Cody take her hand

and lead her to the huge bus.

He punched in the code to open the door. Flush-mounted LEDs illuminated each step. He climbed in first and then held out his hand to help her.

Cody hit a switch and the room warmed to a soft glow.

Kasey let go of his hand and walked ahead of him. "Wow. It might look the same on the outside, but it's totally different on the inside."

"Do you like the colors?"

Kasey walked through the space taking it all in. "I do. Yes, very soothing. It's so much brighter."

"Yeah. They have a new designer and she talked me out of the dark colors I usually have and into the tan and teals. I'm glad she did."

"Reminds me of turquoise and desert sands. It seems so much roomier too. It must be the color."

"A little, but I think having separate chairs instead of everything being a blocky couch really works in here. There's more empty space and wait until you see it with the slide-outs. They did some amazing flipping and folding. This thing even exceeded my expectations." He motioned to the far side of the bus. "Are we clear on this side if I open the slide-out?"

"There's no fence on that side," she said.

He pushed a button and the motor hummed as the room expanded.

"It's like those Transformers Jake loves so much." She spun around in the center of the space. Inlaid glass tile, hand-tooled leather inlay on the overhead compartments, and the floors looked like hand-scraped wood planks. Comfortable, but no doubt high-end.

Cody looked proud of the new digs. "I don't know how manly all this is, but I'm liking it."

"I don't think anyone is going to challenge your manhood." She remembered the exact thought that had gone through her mind the first time she'd photographed him. *This guy could wear a pink tutu and look masculine.*

He opened a double cabinet over the sink and took down a white glossy box.

Does he have the market cornered on those white glossy boxes? It looked just like the one he'd given her last year at the last concert before she left the tour, only this time the ribbon was shiny steel blue, like his eyes, instead of teal.

"You really didn't have to do this." Her name was printed on a small white envelope tucked into the top of the box. She tugged on the ribbon.

Her mind wandered to last year. Jake had taken the long length of ribbon and run through the yard with Shutterbug, not even ten pounds soaking wet yet, running after him. They'd played with that ribbon for a week until it was so frayed it looked like dental floss.

"It worked out perfect that I'm here to actually give it to you. I'd planned to mail it, and you see how well I planned that."

She tugged the silk ribbon free and laid it in her lap, trying to contain the nervous jitters by biting down on the inside of her lip.

Cody sat down next to her. His leg felt warm against hers. She wanted this warmth, welcomed it. He smelled of soap, shampoo, something fresh.

She resisted looking up at him. With her eyes lowered, she gently peeled the white paper from the box. Inside, another box of black velvet was about the size of a watch box. She flipped open the hinged lid, and lifted a gold bracelet from the box.

"It's beautiful." Three charms dangled from it: a camera, a white-gold music note, and a teddy bear. Between each charm there was a silver-and-gold bead.

Cody fingered the teddy bear charm. "This one is chocolate diamonds."

"Like Bubba Bear?"

He nodded. "That's exactly what I was thinking. They don't make red licorice diamonds, but I've put in first dibs if they ever do."

I love red licorice, but chocolate diamonds are a-okay. "I think I may like chocolate diamonds better."

"I was thinking they match your eyes."

She clasped his forearm. "Cody, it's so generous, and so perfect."

"When I saw the teddy bear, and then the camera, I knew I had to get it for you. They reminded me of you. The music note is to remind you of me and those good times we shared." He put his hand on top of her leg and gave it a squeeze.

"I don't need a bracelet to remember. We made some very special memories. Thank you so much."

"You're welcome." He took the bracelet from her. "Let me help you with it."

She held out her arm and he draped it under her wrist and clasped it, then laced his fingers through hers. "Pretty."

"I love it." She leaned over and kissed him on the cheek. A soft kiss, but she yearned to give him so much more. Her breath caught. *You can't do this, Kasey. You're a mom, and he's a man who loves being on the road. It would never work.* She smiled and put her hands in her lap. "It's beautiful."

"As you." He tilted his head like he was trying to think of something to say next.

Or maybe he wanted a bigger kiss too. Why am I torturing myself? She swallowed.

He broke the silence. "So, what's the big plan for your birthday?"

"I'd like to say *nothing,* but Riley insisted on making it a party so she and Von are coming up on Saturday."

"That sounds like fun. Are you sure the guys won't be in the way? We can take this little convoy somewhere else."

"No. Not at all. The more the merrier. Really, it's just a cookout and cake. Very casual. It'll be small . . . well, bigger now, but that's fine because it was going to be just us and cooking out. I've got some things to figure out and Riley's always a balanced sounding board."

"Everything okay?"

"Not quite, but I'll figure it out."

"I should be back by then."

"I hope not. Maybe things will go so well on your trip to see Lou that you won't even know it's Saturday."

"We'll see," Cody said.

"Well, let's hope so, but either way at least you'll settle what's going on in your heart once and for all."

He looked hesitant. Although he'd never shared the details, from the lyrics of his songs she knew that love had burned him a time or two.

Kasey tucked the wrapping paper in the box

and set it on the counter. "Are you going to bring Lou to Arty's for his party on Friday night?"

Cody looked surprised. "You're going to that?"

"Yeah. He wouldn't take no for an answer. He said you were going to be there."

"I told you he liked to have his way the first time we met. Remember?"

"I do recall. It was right there at Arty's estate after the photo shoot. That's how you roped me into photographing your tour."

"Best roping I ever did."

"So, I take it you're not planning to go to Arty's anymore?"

"Nope. Never did say I would. I'm sure you aren't the only one he told I'd be there, though." Cody shook his head. "I hate those big parties he throws. He showed up in Maryland trying to talk me into going. He wasn't too happy with me for turning him down, but I'd already told him I wasn't going. That's just not my scene."

"I should have stood my ground. I let him sucker me right in."

"He's good at that."

"I felt kind of obligated when he said the publisher who did the book we worked on together is going to be there."

"See. He knows what buttons to push. I should've known he was going to invite you when he mentioned they were going to be there.

Sorry. Hell, his parties are so crowded he'd probably never know if you weren't there."

"I've already made arrangements for Jake and everything. Riley's picking him up for a sleep-over at their place."

"If Pete is still here, he'd watch Jake for you. He's great with kids."

"I know. I remember, but no thanks. I already have it planned and Jake is looking forward to it."

"Maybe we should go to the party together. You can ride in my big new bus." He gave her a shifty-eyed wink that bordered on flirty and creepy at the same time.

She opened her mouth to respond, but she wasn't sure if he was teasing or not so she just laughed it off. "Come on. Let's get back to the house."

When she stepped out of the bus, most of the guys were out front making their way to the other bus. Kasey and Cody said their goodnights to the gang as they walked back to the house.

Inside Pete was sitting on the couch strumming his guitar. "Everything's been quiet in here."

Kasey hadn't been worried. Jake was a hard sleeper. They could have rocked a concert and not woken him once he was asleep. "Thanks, Pete."

"Anytime." He got up and left them standing in the living room.

"I'm so glad y'all are here," she said. "It was a really fun night."

"Sweet dreams," Cody said and then turned to leave. He stopped midway out the door. "I could get used to nights like this."

Me too. She locked the door and went to her room.

As she lay in bed, her mind raced. There was a time, before Nick, before she was a mom, that she'd have loved that carefree lifestyle. But that wasn't hers to have anymore. *A small price to pay for the love of a child.* Jake needed a stable home. She'd been able to provide that on her own and that was fine by her. She didn't have to replace Nick in her life, and she wasn't in the market to. Besides, Nick still had a hold on her heart.

Cody was footloose and on the go; that wasn't the kind of life she wanted for her son, but what she'd felt tonight . . . it felt good. It felt like those moments when Nick would make her heart race. Cody was like Nick in a lot of ways and that's probably what had her emotions in chaos. That had to be it.

And just the other day she'd told Scott she'd never have those feelings again.

Be careful what you say about never. Those things always came back to bite you.

Here she was having those very feelings, only not about Scott. He'd be a great dad, but the danger of his job made her nervous, and there was no spark there anyway. After tonight and the sparks she felt being around Cody, she knew more than ever there'd never be that feeling with Scott. It wasn't just her after all. It was them.

❖ Chapter Seven ❖

Sweaty but rejuvenated after an early run, Cody fixed coffee on the bus. It was nice to exercise outside in the fresh air rather than in a gym or on the bus. Getting up predawn to beat the heat wasn't too hard either since he'd been awake most of the night anyway thinking about Kasey. How she fit in with the band last night, just like she had last year. So easy. Like they'd been friends forever.

He stepped off the bus and took the back path around to the patio to see if she was up yet. Through the back windows, he could see her at the kitchen table sipping something from a mug the color of milk chocolate. She looked fresh in a light yellow sweater set and faded blue jeans. Her blonde hair hung straight past her shoulders, and although he couldn't see her eyes from here, he knew them to be about the color of the mug she held between the palms of her two hands.

He tapped on the back-door glass.

She looked up.

"Mind if I join you?" he asked and motioned through the glass panes.

"Not at all." She waved him inside. "Jake's getting his stuff together so I can take him to school." She nodded toward his supersize coffee mug. "That must hold the whole pot."

"Better part of it. Gets you from point A to B without a refill. How'd you sleep last night?"

"I slept like a baby."

"I never know if that's good or bad." He slid into the chair across from her. "I wondered if the diesel of the generators was going to bother you."

"I slept great. Didn't even hear them. This house must be pretty well insulated. Even when the farmers have their equipment in the fields harvesting next door we can barely hear it."

"Well, that's good. So how's that feisty grandmother of yours doing these days?"

"Grem's been kickboxing Father Time, but he's winning. He's stolen most of her memories now too. I'm not sure how much longer we'll be able to continue in-home care. She's having more bad days than good. The last time I was there she called me 'Georgie' the whole time. I have no idea who that is, but I played along."

"That's got to be hard for you."

"Yeah, it is. It's hard to watch someone who was always in charge become frail and confused. Plus, she's the only real family I've got around here besides Jake. Once I got married I never gave it a thought that I might be without Nick someday."

"At least you've been married. Most guys my age have already been married at least once. I thought it was going to happen with Lou all those years ago, but it didn't, and then I focused on my music. Once my music took off the women who came into my life were not really the marrying kind. They were . . . interesting, to say the least."

"Maybe you didn't let the right ones in."

Maybe it's because I've never met someone like you. "I'm pretty sure of that. It was easy to get swept into the crazy thrill of it all. But lots of my friends from that period are getting divorced, and not just divorced, but nasty-divorced. Maybe not meeting anyone was a blessing."

"Don't say that. Marriage is good. One of these days you'll meet the right partner and you'll know it. Everything will just fall into place and you won't waste a second sealing that deal."

And why am I getting ready to go to Raleigh when I know I'd rather be here with you? He wanted to open his mouth and say it. Ask her if there was a ghost of a chance for him to be a part of her life, but he couldn't do it. If she said no, he didn't think he could take it. Safer to keep quiet. "Sometimes my life can be complicated."

"Same here. I'm no picnic. My job had me on the road, and that can be a problem for some relationships. But Nick understood me, and he trusted me. He got it that some days I'd just get in my car and leave to take pictures and not come back for twelve hours. He didn't get mad. Didn't get jealous. Didn't get all pouty. He had an appreciation for my work and our times apart were torture but when we were back together . . . there was nothing sweeter."

"Do you think you'll ever have it again? Scott seems pretty interested in you."

She took a deep breath and looked off. "Scott's a good friend. He'd like to be more and I've tried, but I just don't feel it. It might be that I've had my one true love and if that's the way it is, I wouldn't trade one day of what I had with Nick to have another chance."

"That's really special," he said. "Does someone ever get over losing a love like that?"

"I've asked myself that very question a hundred times. Maybe I don't want to be over it. Jake and I, we're finding a new peace, and I think the slower pace of Adams Grove has helped." She slapped her hands on her thighs. "So, geez, this is heavy talk. What's on the itinerary for today?"

"I'm trying to figure that out. Pete's going to rent a car to go up to his parents' house; it's their wedding anniversary. I'm going to head to Raleigh. I wanted to check with you before I told the guys they'd be here through Sunday. It's a big favor, I know."

"That's fine by me," Kasey said. "Where are you heading Sunday?"

"Texas. Arty got me a commercial. Chevy pickup trucks. Should be fun. I wrote a song for it, but I'm in the commercial too."

"That's perfect casting." She could easily picture all six foot four of him filling up the cab of a big ol' pickup truck, smiling for the camera. He had movie-star good looks. Too bad other than concerts you didn't see much of him. He was private that way, but she did know how much he loved trucks, so it probably hadn't been hard to talk him into it.

I'd have loved to have gotten the contract to do the stills on that. But just as quickly as the thought came, she pushed it aside. Those days were coming to an end.

"All right. Well, I'll probably head out to surprise Lou later this afternoon," Cody said.

"Tell Pete if he doesn't mind waiting until Riley picks up Jake this afternoon, I'll take him up to his parents' house and then I'll shoot over to Arty's. It wouldn't be all that far out of the way and it'll break up my drive."

"I'll let him know." Cody was feeling even less inclined by the minute to go see Lou today.

"I'm ready, Mom," Jake called from the living room.

"Okay. I'm coming." She drank the last sip of coffee from her mug and stood. "I've got to take him to school." She took two steps toward the living room, then stopped and turned. "You wouldn't want to ride along, would you?"

"I'd love it."

"Come on, then."

"Want me to drive?" he asked as he followed her into the front of the house.

She raised a brow. "Not unless you don't trust my driving."

"Hi! I didn't know you were here." Jake looked excited. "Are you riding to school with us?"

"I am if you're okay with it."

"Yeah! Can we ride in your bus instead of Mom's car?"

Kasey said, "Not today. Some of the guys are still sleeping on the bus."

"Oh. Someday?" Jake added, "Please?"

"I tell ya what, one of these days I'll even let you drive the bus on my lap. Is that a deal?"

"Yes. I like that deal." Jake climbed into the car with his lunch box and backpack.

Kasey spoke across the top of the car. "You know you have to keep promises you make to these kids. They don't forget a thing."

"Cool by me." Cody leaned in and whispered to Jake. "Is she a good driver, Jake?"

"My mom's a really good driver," he said. "She got a ticket once though."

Cody closed the back door and got into the passenger seat.

"Only one ticket?" Cody eyed her. "Ever?"

She shrugged, trying to look innocent as she started the car and headed toward the school.

Jake played the role of tour director, pointing out local landmarks as they drove through town. He even explained each of the crops and how the train tracks weren't really used anymore.

When Kasey pulled into the parking area, a blue shirted "helper" met them at the car. She buddied Jake up with another child and collected more students as she headed toward the school leading the train of linked children.

Kasey leaned forward over the steering wheel watching Jake all the way to the door of the school. "He's growing up so fast." She put the car in gear and backed out of the parking space. "If you're not in a huge hurry, and you're hungry, Mac's Bakery has the best bear claws I've had anywhere in the country. Want to pick some up for the guys?"

"They'd love it."

"Great. I'll give you a little tour of my new hometown." She turned down Main Street and cruised up the block. She slowed down in front of the brightly painted orange building. "Do you mind if I stop here for just a minute?"

"No. I'm not in any hurry."

"Awesome." She pulled the car next to the curb in front of the vacant storefront on Main Street.

She got out and peered in the window, then jotted down the phone number from the FOR SALE OR LEASE sign propped in the window.

Cody got out and followed along. "Are you opening a photography studio or something?"

"Maybe a frame shop." She turned and looked at him, her cheeks reddened. "I have to figure something out now that Jake is in school." She peered through the window again.

"But you love those photo shoots."

She turned and let out a breath. "I do, but I love my son more."

"You could get a nanny."

She looked doubtful.

"It's not that crazy an idea. People do it all the time."

"Not people like me."

"Maybe there's another creative solution that wouldn't mean giving up the photography. It's such a big part of who you are. If the nanny isn't appealing, maybe you homeschool Jake on the road, or put him in a boarding school with some flexibility during those times you travel. I have friends that take their kids on the road. There are other options."

"In case you hadn't noticed, I'm not rock-star rich like you."

"You do okay."

"I'll figure something out. I'll do whatever it takes to do the right thing by Jake."

"I know you will. Just don't rush it. Something will work out. It always does."

"I hope you're right," she said as she walked back to the car.

They got in and she drove up to the next block and parked in front of Mac's Bakery. The bright blue awning shaded the arched letters on the glass.

"That smells great," Cody said.

"Wait until you taste the bear claws." She took the keys from the ignition. "Do you want to wait here?"

"Why? You embarrassed to be seen with me?"

She laughed. "Hardly. I just thought you might want to keep your visit to Adams Grove on the down-low."

"No. Don't be silly." He stepped out of the car and walked inside with her. The kid behind the counter was probably in his midtwenties and it was obvious he recognized Cody. His eyes darted back and forth between Cody and Kasey.

"Yes, Derek. It is who you think it is," Kasey said.

Derek wiped his hands on his apron. "Cody Tuggle?"

Cody shook Derek's hand. "Nice to meet you, Derek. I hear you have the best bear claws in the world."

"My dad's recipe. Yeah. They're a town favorite. We sell more of those than anything else. My specialty is the cakes."

Cody shoved his hand into his front pocket. "Can you get us a dozen of those famous bear claws to go?"

"Yes sir." Derek ran to the back and came out with two white boxes. "Here you go. On the house."

"No. No way." Cody peeled off a couple of twenties and placed them on the counter. "Thank you. I appreciate the thought, but I've got this."

"Would you mind autographing something for me? You know, just to prove you were here?"

"Sure. What do you want me to sign?"

Derek looked around, and then grabbed a big circular piece of cardboard that he used underneath tiered cakes. "How about this?"

"Got a pen?"

Derek handed him the whole pencil cup.

Cody took out a marker and began to write and then stopped. "Wait a second."

He opened the box and took a bite of one of the bear claws. He turned to Kasey. "You were right. But then you always are."

To Derek at Mac's Bakery
Best bear claws around!
~ Cody Tuggle

"Thank you so much!" Derek placed the cardboard up on the rack just below where the prices were hung.

As they walked out, Kasey said, "Thanks for being so nice to him. You made his day."

"Made mine too."

When Kasey pulled into the driveway, most of the guys were up and moving around. They'd already rolled some of the bigger boxes out of the trailer and were wheeling Cody's motorcycle down the ramp.

"Want to go for a ride on my bike?"

"No. You've got places to go."

"Come on. It'll be fun. It's a gorgeous day and there's plenty of time before I'll head out."

"I don't have a helmet," she said.

"I've got an extra." They climbed out of the car and Cody took the box of pastries over to the guys. "Best bear claws in the world, says our hostess."

The guys dug in and nodded their approval.

Cody disappeared into the trailer and walked back out with a helmet. "Just a quick ride."

She looked unsure, but finally came around. "Just a quick one and you can't go real fast."

"Promise," he said. He laid the black half helmet on her head and helped her buckle it and then put on his own. He straddled the bike and Kasey put one foot on the back foot peg and swung her leg over like she'd done it a time or two.

He started the bike and the pop-pop . . . pop-pop . . . pop-pop pause echoed through the custom pipes. "Ready?"

"Yes."

He'd kind of hoped she'd be clinging to him like Velcro but she seemed perfectly fine with one hand on the back rail.

He talked to her over his shoulder. "You've ridden before."

She leaned forward. "Don't get that many gigs shooting cars and motorcycles without riding a few."

Cody lowered his arm and let it hang on the outside of her leg as they rode through the scenic countryside. It felt good to let go and just ride. Kasey was the perfect passenger. Totally neutral through all the curves and he liked it when she giggled when he patted her thigh just to let her know he knew she was there.

They only passed a few cars on the ride. He'd promised to keep it short but he could have ridden all day with her on the back of his bike. He turned left at the end of the next road and all of a sudden, Kasey freaked out.

"No," she slapped his shoulder. "Don't go this way."

"Why not?"

"Scott's mom lives down this way."

"So?"

"So, I don't want to start any gossip."

Gossip in general, or just gossip about you and me? Cody turned around at the next wide spot and headed back to her house.

Kasey stood on the pegs of the bike and lifted herself up and off, stepping down as she unhooked the helmet. “That was fun.”

It was until you went paranoid on me. The Jake thing he could understand, but maybe it wasn’t about the kidnapping and more about just who she was. “Thanks for coming along. You’re an old pro. I thought I was treating you to something new.”

“Well, it was new with you.”

“We’ll do it again sometime. I’d love to take you for a ride down my favorite path at home. It goes by an old grist mill. Really pretty.” Only he somehow doubted she’d ever agree to really do it.

“Sounds beautiful. I’ll bring the camera.”

“Of course you will.”

She stood there for an awkward moment. “I guess you probably ought to head on down to Raleigh now.”

“Yeah. Might as well shove off.” *So why aren’t I moving?*

Kasey shrugged. “Wish me luck at Arty’s tonight. If he asks about you, I’ll say that I just talked to you and you said you were getting married and leaving the music business.”

Cody whistled. “Yeah, do that. It’ll send him right off the deep end. Be sure to have your camera ready for that shot.”

“Count on it.”

He pushed the bike back and turned it toward the road, then took off.

When he got to the end of the driveway he could see her still standing there staring at him.

What are you thinking right now, Kasey? I sure would love to know.

❖ Chapter Eight ❖

Just as Cody reached the stop sign on Route 58 and Nickel Creek Road, huge raindrops fell with the weight of malt balls and they were coming fast. A lightning bolt flashed, followed by an immediate crack of thunder. A little too close for comfort.

It's got to be a sign.

He turned around and headed back to Kasey's house, squinting against the pummeling rain. She must have heard his motorcycle because when he turned into the driveway she was already motioning from the front door for him to pull around to the garage.

He drove the Harley into the garage bay and gave it one rev before he shut it down and took off his helmet. "Where the heck did that come from?" His shirt was soaking wet so he took it off too and draped it over the handlebars. "I guess that road trip wasn't meant to be."

"You aren't letting a little thing like rain stop you, are you?"

"You're giving this visit more potential than

it deserves. It's fine. There'll be another time."

"Or not." She walked over to a cabinet next to the door and then tossed a key chain to Cody. He snagged it in midair.

He looked at them. *Ford keys?* "What's this for?"

"The car in the other garage behind the house."

"Why are you so determined to get me out of your hair?"

"It's not that. You helped me. I'm helping you." She walked toward the garage door. "Follow me."

He unsaddled from the bike and took her hand. "Ready?"

"Yes." She took off running with him at her side. "That is the coldest rain," she squealed.

"Yeah, it is. At least *you* have your shirt on." He tugged her along faster toward the backyard.

She grabbed the handle on the carriage house garage and Cody helped her open the door.

A blue tarp covered a car in the middle of the space. This garage must have been intended as her husband's man cave.

She lifted one corner. "Help me uncover it."

He grabbed the other side of the cover and they walked it forward. The baby-blue Thunderbird looked showroom ready. "It's a beauty." Cody stood back, admiring it.

"I used to love riding in this car with Nick. I come out and start it once a week for good measure. Other than that, it's just sitting here."

He looked at her like she was crazy. “Kasey, I can’t drive this car. I bet it’s never been in the rain.” He hadn’t seen an old Thunderbird this nice since he took his ’39 Chevy down to the Barrett-Jackson auction to raise money for Wounded Warriors. “Nineteen fifty-seven?”

“Good guess. You know your cars. It’s fine to drive it in the rain. It’s a dependable car, and Nick drove it all the time. He loved this car. I think sometimes he drove it in the rain just as an excuse to spend more time shining it up.”

He walked around to the side and opened the door. “Man. You just don’t see them like this every day.”

“There’s another one almost just like it right here in Adams Grove, believe it or not.”

“Really?”

“Yeah, except it’s not stock like this one. That one has satellite radio and power everything. Scott Calvin has one. He was driving it the day we met.”

“What are the odds?” *Even just hearing that guy’s name bugs me.* He closed the door. “I’m not sure I feel right about driving this. I appreciate it, but I’ll wait.”

“In the grand scheme of things it’s just transportation. It won’t rust. It’s just sitting in here gathering spiders. Drive it. That’s what it was made for.”

He opened the driver’s side door and sat inside.

"She's a beauty." He was so tempted. Not even because he wanted to see Lou, but because it would be fun to drive this machine. "You sure?"

"Yeah. I'm sure. I know it's not too low-key, but then you never are."

He nodded. "True. Thanks. I'm going to go get changed into some dry clothes first though."

Kasey stepped out toward the driveway and peered outside. "I thought I heard someone drive up. Riley's here."

Cody got out of the car and put the keys in his pocket. "I guess this is it for a while then?"

"Guess so." She stepped back. "I really hope it all goes well with Lou and that y'all have so many fireworks you set off a smoke alarm."

"Wow, you know how to put pressure on a guy."

He walked back to the bus wishing he were going to be the one riding with Kasey to northern Virginia instead of Pete.

"Not a good day for a bike ride, is it?" Pete teased.

"Not so much."

"Kasey and Riley are getting ready to go pick up Jake. She said she'll be ready to roll as soon as they get back."

"Thanks. I'll be ready," Pete said.

Cody closed the door to his room behind him. Trying to think positive about the trip, he tossed a change of clothes in his duffel bag. He changed into a charcoal gray shirt with diamond-shaped snaps and tucked it into his jeans. Then, he grabbed his custom Bailey guitar and pushed the cowboy hat down on his head, before heading back out to the garage to get the T-bird.

He backed the car out into the driveway and adjusted the mirrors, then punched the manual buttons to find a radio station. The first one he pushed was a sports talk show. *Good taste, Nick. Women. Cars. Radio stations. We probably would have been friends.* He typed Lou's address into his phone for directions.

Right at a two-hour drive. Not bad.

Once he got on the interstate it was smooth sailing. The car handled nicely and it was kind of a cool feeling to know that the nods and looks he was getting were for the car and not for him.

He took the US-64 bypass exit toward Raleigh, and now that he was starting to get closer he found himself feeling a little nervous about being on Lou's turf.

Maybe you really can't go back. When he and Lou were a couple, times had been lean. He was just barely making ends meet playing smoky bars and doing session work whenever he could get it. Back then going up to the local ice cream shop for a lime sherbet freeze was a celebration. One they didn't afford often. Mostly it was at home with the generic stuff. Still good memories though. *We've come a long way.*

That was a good memory, though. He hadn't had

a sherbet freeze in years. He swung the car into the next strip mall and parked in a spot toward the middle of the lot so no one would bump the car.

Feeling good about the idea, he tugged his hat down and jogged up to the grocery store. He took a cart and started heading for the frozen food section to get lime sherbet, then over to the soda aisle for a bottle of lemon-lime soda. He passed up the brand name and went for the generic store brand. That's all they could afford back then. It seemed like a fun thing to do, and a nice memory to relive.

Aisle six had no one waiting so he wheeled the cart up to the counter and put his things on the belt. The woman ringing him up never even made eye contact with him. She looked like she wasn't having a very good day the way she swept the items across the scanner and then dropped them into the plastic bag.

"Do you mind if I get a paper bag for that?"

She looked up at him like he'd asked her to strip and dance naked on the belt.

"Do you *have* paper bags?" he asked.

She sighed, locked the register, and slogged around the end of the next aisle to get one.

"Thank you so much. I really appreciate it. You can just put the plastic bag right inside there." \ He smiled his famous smile and she softened a little. "You're an angel."

That did it. She smiled.

He handed her a twenty and she counted back his change.

"You have a great day, ma'am." With the grocery bag tucked in the passenger seat, he started the car, reset the GPS, and turned back on the main road. He'd been driving for about fifteen minutes when the GPS indicated a left turn ahead. He took the left into a heavily treed neighborhood.

A really *nice* neighborhood. Deep paved ditches lined both sides of the road with huge trees and fancy light poles along a sidewalk lining both sides. The houses were huge. He cruised by at least twenty that each had to be on at least five or six acres. Most of them were fenced and many had horse barns in the back. The neighborhood wasn't new; it had the look of a community that had history. The size of the trees told a story of generations of people, wealthy people, living here.

The GPS directed him to make a right turn ahead.

He took the right and he was at the address she'd given him. The house was grand. Not that he didn't want her to have done well, but this place was impressive. Arty had told him about that guy she married. Old Mr. SpaghettiO had asked her to marry him with a ring in a bowl of spaghetti, or something like that. He must have had one heck of a job and she must have really taken him to the cleaners when they divorced to be able to afford this alone. That was a little unsettling.

He drove to the end of the street and turned around. This certainly wasn't the kind of neighborhood where you parked on the side of the street. The security force would want to know what the heck he was up to.

This has to be wrong. But as he got within range of the address again, he saw her SUV pull into the driveway and enter the garage.

Although the house was nice, it certainly was no comparison to his house, or even the ranch. But it gave him the unsettled feeling there was more about her that he didn't know.

Why had he expected her to stay pretty much status quo all these years? Had she said something to make him think that or did he make the assumption? Was she just that modest? If so, he sure didn't need to worry about her being a gold digger, not that she ever was.

It was weird that in his mind he'd pictured her in the same old apartment she'd been living in when they broke up. Why would her life have stood still? He shouldn't be surprised, but he'd be lying if he said it hadn't set him back on his heels a little.

Quit overanalyzing it, man. Just go up and surprise her before you talk yourself out of it. You didn't drive two hours to turn around and go back.

He pulled into the driveway and grabbed the bag from the passenger seat. He felt as nervous as the young musician who had stuttered his way through asking her out the first time. She'd been so pretty, and he'd just been a struggling guy with a dream.

The natural stone-paved walkway made his boots sound loud as he made his way up the stairs to the front door. He hit the doorbell and positioned the bag behind him.

His heart beat a little faster as her footsteps neared and then she opened the door.

He took off his sunglasses and watched it register on her face who was standing in front of her.

"Surprised?"

"Completely," she said. "Come in. What are you doing here?"

She stepped back from the doorway and he followed her inside.

I was kind of expecting one of those movie moments where you rushed into my arms because you were so excited. That was barely a good greeting if I lived in the neighborhood and stopped by, much less drove two hours to surprise you. "Our show got rescheduled because of the flooding down in Virginia Beach. You've been so nice to fly out the last few times to the concerts. I thought it was only fair for me to make time to come to you for a change." *Okay, now I'm just rambling.*

She stopped by the stairway. "Now, I'm

completely surprised." She looked like she wasn't quite sure what to do, and then a whistle sounded from the kitchen. "I was just making a cup of tea. Want some?"

"Tea? I don't think so." He lifted the paper bag up to his hip. "I brought the stuff to make lime sherbet freezes."

"You did not." She gave him a sideways glance. "Did you really?"

"I did." *Oh God, this sounds so hokey.*

"Come on back. The kitchen is this way. That sounds great." She led the way through the foyer to the back of the house into the kitchen. A tea kettle spewed steam.

"This place is really nice," Cody said. "I know we said we weren't going to talk about the past, but just how long have you been divorced?"

"I don't think that was the part of the past we meant was off-limits." She laughed. "I didn't even have time to change my name on all my credit cards. The easier question would be how long was I *married*."

"So how long were you married to Mr. SpaghettiO?"

"Mr. SpaghettiO? His name was Jack Russo. How do you get *spaghetti* out of that?"

"Arty told me the guy proposed to you with a wedding ring in a plate of spaghetti. Spaghetti and rings. SpaghettiOs."

"You're such a goober." She shook her head.

"And Arty is an ass. That's not the way it happened, but it only lasted three months. So I'm surprised he even told you anything about it."

"Three months? That's barely a relationship, much less a marriage."

"I know. It was wrong from the get-go. I knew it. I shouldn't have married him. We'd both jumped into it for the wrong reasons."

Cody pulled the sherbet and soda out of the bag and placed it on the island.

Lou twisted the bottle and laughed. "Generic. Man, you went full in, didn't ya?"

"Like old times. Wanted to do it right."

"You sure did." She took two tall glasses out of the cabinet and placed them in front of Cody.

"Got an ice cream scoop?"

"Sure do, in the drawer right there in front of you."

He dished up a couple scoops of sherbet into each glass.

Lou opened the bottle of soda. "This was really a thoughtful surprise."

She poured soda slowly into the glasses. The foam rose to the top. Lou looked at Cody. "This is the best part."

He leaned forward and took a sip, letting the sticky lime bubbles cover his top lip.

She gave him a peck on the lips. "Like this," she said, licking the tasty stickiness. "Like old times."

No. It wasn't the same. That was a sisterly kiss. Can't say I didn't try.

She handed him a glass. "Let's sit in the den."

Cody followed her into the next room and sat on the leather couch. "Nice place. Russo, spaghetti or no, sure did treat you right. This house is amazing."

"Oh, we never lived here in this house together."

"Oh, I just assumed . . ."

"No. I can thank Arty for this place, and your success too, but that's part of the past we said we'd leave in the past."

Can't thank me for this. "What do you mean—"

The phone rang and Lou jumped up from the chair. "Sorry. I'm expecting a call. I've got to grab that."

"Sure." He sat there for a minute. The phone conversation in the next room didn't sound like it was going to be quick, so he got up and wandered through the rooms downstairs. The art was nice. The furniture expensive.

A sound at the front door behind him made him turn. Lou hadn't said she was expecting anyone.

Isn't this awkward?

The door swung open, and a young brunette girl walked in wearing skinny jeans and a light blue blouse. The heels on her pointy-toed shoes had to be at least three inches high but she was still a short little thing, and pretty. Very pretty. She dropped her keys on a metal platter right next to the door and then looked up and caught his stare.

"What?" She cocked a hip and then recognition flashed in her eyes. "Hey, I know who you are. You're Cody Tuggle."

"Yeah. I am. And you are?"

"Amy, and wondering why you're in my house?"

"Nice to meet you, Amy." *Roommates. Maybe that explains the grand digs.* "Lou's in the other room. On the phone."

The girl rolled her eyes and let out a huff. "She's always on the phone. Hope you're not in a hurry."

She breezed past him toward the kitchen. A sugary-sweet aroma trailed behind her.

Cody fell in step. "What's in the box? It smells great."

She laid a white box down on the counter. "Pecan pie. It's kind of my specialty. I work over at the bakery part-time. How do you know my mom?"

"It was a surprise visit." *Mom?* "Your mom? Who's your mom?"

"Who are you here visiting?"

"Lou."

"That's my mom." Amy flashed him a no-duh kind of look. "How do you know her?"

"We used to date." *This girl can't be Lou's daughter*. "Lou's too young to have a daughter your age. How old *are* you anyways?"

"You'll score big points with her for that comment. She loves trying to act my age." The girl seemed flattered. "I'll be seventeen on the ninth."

He didn't have to be a math major to do that calculation in his head. He knew exactly who had been sleeping in his bed when that girl has conceived. Now that he looked closer, she did resemble Lou. He felt the blood pounding in his temples as the realization from his brain struck a nerve.

"Sorry, I was—" Lou stopped so abruptly she nearly fell forward. The color drained from her face.

As casually as he could manage, Cody said, "I just met Amy."

"I can't believe you didn't tell me, Mom."

"I was thinking the same thing." The words bit, and the betrayal from seventeen years ago when she broke his heart paled in comparison to this. "I didn't know you had a daughter."

She avoided eye contact with him. "Amy, I thought you were going out of town straight from school."

"Don't worry, I am. I'm not going to mess up your little date."

"You're going to be late."

"I've got plenty of time, and so what if I'm late. What's the big deal?" The girl looked between them. "Is everything cool?"

"Yes. It's fine."

"I have to go. I just forgot to get the gas card from you."

Lou dipped her hand in her purse and handed Amy the gas card and some cash. "Don't speed."

"I won't." She picked up the pie and headed for the door. "Nice to meet you, Cody." She left the room and the air between Cody and Lou hung so heavy that Cody felt like he couldn't even breathe it.

A tumble of confused thoughts and feelings assailed him.

Lou straightened, but her voice held a slight trace of hysteria. "You said we weren't going to talk about the past."

"Yeah, but she's right there. Why didn't we ever talk about this? That's not SpaghettiO's kid."

"Don't call him that," she snapped.

"Why are *you* so upset?"

"Because. It's the past. I don't want to relive it all again. I've moved on and things are good. I want them to stay that way."

Cody leaned against the counter to steady himself. "You should have told me. I could have helped."

"You did. Look around you. We're very comfortable. Arty has made sure of that. I appreciate it."

Appreciate it? What the hell does that mean? "This isn't about Arty. It's about Amy. I had a right to know."

"This was a mistake. I knew it was." She sighed heavily and squeezed her eyes shut for a two-count, then steadied her voice and looked him in the eye. "You didn't have a right. It was over. Arty took care of everything." She fingered the glass on the counter. "You probably should just go."

He stood there staring at her. Was there anything else to say? He didn't even know where to begin. He took one step back. "Yeah. Okay." *I have a daughter?*

Cody stormed out of the house and slammed the door.

He paused on the front porch for just a moment feeling totally out of it. The Thunderbird in the driveway reminded him how this all began. He got into the driver's seat and pulled out of the driveway. As he idled down the street, a bright yellow Mustang passed by. Amy tooted the horn and waved.

She didn't act like she knew either. Lou, how could you have kept this from me? From her? I'd have been a good father. I loved you so much.

He pounded his hand against the steering wheel.

The shock was beginning to dissipate, but it was just as quickly transforming into anger. Arty. Why was Arty such a damn manipulator? That's why he got paid the big bucks, but this wasn't his career. It was his life.

Images of a much younger Arty Max filled his

mind. He could almost hear his smooth-talking voice as clear as he had all those years ago. He'd said, "Don't let that girl ruin your dreams, boy. She left you. She doesn't believe in you or understand the sacrifices you've made. Leave her or leave the dream. What's it going to be?"

Sacrifices. Yeah. I had no idea what you meant back then. I thought you meant all those weeks on the road in a van playing dives and singing over bar fights. Shit. If only.

Arty had acted like he was there for him through those months he was so down about the breakup with Lou. He'd even had Cody move into his place for a couple of months while he worked on the new songs. Every time he'd thought of trying to renew things with Lou, Arty had reminded him what a foolish idea that was. Turns out there was a whole lot more to what Arty was trying to protect than his artist's heart. He was probably behind Lou keeping everything a secret. It would be just like him to stick his nose in where it didn't belong.

I shouldn't have listened to him. I should have talked to her. Kept in touch. But then again, his songs had said it all. He'd poured every bit of emotion he had into those songs. They'd paid off nicely too. He'd hung his heart on his sleeve and people were right there with him, hearing their own heartaches in his songs. Lou had to have known how he felt. He was sure she did, even if she'd never called or tried to contact him.

He'd broken promises. He'd put his dreams first, but they were young. All she'd wanted was a family. Well, it looked like she got what she wanted and decided to do it without his help. Even so, if Arty had taken care of all of that like she'd said, he had no right to keep it from him all these years.

As he got closer to Adams Grove he knew he wasn't going to sleep until he sorted this out with Arty. He should fire him. It was the ultimate betrayal. *Hell, if he could set Lou up like that and use my money without me knowing, no telling what he's been scamming off the top all these years.*

The old Thunderbird wasn't known for its speed, and that was probably lucky for him right now. He'd already driven an hour out of his way, but that didn't matter now. He needed to face Arty tonight. The static on the radio was about the best Cody could get with AM on this stretch of road and that couldn't drown out even half the stuff reeling through his mind. He wished he'd driven his motorcycle. He'd have cut this trip in half, and wouldn't have to stop for gas, because this little ride was a heckuva gas guzzler.

He took the next exit off the interstate to refuel. As he stood there, he couldn't help but get madder. His success had turned Arty Max into one of the most sought after agents in the country.

Arty might own fifteen percent of my career

but he has no right to the details of my life. How could he have kept this a secret all of these years?

He tugged the receipt from the pump and twisted the gas cap back in place. He was pissed at Arty, but Lou wasn't free of fault either. What a fool he'd been then—and now.

Cody got back in the car and pushed it to its limits all the way to Arty's estate.

❖ Chapter Nine ❖

Kasey was glad she'd been able to freshen up and change at Pete's parents' house before she headed back south toward Arty's estate near the Blue Ridge Mountains. That sure beat stopping somewhere on the way. The two-and-a-half-hour ride to northern Virginia with Pete had flown by and meeting his parents was fun. His mom had insisted on having her stay for dinner, and since Arty's party didn't even start until eight, it had worked out perfectly. Pete's dad was just as big a flirt as Pete and it had been neat to see them interact. It made her wish she'd had parents like his, but then she'd never had an adult relationship with her own parents. Once she went off to college Mom and Dad had headed off to Europe, and after several long trips there, decided to make their life in Spain. Other than money and the occasional card from one place or another, they really seemed more like distant relatives these days. Grem and her stuffy house had really been all the family she'd known for the past ten years.

I'll never let Jake think that way of me.

The ride to Arty's was an easy one and now that she was recognizing landmarks, she knew she was close.

Arty Max had a reputation for representing top acts and his property was just as flashy as the talent he managed. The road back to the estate was long and windy just like she remembered it, only it looked different in the dark. The whole road was lit with so many lights that it made her feel a little like she was driving down a runway. Around the next corner there was a makeshift guard shack.

She slowed at the giant stop sign.

A guy with a clipboard stepped to her window. "Your name, ma'am."

"Kasey Phillips." It wasn't a clipboard, but rather an electronic tablet.

He swept his finger across the screen, scanning the list. Then he walked around to the back of her car. It looked like he'd taken a picture of the license plate number. She watched him come back around to the side of the car. He handed her a ticket. "Thank you. You can take this road straight back and then follow the blue lights. A valet will be there to take your vehicle."

"Thank you." She rolled up her window and drove on. One way in and one way out. They had this under control. When she got to the end of the blue-lit path, the valet ran to the side of her car and opened the door to help her out. "Ms. Phillips?"

"That's me," she said.

He handed her a valet ticket then lifted a leather tote bag. "I'll put this in the backseat of your car for you. The bag and contents are a welcome gift from Arty Max. You can follow the path to the house. Enjoy your evening."

These guys were on the ball. "I will."

He pulled away from the curb and two other valets helped others with their vehicles as she started to walk away.

Lanterns lit the grounds like giant fireflies and music filled the air. The music seemed to come from the direction of a huge tent that was set up just outside the front of the house.

Country music. Probably new talent Arty'd just signed getting some exposure, and whoever they were, it sounded pretty good.

She ducked inside the tent. A few people mingled at tall bar-height tables that lined each side of the stage. A lit marquee listed half a dozen names. She recognized only one of them. CDs were stacked next to the marquee, free for the taking. Arty was pimping them in a big way, but then that's what he was known for. A young woman stood in the center of the stage singing with only an acoustic guitarist, and she sounded great. Not something just anyone could pull off.

Kasey wished she had her good camera equipment with her. It would've made an awesome picture. The brunette beauty had the look and the chops. Arty sure seemed to know how to pick them, but she didn't see any signs of him out here. She took her small camera from her purse and took a couple of pictures.

A bartender served drinks near the entrance looking bored, and heavy hors d'oeuvres filled tables nearby. The few guests who were out here listening were probably record-label types and the girls on their arms were about half their ages.

She wished now that she'd done the selfish thing and had Cody come with her. She always felt so awkward at these kinds of parties by herself. She headed for the house hoping Arty would be inside.

A small crowd gathered there. It was a mix of everything from evening gowns to blue jeans. She was somewhere in the middle in her black pants and dressy blouse, and that suited her fine. Good jewelry was always a blessing. Having Grem as her personal style consultant in Kasey's formative shopping years had given her a champagne taste for the good stuff, but she'd mastered dressing up and down with accessories instead of closets full of clothes over the years out of necessity. With the amount of travel and varied activities the photo shoots called for, accessorizing was a must. Plus, she'd much rather have an extra suitcase of camera equipment than clothes.

A waiter stopped and offered her a glass of wine, which she accepted. She took a sip and glanced around the room for a familiar face. Several people congregated around a fountain of chocolate, dipping fruit with silver tongs and trying not to make a mess. It looked like a hassle, but there were also rows of gold-rimmed china with fruit that had already been dipped. She chose one of those instead.

Arty stood across the room holding a glass of brown liquor, swirling it in the air as he talked with his hands like he was known to do. She suspected if someone tied Arty's arms behind his back, he would fall mute.

By the expressions on the people listening to his story, that might be a welcome gift right about now.

Kasey recognized a couple photographers clearly here to work the party. Although she'd been invited as a guest tonight, she'd have been much more comfortable if she had been here to photograph rather than mingle.

She heard her name, and turned around.

Arty had spotted her. He was waving his arms in the air and calling out to her, motioning her over.

She smiled and worked her way across the room.

Arty introduced her to the group. "Sit," he said

as he gestured to the huge half circle of leather he called a couch. The publisher of the book she and Cody had done for the tour was there and it was the first time they'd met in person.

"We love what you did with the photographs for the tour book," he said.

"Thank you. It was fun to do."

"Where is Cody? Isn't he going to be here tonight? Did you know your book is up for an award this year?" The publisher scanned the room, then leveled a stare at Arty. "I thought you said he'd be here."

Arty looked flustered. "He was going to try to fit it in, but he's on the road. Doubtful."

Kasey knew Cody would love to see Arty squirming right now. She was so tempted to take a picture.

"I'll tell him when I see him," Kasey said.

"Please do. We'd love to hire you to do a couple other tour books for us." The publisher handed her his card. "Let's get together and talk about it."

She knew Arty would kill her if she squashed the offer right here so she accepted the card knowing full well she wouldn't be able to do another job like that now.

The book guy turned to talk to someone else and Arty sidled up to her.

"You've spoken to Cody?" he asked.

"Yeah, saw him this morning." She was enjoying making Arty feel a little uncomfortable under the circumstances. Her phone vibrated and fear pricked her nerves. "Excuse me. I need to take this call." She glanced at the display. It was Riley. She answered the call and moved quickly toward a door to go outside where she'd be able to hear.

"Is everything okay?" Her voice shook.

"It's fine. I didn't mean to scare you. Jake wants to check on you. Do you have just a minute?" Riley asked. "It's noisy. Are you already at the party?"

"Yeah. I am." Kasey let out a breath and placed her hand on her racing heart. "Thank God, everything's okay. Of course I'll talk to him." She shifted the phone and walked over to one of the garden benches. Jake came on the line and they spoke for a few minutes. He didn't seem the least bit worried about being away from home and that was a relief.

"I love you ten and five, Mom."

Those had been the biggest numbers in his world when he first started saying it. Now it was just their little secret code. She loved it when he said that. "I love you too, Jake."

The door she'd walked out of had locked behind her so she walked around until she found an unlocked entrance and ducked back inside. It was a little like being in the middle of a carnival on a weekend now that more people had shown up. The bartenders were tossing bottles and serving up drinks with all the flair of a Vegas bar, and the music from outside comingled with an acoustic set being played inside.

Kasey went to get a refill, but two people arguing in the hall caught her attention. A brunette had her back to Kasey and Arty was clearly not happy with her. Whoever the girl was, she sounded like she didn't want to be here tonight. Kasey couldn't blame her really. It wasn't her kind of thing either, but Arty probably expected all of his people to show up and make the effort. Evidently, something wasn't going according to plan.

She saw him catch her staring. She slowly turned, pretending to have been scanning the room. *That was embarrassing.* A tall man walked over to her with a longneck beer and struck up a conversation. Someone tapped her on the shoulder. She turned around to find one of the guys she'd done shoots with several times over the years.

"It *is* you!"

Kasey brightened. "Andy Lawrence. It's great to see you."

Andy glanced at the guy. "Am I interrupting?"

"No. We were just chatting." She turned to the stranger. "Will you excuse me?"

He nodded and Kasey turned back to Andy. "It's great to see you," Kasey said. She rose on tiptoe and gave him a hug and whispered into his ear.

"You couldn't have had better timing. Thanks."

He smiled. "Haven't seen you in way too long. How's business?"

"Great. I didn't know you knew Arty Max."

He laughed. "Once Arty decides you can get him some airtime or press, he kind of makes you a friend whether you like it or not."

She nodded. "I know what you mean."

"I saw the pictures you did of Cody Tuggle. They were smokin'."

"Thanks. That means a lot coming from you." Andy's camera hung over his shoulder. "You're shooting tonight. Great."

"Yeah. Told him I'd take some candids while I was here." He took a step back. "Smile for me."

She raised her glass, and let him take a picture of her. *"Cha-ching."*

"I like the sound of that. I hope tonight brings some *cha-ching* in. Jobs have been a little tight lately." He looked at the picture. "Thanks. That's a good one. I'll send you a copy." He looked past her and turned back with an apologetic expression. "Oops. There's Dustin. I gotta run. We need to catch up sometime."

"I'd like that." He moved through the crowd and she saw his flash go off as a crowd of people surrounded Arty's latest act.

She glanced at her watch. It was almost nine thirty and the quiet little gathering she'd walked into was now a high-pitched thrum of action.

She'd done her duty. She'd made nice with the book people, and Arty saw her. She could leave at any time, and now seemed like the perfect moment to make her exit.

❖ Chapter Ten ❖

The tires squealed as Cody swerved through the familiar curves of the road back to Arty's estate. He accelerated out of the second one a little too tight and then he slammed on his brakes to avoid rear-ending a long line of cars.

How did I forget about that damn party tonight?

He'd been so focused on giving Arty a piece of his mind immediately that he'd forgotten all about the stupid party, but he'd come too far to turn back now. If he didn't settle this tonight, he'd surely explode.

Cody threw the shifter into reverse and turned around. From the main road he took the second entrance that only a few people knew about that led down to the barn. It wasn't well-marked, but the feed trucks used it and it led right back out to the house. He forced himself to slow down on the pitted gravel bed road. Once he passed the barn and got near the homestead another line of cars waited to be valeted.

By the time he'd handed off the car and neared the main house it was clear there was no way inside without passing through a long line of cameras, and he was about at the end of his patience. Cody recognized the song playing in the big tent out front. It was Dustin. The kid was probably on cloud nine. Cody remembered when he was first starting out. Those tent gigs were as exciting as all get-out. The first taste of celebrity. It was like a drug and Arty was the king of doling it out in doses that kept you inspired to work your ass off.

Cody veered off to the left of the front door toward the row of cottages. He knew the way well. One of those cottages was named after him, and he'd stayed there plenty of times over the years. The side entrance into the main house was just on the other side of the back gardens down a lit path.

There wasn't a soul out here. He opened the glass-paneled door and slipped inside with the other guests. At six foot four, blending in with the crowd wasn't all that easy. For once it would have been nice to be average height. He stayed to the outside of the crowd, looking across the top for that weasel of an agent of his. At least if he was in here he could get him into the office for a semiprivate conversation.

A server offered him a drink from her tray, but Cody refused. He pushed his hands in his pockets and kept an eye out for Arty.

"Cody! My man."

The slap on his back caught him off guard. Cody spun around to face Arty.

"I thought that was you, but you swore you weren't going to be here. So glad you had a change of heart," Arty mused.

It was all Cody could do not to coldcock him right here in the middle of the room. His blood boiled. "I need a word with you."

"What's the matter, buddy?" Arty motioned to the group of people to his left. "This man right here. He's a good man. And you, my friend," Arty motioned to a man in a blue shirt and his platinum blonde arm candy, "you two are staying in the cottage that his fame built. Wait until you hear the next album. Amazing. Maybe I'll sneak you a little demo to listen to while you're here."

You're so full of shit. I haven't even given you any material from the new album yet. Tell the people what they want to hear. That's just the way you roll, isn't it? Cody tried to restrain his anger but every muscle in his body clenched.

"It's so nice to meet you," the man said. His wife stood there practically weeping from nerves, unable to even utter a word.

It happened all the time and it still made him uncomfortable when people acted like that. Didn't they realize it was just as awkward for him as it was for them to meet someone new?

"Nice to meet y'all," Cody said, then turned back to Arty. "I need to talk to you. Now."

"Sure. Let me find the editor." Arty craned his neck searching.

"Now, Arty."

"Shh." Arty gave him a look. "Not so loud. You're not going to make a scene, are you? Just hang on a minute."

Cody grabbed Arty by the collar of his jacket and pushed him toward the office.

"What the hell are you—" Arty tugged away from Cody's grip.

"I asked nicely. I said we need to talk."

"Fine." He straightened his suit jacket, and placed his empty glass onto a waiter's tray as he walked by. "What's got you all riled up?"

Arty walked under his own power into the office, but Cody was hot on his heels.

"Want to know what's got me riled up? You, damn it." Cody leaned back against the door to close it, then moved toward Arty.

Arty was no fool, he was already slithering around to the other side of his desk like the worm he was. "Me? What the hell? I'm just throwing a party. A party you said you weren't coming to, if I recall. What's the problem?"

"You lying sack of sh—"

"Whoa. You just need to calm down."

Cody lunged across the desk with his finger just inches from his pointed nose. "Why didn't you tell me? What else have you kept from me all these years?"

Arty bobbed out of direct alignment with Cody's loaded finger. "What are you talking about?"

"I went to see Lou today." Cody watched the color drain right out of the man's face. "Yeah. I know."

"Lou?" Arty's breathing got heavy like he'd been running, and if he was smart he would've been.

Fury almost choked him. So much that he could barely get the words out. "Don't play stupid with me. You know who she is."

"That's who you went to see?" He lowered his head and mumbled, "I ought to have Annette's ass for this."

"This isn't about Annette, Arty. It's about you. You. Your lies."

"I told you to leave the past where it was. She was bad news the first time." Arty's voice got calmer. "Trust me. She's not worth causing a scene over. Calm down. Sit." He motioned Cody toward the chair on the other side of the desk. "Sit."

"Don't play that psycho-calm crap on me. You never told me she had a daughter."

"Annette should have stayed out of this. She knows how I feel about dredging up things from the past."

"Annette? Arty, you're the one who lied to me. These are things from my past. Things I had a right to know about."

"I didn't lie." Arty shook his finger. "No. I didn't. I just didn't get around to telling you, or did I? Are you sure I never told you she had a kid?"

"I think I'd have remembered something like that, Arty." Cody picked up the award he'd won for song of the year, the one he'd written after that breakup.

Arty looked at him as if daring him to do anything to the coveted award.

Cody threw it across the room, causing the picture on the wall to crash to the ground. "You had plenty of time to tell me she married Mr. SpaghettiO. I guess the rest just slipped your mind."

"That was my award!"

"No . . . It was my award. I earned that."

"Calm down. You're making way more out of this than it's worth."

"I thought you didn't like Lou, but really you just didn't like her being around. You paid her to stay away from me?"

"No. I didn't."

"I saw the house. That's one heck of a payment plan." He ran his hand across his chin. "She said she appreciates how comfortable we've made her all these years. Basically, you could say you're the reason we didn't stay together."

"No. *You're* the reason y'all didn't stay together. Remember, you wanted to be on the road. I got that for you. Your dream. I made it happen." Arty plopped down into his desk chair. "You'd be nothing if I hadn't helped you. Lou wasn't helping you get it. Anything not helping is hurting. Just sayin'."

Arty's cool mocking hung in the air.

Cody's jaw pulsed. "You never liked her."

Arty cocked his head and gave a glassy stare. "Oh, my friend, that's where you're very wrong. But what I did do was save your sappy, lovelorn ass more angst than you had. You should probably be thanking me."

"For lying? Keeping secrets about Lou's daughter? Paying for that house? How did you even do that without me knowing the money was gone? Hell, what else have you skimmed off the top?"

"Hold it right there, Cody." Arty stood and straightened his jacket. "I never took a dime from you."

"Don't lie anymore. It's over. I know. I met Amy today. Lou told me you paid for the house. It's a nice house too. You must've felt guilty as hell. But Arty, it wasn't any of your business. You had no right. You own part of my career, but not my life."

"I had every right."

"There's a line."

"What's the difference Cody? It was over. She was no good."

"I had a child." Cody licked his lips and tried to hold back the tears. "I'm a father."

"What?"

"What do you mean, *what?* Just because I didn't know about it doesn't make it untrue. How could you not have told me I had a daughter? You let me go all that time thinking I broke that girl's heart. You told me she'd moved on, gotten married. You led me to believe she was happily married and you knew that wasn't the case, didn't you?" Cody slammed his fist into the back of the chair. "Damn you, Arty."

"But you—" Arty started.

"And you paid her all these years. Jesus, Arty. What kind of jackass do you think I am? I'd have done right by them. It was not your place to do this."

"I was thinking of your career."

"Like hell. You were thinking about your wallet."

"Cody. Stop. Listen to me." Arty cleared his throat. "She's not your daughter."

"I don't know how I'm supposed to fix this, but I will."

"Cody, you're not her father."

"I met her. She told me her birthday. I can do the math. And Lou said she had you and me to thank for that fancy house."

"She's *my* daughter," Arty said.

❖ Chapter Eleven ❖

"*Your* daughter?" Cody shook his head. "No. Stop screwing with me. That's impossible."

Arty laughed. "Possible, and fact. I paid for that house with my money. Fifteen percent of your money, to be precise, that I earned by representing you. By making you the star you are today. I don't need to steal from you. Look around. I'm just as rich as you are. She's mine."

Cody cramped forward like he'd been sucker punched. "No."

"Yeah."

"No." Cody stepped back. *This can't be happening.*

Arty pointed to his hair. "Amy's hair is brown, and her eyes . . . brown just like mine. Not too likely you and Lou would have a brown-eyed daughter. And Lou even named her after me. *A* for 'Arty,' *M* for 'Max,' and *Y* for 'Why the heck didn't we use protection?' *A-M-Y*. Amy."

"Uh-uh. No. She'd never have slept with a conniving shit like you."

Arty shook his head. "Watch it, Cody. I know you're pissed, but we've got a long history. Don't say something stupid." He slid open his desk drawer and pulled out a picture and sat it on his desk.

Cody snatched it up. Then looked back at Arty. *She's not my daughter.* A much younger Amy sat next to Arty in the picture. With them side by side it was pretty clear there was a relation there. Arty wasn't lying. Even he couldn't make that corny crap up. Cody could see it in his face. "How could you, man? You knew how much I loved that girl. She was my whole life back then, as much as the music." He threw the picture down on the desk.

Arty stood and walked back around the desk. "She'd have dragged you down. If she'd been all that, she wouldn't have fallen into my bed so easy."

"You slept with her while we were together. Man, that's—"

"I'm sorry, but frankly I probably saved you from a worse heartache than you got. Think about the earnings you'd have lost in a nasty divorce somewhere down the road."

Cody turned his back on Arty. *I'm not sure which is worse. Thinking I had a daughter I didn't know about, or finding out you slept with the woman I loved and fathered a child with her right under my nose.*

"I know it's not what you wanted to hear. Trust me. She's no good. I probably did deserve her, but thankfully we both dodged that bullet."

"You didn't do me any damn favors." Cody straightened and then turned and swung on Arty, landing his fist right in Arty's gut and sending him ass over elbow to the floor. “Yeah. That’s one thing we agree on. You’re sorry.”

“Fine, man. I deserved that one,” Arty said. “Now can we leave this mess in the past? Get the hell out of here before you do something we both regret.”

The door of the office swung open.

Why did I think I’d be the exception to your nasty underhanded ways? I was a fool. “I don’t regret one thing I’ve said or done. You deserve more than that. I ought to beat the hell out of you with my bare hands right here and now until you realize what an awful human being you are.” Anger singed the corners of his control.

Cody took a lunge toward Arty just as three guys came running into the room.

“You okay, Arty?” asked a beast of a man with biceps as big as bowling balls.

Fists clenched, Cody kicked the trash can next to Arty’s desk clear across the room, sending a shower of papers that fluttered across the floor. “You’re not worth my damn time,” Cody said, then turned to the people at the door. “It’s fine. Nothing to see.”

Arty stood and straightened his suit. “It’s fine, guys. We’re just finishing up. I’ll be out in a minute.”

People in the main room gathered around the door, craning to see what was going on.

Cody swept past them and then excused himself

through the throng of people hanging around the door trying to catch a little bit of the drama he'd been doling out. He could barely absorb everything that Arty had just said. This time the guys with their cameras were armed and ready for him, peeking through the bushes and snapping as he walked by. Cody raised his arm to cover his face. "No story here, guys. Move along."

Kasey's T-bird was still where he'd left it, just like he'd asked, when he got to the valet and pressed a hundred-dollar bill into his hand. "Thanks."

The young valet ran up to the car at Cody's heels. "Thanks for the tip, but could you sign my hat too?"

Cody was in no mood, but he'd always promised he'd never be an ass to a fan. "Sure. You got a pen?"

The boy took a marker out of his pocket and handed over his tan Stetson.

"Under or over?" Cody asked.

"Right on top!"

"What's your name?"

"Jace. *J-A-C-E.*"

Cody scribbled his signature on the guy's hat and handed it back to him. "Here ya go, Jace. Thanks for your help."

"Thank you!"

Cody gave Jace a nod as he turned the car around and headed back toward the main road.

When he pulled onto the interstate, heavy raindrops began splattering against the windshield.

"Could it get any worse?" But it did somehow seem appropriate for how he was feeling right now.

What is it about my whole world crashing that gets the creativity going? He could already hear the melody of a new song forming in his mind.

The rain came down so hard he could barely see, and rather than risk wrecking Kasey's car, he got off at the next exit and went into a truck stop. He sat in a back booth and sipped a cup of coffee, replaying the day in his mind. He flipped over the paper place mat and began writing down the chords and the few phrases that were already coming to him rapid-fire. The piece of pie the waitress had talked him into sat there untouched. His stomach was in no shape for consuming anything tonight.

"The biggest betrayal of all," he wrote.

How could she have slept with Arty? Another band member would have been bad, but my own agent? He was supposed to have my back.

His phone rang. He glanced at the display. It was Lou, so he didn't bother to answer. Shortly after, at a little after eleven, she texted, I'M SORRY.

Arty must have called her. Lou must have figured he was a total idiot to have thought Amy was his child. Another text came through. CAN WE TALK?

He turned off the phone and put it in his pocket.

The waitress wandered over with a pot of coffee. "Top you off?"

"Thanks."

She dropped two creamers on the table. "You look familiar. You been in here before?"

"No. Just passing through."

She stepped back and turned her head. "I'm usually pretty good with faces." She glanced down at the paper. "You some kind of writer?"

"Yeah." That wasn't a total lie. He wrote songs.

She grinned a big overwhitened smile. "I'm going to write a book someday. Fiction, but based on my life."

If she sat down and started telling him her story he was going to kill himself. "Good luck," he said, trying not to encourage her. Thankfully, the bells on the door tinkled as a family of four came in. *Saved by the bell, literally.*

"Holler if you need anything." She scurried off to seat the customers.

Cody stared out the window. The rain was finally starting to slow down. He took out the bills from his front pocket and placed some money on the table, then folded the place mat and tucked it into his pocket.

He drove back to Adams Grove, but he wasn't up to talking to the guys tonight and they'd have twenty questions if he showed up there now. He passed Nickel Creek Road and headed toward

Main Street. It was peaceful. Nothing was open and only a few lights from the upstairs apartments over the shops gave any indication anyone was around at all. He pulled the car into the parking lot next to the market, and cranked down the window. The air had cooled down and the frogs were loud enough to be background to his vocals—which was really saying something. It was the loud kind of quiet that reminded him of being home on his ranch in Nashville.

He wondered if Kasey had been at Arty's when he showed up. There had been so much going on in his head that he wasn't thinking straight and now he regretted having shown up at the party, not only because of the scene he'd made, but the blow of the whole situation still had him reeling.

How could you have done that, Lou? The people he'd trusted with the most important things in his life—his heart and his music—had both betrayed him.

He took out his phone and deleted the messages from Lou. Old text messages from Kasey still littered the log. He hadn't ever deleted them.

Wonder if she's home yet? The phone showed that it was just after one. Arty's parties usually didn't run long. They were like bottle rockets: big, hot, wild excitement, but fizzled out before anyone got bored.

Flipping through the old texts between him and

Kasey made him grin. He loved how she always ended each note with a smiley face.

He pressed the key to start a message. His thumb hovered over the letters.

It would be a lot easier to know where to start if he knew whether she'd still been at the party or not when he got there. Heck, for all he knew the altercation with Arty was already on the news. He wasn't sure how much folks had heard or seen, but that didn't matter. The press would make up a good story to fill in the blanks. He'd lived through that enough times in the past. Amazing how fast bad news traveled, but then again if that were the case he'd have already heard from Annette.

He double-checked the messages. Nothing from Annette. That was good news. He looked at the Twitter feeds. Only a couple comments there. Maybe it would blow over.

He typed into the keypad. HOPE YOUR NIGHT WAS BETTER THAN MINE. JUST WANTED YOU TO KNOW HOW MUCH I APPRECIATE YOUR FRIENDSHIP. He read it, then deleted the second sentence. *No sense sounding like a complete sap.*

HOPE YOUR NIGHT WAS BETTER THAN MINE. Better. He clicked Send, then lowered his head into his hand against the door jamb.

A chord sounded, alerting him of a reply.

Kasey? He looked at the text. HAD TO BE. I

DIDN'T FIGHT WITH ARTY. WHERE ARE YOU? she'd texted back.

He typed, ADAMS GROVE. YOU?

HOME. YOU OKAY? ARE YOU ON THE BUS?

She knew. Well, he didn't know what she knew, but she'd known it hadn't gone well. NO.

NOT UP TO TALKING TO THE GUYS.

His phone rang.

"Why are we texting like teenagers?" she asked.

That is kind of stupid. "I don't know. I guess I started it. I thought you might be asleep."

"I'm not. I was worried. What happened?"

"It's a long story."

"If you're not up to talking to the guys, you can stay in my guest room. I won't even ask any questions. Jake's with Riley. I'm alone. The buses were dark when I came in. Just pull the car into the house garage. No one will even notice."

"You sure you don't mind?"

"Positive. I'll put the garage door up for you."

"I'll be there in a few minutes." He started the car and drove back to Kasey's house. She was right. The buses were dark, and if anyone noticed, they didn't bother to come out to get an update. He pulled into the garage.

Kasey stood in the doorway between the house and the garage holding a beer. She clicked the garage door remote and the door slowly began to close as Cody walked toward her.

He shook his head and shrugged. She looked

cute with her hair up in a ponytail and wearing sweatpants and an oversize T-shirt with CALL ME, DARLIN' across the front.

"Hey, darlin'," he said, but even he recognized the lack of joy in his own voice.

"Huh?"

He nodded toward her chest.

"Eyes up here, cowboy." She pushed the door wider, then realized he was commenting on the words on her T-shirt. "I guess it's a good sign that you still have your sense of humor."

"Thanks for taking me in," he said as he climbed the steps.

She handed him the beer. "Thought you might need this. You hungry?"

He shook his head.

"I made you a PBJ, no crust."

"You remembered?"

"Of course I remember." *Why do I remember that? I couldn't tell you what kind of sandwich Scott would want, and I spend a lot of time with him.*

He took his hat off and set it down on the counter.

"Do you want to talk? Or just go to bed?"

I'd like to take you to bed and do things to you that would make me forget I'd ever gone to see Lou or found out about the whole sordid past.

Kasey cocked her head. "To sleep."

She'd read his mind. How'd she always seem to do that?

"Come on," she said. "Let's go sit in the living room."

He followed her into the living room and sat on the couch in the dark. He set the beer on the table beside him.

"Need a friendly hug?" She sat next to him not bothering to turn on the light.

"Yeah." He held his arm out. She scooched over next to him under the crook of his arm. He wrapped his other arm around her and held on tight.

"You don't have to say anything unless you want to," she whispered.

He laid his cheek on top of her head. They sat in the dark. It was quiet except for the soft echo from the buses' generators outside.

Cody squeezed her tight for a moment. "You were there. How much did you hear?"

"I heard the fight in Arty's office."

"What happened after I left?"

"Arty played it off as a misunderstanding. He said y'all were cool, and encouraged everyone to forget about it."

"Humph. We're far from cool."

"I left right after you did, and there were a lot of people waiting to get their cars from the valet."

"What a disaster." He rubbed his eyes, then pushed his hand through his hair. "All in one day

I went from trying to give an old relationship a second chance, to thinking I had a daughter, to finding out that I don't have a child but my sleazeball agent and the girl who broke my heart do. Un-freakin'-believable."

She laid her hand on his arm.

"I never knew. Never suspected a thing."

Kasey pulled her feet up on the couch. Cody hooked his arm under her knee and tugged her close. "I can barely get my head around this. I went over to Arty's place mad as fire. I thought he'd kept my daughter a secret from me all these years. You can't believe the emotions that were bouncing around. I was proud to be a father. Hurt I hadn't been there. Worried that I hadn't been there for my child. Embarrassed that I somehow didn't know. Mad that Arty had kept it from me."

He reached over and took a sip of the beer. "Thinking I was a father. Thinking I'd missed out on one of the biggest gifts in life. Those feelings were swirling faster than the tires on that T-bird."

He sat quiet. She was a good listener. She hadn't even said a word. Was she as shocked as he was? Did she think he was a fool? No. Her touch told him otherwise.

❖ Chapter Twelve ❖

Kasey knew about betrayal in the worst kind of way, and she wouldn't wish that feeling on anyone. The best she could do right now was listen. So she did.

Finally, Cody shook his head and looked into her eyes. "How can this be how it's supposed to be?" He looked away and took another sip of his beer.

"I've lived for all these years believing that I was the reason Lou dumped me. That I hadn't handled things right. That I'd done a disservice to her by not staying home and getting a regular job. That I followed my dreams at the price of leaving her behind. I've been so wary of trusting a relationship ever since then. And now. Now, I find out it's all a lie?"

"I'm sorry she hurt you."

"Again. She hurt me again, but Arty did too."

She shifted closer.

"I was clueless. Even now, knowing the whole story, I don't see how it happened."

"Sometimes there aren't logical explanations, Cody. You could rack your brain trying to figure it all out and it still won't make you feel any better."

"I used to want a family. It was either-or back then, and I chose the music. Felt guilty for it too.

Maybe I could've had both. If not then, why not now? I don't have to work so much—maybe if I had a family I wouldn't."

She sucked in a deep breath. It always sounded easier than it was. "Or you might. You love your music. You come alive on stage. You'd have to make some compromises. Raising a child isn't easy, and it sure as heck isn't a part-time gig."

"I used to think music was enough; anything else was a bonus. I was wrong. I want more." He nodded. "I do. I want more."

"You can have more." Even in the dim room he connected with her gaze. "You're Cody Tuggle. You can have anything and anyone you want."

He laughed and shook his head. "That's not true. That's what people would like to believe, but it's all smoke and mirrors. Besides, love isn't like that. It doesn't matter who you are or how much money you make, it has to be from the heart."

"You've really been thinking about this."

"Yeah, I have." He took her hand in his and held it in his lap. "You've had that real love. You know."

She placed her hand on his heart. "I do know real love. Cody, I know you're hurt, but for all of that to have happened, it couldn't have been the real deal. You'll have your one true love. It'll happen for you."

"Man, I hope so." He reached his hand to her

cheek. She didn't pull back, and his breath quickened. He leaned forward and placed his mouth gently over hers.

Whoa. That's just his emotions in overdrive. Don't get sucked in. She placed her hands on his chest and slid away. "You've had a tough night." She grabbed his beer can and headed to the kitchen.

Kasey dropped the beer can in the trash and stood in the dark kitchen.

Until that very moment she hadn't admitted to herself that she'd felt a real attraction to Cody . . . but that kiss. Sure, Cody Tuggle was hot. Women all over the world swooned at the sight of him, but that kiss hadn't just created a spark. That was an all-out sound-the-alarm blaze.

She inhaled slowly through her nose to try to steady her breathing. Part of her wanted to move right into something she hadn't even fathomed since Nick was gone, and the other wanted to be Cody's supportive friend. *You can't be both, Kasey.*

She was dying to know every single detail of what went on tonight, but she'd promised not to ask questions. Determined to be a good listener, she'd kept her questions to herself, but whatever happened at Lou's house had sent Cody into a tailspin.

None of the pieces seemed to fit completely, but it didn't surprise her that Arty would have done something skeevy like sleep with Cody's girlfriend. He seemed that type.

She didn't bother offering him another beer. Thank goodness she hadn't had one, else she may not have been able to keep her wits about her in this situation. She went back out to the living room. He still sat there on the couch.

"Thanks for letting me just talk tonight." He sounded exhausted.

"I'm glad I can be here for you."

"You don't owe me anything, Kasey."

I didn't mean it to sound the way it came out. "I know. I want to be here for you. Why don't we call it a night? Sometimes things look better after a good night's sleep." Her heart ached for him over what he was dealing with tonight. "The guest room is made up. Make yourself at home."

He got up and started walking down the hall, then stopped and turned. "Hey, Kasey?"

"What?" *Please ask me if you can sleep in my bed.*

"I love how you end all your text messages and e-mails with those smiley faces. Just wanted you to know that."

She watched him walk down the hall into the guest room and close the door. Where did that come from? Being the smiley in Cody Tuggle's day wasn't a half-bad compliment. Now if she could sleep knowing he was just down the hall. That would be a miracle.

• • •

The next morning she woke to the smell of bacon. She rolled over and stretched. That had never happened in this house before. She got out of bed, brushed her teeth, and ran a brush through her hair. Her stomach growled as she walked into the kitchen.

"Was that your stomach?" Cody stood in her kitchen, in blue jeans and no shirt, cooking. *This has got to be a lot of women's fantasy. Lord, help me.*

She stepped next to him. "It was. What are you doing?"

Cody held the spatula up in the air. "Making you breakfast."

"With what? I know that I didn't have bacon or eggs in my refrigerator."

"Ahh. But I did." He slid the small frying pan from the burner and moved crispy pieces of fried bacon from the pan to a paper towel one by one. "The luxury of living on a custom coach for so many months. I raided my refrigerator when I realized my only choice was going to be fruit ring cereal."

"You got something against cereal?"

"No. You got something against bacon and eggs?"

"Only the part where you have to cook them." She walked over to the refrigerator and got the apple juice out and poured two glasses. "I forgot you were a good cook."

"And I thought I'd impressed you when we were on the road together."

"You did!"

"Out of sight, out of mind."

"You're kind of hard to forget." She snagged a piece of bacon from the paper towel on the counter and then sat down at the table as he finished cooking. "This bacon is perfect. Every time I've tried to cook bacon I fill the house with smoke and it tastes like rubber fishing worms."

"It can't be that bad."

"Trust me. It's bad. I've had to come to terms with it. Cooking is just one of those things that I'm never going to master."

"I could teach you," he said.

"I'm a lost cause. Maybe you can lend me one of your people to cook."

He looked at her, nonplussed. "I look like the I-got-people type? Really? Damn, that's disappointing."

"I didn't mean it like that. It's no secret you're famous, so I just figured." She bit down on her lip and felt the color flood her cheeks. "I'm sorry. But, I mean, you have a plane. Having people just seemed like a sure thing."

"It just so happens I do a lot of my own cooking when I'm at home, unless I'm having a party or something, but you're right. I have people. Someone has to hang around the house while I'm on the road since that's about half the year."

"I guess that would be true."

"They take care of my dogs, make sure things get taken care of. Houses don't do well empty."

"A German shepherd, right? Named after the guitar."

"Yeah. Gibson. I have a border collie named Rose too."

"What's your house like?" She regretted it as soon as she asked. It sounded so trite.

"I don't know. Like me, I guess. Lots going on in it. Hard to explain. I'll show you sometime."

"I'd like that." He probably wanted some things private. All she knew was that he lived somewhere near Nashville.

"Want a cooking lesson?"

"Right now?"

"Sure. Do you know how to make an omelet?"

"You've got to be kidding. I can barely make scrambled eggs."

"Easy." He put a small Teflon pan on the stove. "For a girl who doesn't know how to cook you have some of the best pans on the market. I was shocked when I started looking for pans."

"Nick bought those. He did most of the cooking."

"I happen to be an expert omelet maker. What's your favorite kind?"

"Ham and cheese, and it just so happens I do have both of those things in the refrigerator."

"Great. Fetch them up. The milk too."

She gathered the items from the refrigerator and set them on the counter.

"This'll be so neat if I can do it. I felt like such a loser on Jake's first day of school. I wanted to cook him breakfast, but I knew I'd make a disaster of it and stress him out." She swept her hair behind her ear. "The other mothers would probably die if they knew I feed my child fruit ring cereal every morning."

"Don't feel like a loser. Your mom wasn't around. Mine was. I used to love spending time in the kitchen with her. Still do."

"You're close with your mom?"

"Very. You'd love her."

If she raised a sweet man like you she has to be great. "I'm sure I would."

Cody made the first omelet, ending it with a flip in the air before he slid it off onto the plate in a perfect half circle.

She clapped. "You *are* an expert."

"Let's do yours together."

"Okay."

He led her through it step-by-step and it was turning out fluffy and perfect. "I'll be in good shape as long as you want to spend every morning coaching me. Think we could do that via iPhone or Skype?"

"Sure. Here, let me help you flip it." He stepped up behind her and wrapped his arms around her. His bare skin felt warm against her body.

Cody flipped the omelet and they caught it in midair, then Cody took control of the frying pan and slid the omelet onto the plate.

She carried both plates to the kitchen table. “Looks like one of those fancy restaurant dishes.” She took a bite of the eggs. “Tastes even better. Thank you.”

“You’re welcome. I thought it was the least I could do after I kept you up half the night with all my drama.”

“Don’t be silly. It was fine. I mean, it was fine for me. You’re the one who went through all that.”

“I know. I didn’t mean to impose it on you though. I feel like I need to kind of step back and tell you the whole story.”

“You don’t have to,” she said.

“I want to.” Cody started at the beginning with the surprise sherbet freezes.

“That’s so romantic.”

“I think I enjoyed it more than she did.” He explained the whole evening, and the mixed bag of emotions he juggled through the hours.

“No wonder you were so upset.” She shook her head. “I can’t believe they never told you. I’m more surprised no one from the entertainment rags ever picked it up. That’s just the kind of stuff they love.”

“Yeah. They’ll probably snatch it up now. No thanks to me.” He sighed, then gave a resigned shrug. “It was stupid of me to face off with Arty. I was so upset about everything that I'd completely forgotten about the party, but I should have turned around when I got there and realized what was going on."

"Well, on the bright side . . ."

"There's a bright side?"

"Sure. There's always a bright side. You don't have to wonder if you and Lou were meant to be. I think that's kind of an expired offer now."

"Yeah. I kind of had a feeling it wasn't going anywhere. I guess now I know why." He pushed his plate to the center of the table and leaned forward. "Tell me about your relationship with the sheriff."

"He's a good man, and he's been a true friend. But I don't have those feelings." She almost said she didn't think she'd ever have those kinds of emotions again, but the truth was she'd had more feelings with Cody today than she'd had in a long time. Saying she'd never be in love might just be a flat-out lie. Of course, it couldn't be with Cody. He was a star. She was just—what the heck was she anymore? A widow. A mom. A woman with her career in limbo. Not a prize these days.

"So it's not serious?"

"He'd like it to be, but, no. I can't."

"And he knows that?"

"He knows." And now, she knew more than ever that if she did ever have a relationship, it wouldn't be with Scott.

It was somehow freeing, almost a little thrilling, the way Cody had made her feel the last couple of days. Maybe she really would share her life with someone again. But if she opened herself up to Cody, could she ever be enough for someone like him?

❖ Chapter Thirteen ❖

At noon, Riley and Von showed up with Jake for the birthday get-together. Kasey hoped Riley had made her famous red velvet cake, with the creamiest frosting this side of the Mississippi. It'd always been her favorite, but you never knew with Riley. She could get a wild hair and try out something new on you at the oddest times. She didn't have the commitment to tradition that most people did. One year she'd surprised them all with shrimp and grits for Thanksgiving dinner. Nick had almost come unglued. In his mind it was law that turkey be served for Thanksgiving, and although the meal was excellent, they'd had to stop at the market on the way home and buy one to satisfy Nick's expectations.

Kasey ran outside to greet them.

"Mom!" Jake ran toward her. "We had so much fun and we went to the old house and Von took me to get ice cream and we stayed up late making your cake and I got to lick the beaters and we made a fort and I beat Uncle Von at basketball too."

"Weren't you just gone like less than twenty-four hours?" she teased Von.

"Hey, we had some fun. What can I say? Other than I'm exhausted. How do you do it?" Von walked past her carrying the gold cake taker that had belonged to Riley's mom. They'd shared many a layer cake thanks to that thing over the years.

Riley tugged Kasey to the side and whispered, "I see the tour buses are still here. Why doesn't cool stuff like this happen when I'm watching the house for you?"

"Maybe you aren't wishing on the right lucky stars." Kasey couldn't help but tease Riley just a little. Riley was always wishing on lucky stars and anything else that she might consider lucky that day, and Kasey could never keep up with the long, changing list.

"Oh, real funny. You mean the stars in the sky versus the stars . . . on the bus?"

"It didn't have anything to do with me or wishing of any kind really. We can both thank that storm for him being here."

"Back up the bus, Missy." Riley grabbed Kasey's arm. "When did you treat yourself to that?" She twisted Kasey's wrist to get a better look at the beautiful bracelet.

"Isn't it adorable?"

"Adorable? No. Amazing and beautiful, yes!"

Kasey spun the charms to the top so Riley could see them. "Look. A camera, of course, and Jake's Bubba Bear, and a music note to represent my time on Cody's tour." *To remember him.*

"Wait a second." A challenging smirk spread across Riley's face. "Did Cody give you this bracelet?"

She glanced up and grinned wide. "A birthday present."

"I can't believe you didn't tell me as soon as he gave it to you. Did you have this yesterday when I picked up Jake?"

She nodded. "I did. At first I thought I shouldn't accept it. I mean, it's expensive, but he'd put so much thought into the charms and all. I couldn't say no. Besides, I love it."

"I guess you do. I love that guy."

"You barely know him."

"I plan to get to know him a lot better now that he's hanging around you so much." Riley leaned in and looked at the charms again. "The little bear is my favorite."

"Chocolate diamonds." Kasey smiled. "Like my eyes, he said."

"Holy shit. Did he really say that?"

Kasey nodded.

"Hey, Von. What color are my eyes?"

"Green, why?" He walked over and put his arm around Riley.

"What color are Kasey's, and don't look."

"Blue," Von said, but it came out more like a guess.

"They're brown." She looked at Kasey. "That's my point. Von was the best man in your wedding and has known you for how many years?"

Von shrugged. "Ten, twelve?"

Riley lifted a brow. "He doesn't know your eyes are the color of chocolate diamonds, but Cody Tuggle does?"

"So, maybe Cody is an eye guy. Quit reading more into it. Right, Von?"

Von stepped back. "Don't bring me into the middle of this. I'm heading out back to start the grill if that's okay with you two. How many? Are Scott and his mom coming?"

Kasey shook her head. "No. Scott had to work today, so they can't make it, and Cody's guys all went to town, so it'll just be us and Cody."

"Got it. That makes it easy. Doesn't even matter if I burn your food."

"Not funny. It's my birthday. You're supposed to be nice to me."

Riley gave him a peck on the cheek. "Go play with fire, caveman." Then she turned back to Kasey and said, "So how long are they going to be here?"

"They're leaving tomorrow for Texas to shoot a commercial."

"That's a long ride."

"It's not so bad in those big luxury buses."

"Do you think he'd show us around?" Riley asked.

"I'm sure he'd be happy to. Besides, he promised Jake he could sit in the driver's seat today."

"What if you end up in a torrid love affair and go on the road with him? And I don't mean as his photographer either." Riley pursed her lips.

"That's not going to happen."

"How do you know?"

"Because I know. He's on the road all the time. He's famous. He's rich. He's out of my league."

"He is *not* out of your league. You're amazing."

"And you're biased because you're my best friend."

"I'm not biased." She rolled her eyes. "Fine, I might be a little biased, but I know you deserve someone in your life. Nick's gone."

"You don't have to remind me. I've missed Nick every single one of those days."

Riley hugged her. "I know you have, but moving on doesn't take away from what y'all had. You're too young to be an old maid."

"Thank you. I think? Shh. Here he comes," Kasey said as Cody walked off the bus and headed toward them. *Damn those butterflies.*

Riley leaned in. "No one can get that close to my best friend without me getting to know him very, very well."

She nudged Riley. "Don't you start in on the twenty questions with him."

Kasey knew that look in her best friend's eye. She tweaked Riley's arm. "Promise me," she said under her breath but Riley was already on the move.

"So?" Riley walked toward Cody. "It's great to see you again. How have you been?"

"Doing fine," he said to Riley, but Kasey could tell, even from this distance, that he was putting on a happy face. This stuff with Lou and Arty had him feeling low. No one else might notice, but she could see it.

Kasey walked over, hoping she could keep Riley from saying anything too embarrassing.

Riley looped her arm around his well-muscled bicep. "We were just heading out back to start the grill. Join us?"

Grill? Kasey flashed a warning look at Riley. *Poor Cody had no idea what kind of grilling he was in for with Riley.*

With everyone full on lunch and cake, Jake was the only one with any energy but once he brought his football out, Cody and Von were easy to talk into a game of catch in the yard.

Riley and Kasey cleared the dishes as the guys horsed around outside.

"Did you go look at the building on Main Street?" Riley asked as she put the last plate in the dishwasher.

"I did, but I don't know that I need to have a

building to frame pictures. Maybe I can do that from here. I could even turn the carriage house into a dedicated space for it."

Cody walked in with Von. "Uh-oh," Von said. "It's never good when these two put their heads together. It usually means more work for me."

Riley smirked. "Not this time."

"That's a first," Von said to Cody.

Cody sat at the table. Jake came running in from the yard and jumped right into Cody's lap.

"Oomph," Cody said.

Jake giggled. "Can you take me to see the bus now?"

"You got it," he said.

Riley spun around. "Can I come too?"

"Sure. Come on."

Jake grabbed Cody's hand. "Come on. We can cut through the house."

Cody let Jake drag him through the house and Riley leaned over and whispered to Kasey as she walked by, "Aren't they sweet together?"

"You coming, Kasey?" Cody called out.

"I'll be out in a second." She started the dishwasher, and by the time she walked outside Jake was already sitting in the driver's seat of the bus. He honked the horn and just as she waved, Scott pulled into the driveway in his sheriff's car.

She walked out to meet him. "Hey, Scott. This is a nice surprise. You said you had to work all day."

He glanced over at the bus as he got out of his car. "Where's the other one? Cody leave town?"

"No. The guys drove up to Roanoke Rapids for some supplies."

The door opened on the bus and Jake yelled out to Scott, "Hey, look at me! I'm driving."

Kasey waved enthusiastically. Scott barely gave Jake a nod. It wasn't like Scott to act so uninterested.

Scott turned and looked her square in the eye. "Heard about Tuggle's outburst at that party last night. I didn't know y'all were going together."

His tone smacked of sarcasm. "We weren't. We didn't. It was a surprise to me when he showed up there too."

Scott didn't look convinced. "What happened?"

"They had an argument. It was practically over before anyone realized it was happening."

Scott lifted his chin toward the bus. "Why do those star types think they can get away with that kind of behavior?"

"It wasn't like that, Scott."

"If it was such a little argument, why is it on the news?" Scott looked smug.

"I didn't know it was." *Cody must not either. He'd have mentioned it for sure. His publicist usually called as soon as something like that happened.* "Reporters love a good scandal, and if there's not enough excitement they'll amp it up. It happens all the time."

"I'm not so sure about that."

"Well, I was there, and I'm telling you it wasn't that big of a deal."

"Are they still planning to leave tomorrow?"

Before Kasey could open her mouth and respond, Riley came down the stairs of the bus and joined them. "I swear I could live on that thing," Riley said. "Have you been in there?" she asked Scott. "That's nicer than most people's houses."

"Probably cost a lot more than most people's houses," Scott said.

"How much does one of those things cost?" Riley asked.

"I have no idea," Kasey said. "It has to be a lot."

Cody climbed down from the bus with Jake up on his shoulders, and then grabbed his hands and flipped him down to the driveway.

"Do it again!"

Kasey called Jake over. "Come on, buddy. It's all fun until someone gets hurt."

"Good to see you again." Cody reached out and shook Scott's hand.

"You might not say that in a minute."

Kasey straightened. "Scott?"

The other bus pulled into the driveway.

"Excuse me a sec." Cody walked down the driveway at a fast clip toward the bus.

Scott started to say something then stopped. His jaw tensed.

Kasey wasn't sure what was on Scott's mind, but her heart was picking up its pace in reaction to his mood, and she had a feeling something was about to go terribly wrong.

❖ Chapter Fourteen ❖

The last thing Cody needed was for one of his buses to clip Calvin's cruiser. He jogged over and guided the driver, then waved him off when he was in a good spot to shut it down.

Pete came barreling down off the bus. "Cody. We need to talk."

"What's the matter?"

"It's Arty."

Cody raised his hand. "I'm not taking his calls."

"No. You've got to—"

"Look, you don't know what all is going on. I said I'm not taking his calls. End of discussion." Cody turned to walk away, but Pete grabbed him by the arm.

Cody gave him a have-you-lost-your-mind look.

Pete's jaw set and his eyes widened. "Listen to me. No one is taking Arty's calls."

"Good. Then we don't have a problem." Cody strode off. He was in no mood to talk about Arty Max.

Pete jogged two steps forward to catch up with

Cody. "We don't have a problem," he said. "But *he* does. He's dead."

Cody stopped so quick that his body lurched forward before he turned around with his mouth hanging half-open. "What?"

"It's all over the radio."

Cody raced back over to Pete. "What happened? I just saw him last night."

"Yeah. That's all over the radio too. Sounds like y'all had one hell of a fight."

Scott walked up behind Cody. "I need to talk to you," he said.

Is anyone going to give me any good news anymore? The last thing I need is a smitten cop with a confidence problem on my ass. "I just got some bad news. Can it wait?"

Scott put his hand on his hip just above his gun. "No."

Whatever. "Fine. What ya got?"

"Arty Max—"

Cody cut him off. "Yeah. I just heard he died. I can't believe this. Do you know what happened?"

"Some folks want to talk to you about that," Scott said.

"Me? Okay, sure. He seemed fine when I left. Was it a heart attack?"

"No. It definitely was not a heart attack."

Cody glanced over at Pete, then back to Scott. "What are you saying?"

"I'm saying someone killed him. We've got some questions for you."

Cody jerked his head back. "Wait. What? Killed?"

"Apparently so. Can you come down to the station with me?"

"Yeah. Absolutely. Did it happen at the estate?" *Holy shit. Dead?*

"Let's talk at the station."

Cody fell in step behind Scott. "I can't believe this. That place is a fortress. There are cameras everywhere. No one could sneak in unnoticed. Do they have a suspect?"

Scott's eyes narrowed. "You?"

Cody took a step back. "No. You can't be serious."

Kasey ran up to them. "What's going on? One of the guys just said Arty's dead? We just saw him last night."

Scott motioned Cody toward the car. Kasey jogged alongside to keep up with their long strides.

"You're not going to make me sit in the back seat, are you?" Cody asked.

"No. Just get in."

"What is going on?" Kasey asked.

"Just need to get a few questions answered," Scott said.

Don't be an ass to her. Cody opened the passenger door and propped a foot on the door sill.

He made eye contact with a confused Kasey over the top of the car. "Someone killed Arty. They want to ask me some questions. It's fine."

"What?" Kasey ran to Scott's side. "Why do you want to talk to Cody? I was there too."

"The county police have listed him as a person of interest."

She folded her arms and lowered her voice. "And how did you get involved?"

"I let them know where he was. I had information about the case. That's my responsibility."

Cody sat in the front seat, but he could still hear them.

"What?" Kasey stood still. "Why didn't you come and talk to us first?"

"I'm just doing my job, Kasey."

"It's fine." Cody motioned through the windshield to Kasey. "He's doing his job." Kasey was probably thinking the same thing he was—that Scott was enjoying this tough cop act a little too much. The sooner he got this over with, the better. *He'd love to get me out of the picture, or at least out of his town.*

Kasey walked to the front of the car and pointed at Cody. "I'll follow you over there," she said.

"No. It's your birthday. I'll get back. Go on and have your day."

She didn't look convinced.

"Please," he said. *Don't ruin your day. Hell, by the look on her face it was a little too late for that.*

Cody watched Kasey from the side mirror as they drove off. *What's going through your mind?*

It was awkwardly silent in the car. Cody was thankful that it was just a short ride to town. He wondered if Scott would be the one talking to him. Would that even be legal with his relationship with Kasey, and apparent dislike for him? *But then again, with him being the sheriff I guess he makes the rules.*

Scott parked by the rear entrance of the station and got out. Cody followed alongside into the building and down a long colorless hallway to an equally bland interrogation room.

"Have a seat," Scott said.

Cody sat in the cold metal chair and placed his hands on the table. "What happened?"

"I'm hoping you can help shed a little light on that."

"Arty was very much alive when I left."

"But you argued?"

"Yeah. We argued, but I don't think that's important in the scheme of things now."

"What did you argue about?"

"It was personal."

"Folks are saying you were pretty mad. Might have even thrown around a couple threats."

"Yeah, I did, but Arty and I have been working together for years. It's not like it was the first time we'd ever argued and no matter how mad I was, I sure as hell wasn't going to do anything to him."

Cody sat back in his chair. "Do I need my lawyer?"

Scott mimicked Cody's body language. "Guess that's your choice. Do you have an alibi?"

"Yeah. I do."

"Let's timeline your night. Start me off when you left Arty Max's estate."

"I got there about nine and was out of there by nine twenty. I'm sure the valet will remember. There was a hundred bucks in it for him."

Scott took notes. "I'm sure he'll remember that."

"His name was Jace. I signed his hat."

"Nice of you," Scott said, but the words sounded condescending coming from him.

"I was at a truck stop at around eleven. Not sure what it's called, but I could look at an atlas and figure it out. Actually, I have a placemat in my coat on the bus. I can get you the name." Cody ran down the evening, at least up until the part where he was in the parking lot here in town. He didn't care to tell Scott about being with Kasey. It wasn't any of his damn business and if he had to guess, Scott's reasons for bringing him in were more personal than business.

I have to ask. "Can I ask you how exactly you're involved with all of this? I mean we're a couple of hours away from the mountains."

Scott put his pen down. "I saw the news. Knew you were in my town."

His town?

"Gave them a quick call to see how I could help."

Help them or help me? Help get me out of the way is how it feels. Am I just being paranoid?

Scott picked his pen back up. "So, you're sitting here in Spratt's Market parking lot. Anyone see you?"

"I don't know. Maybe one of your deputies since it's right next door. Are there cameras around here?"

"Nothing over there worth spending the money on to protect with that level of security."

Great. "I went back to Kasey's house from there."

"Anyone besides your band members see you?"

"Kasey."

"At one in the morning?"

"Yeah, I was back at her house by one fifteen or one thirty," Cody said. Scott's tone was starting to irritate him. He probably should've just called his lawyer and let them handle this.

Scott lifted his chin. "She saw you come back and get on the bus?"

"No. She saw me pull into her garage and walk into her house." *That will shut you up for a minute.*

"I see. Until?"

Cody pulled his hands up and bounced his fingertips together. "Until you showed up."

It would have been hard to miss the hitch in the last breath Scott took. "I see." Scott practically choked out the words.

Cody watched Scott's throat redden. *Sorry, man. You asked.* "I was in the guest room." He'd have loved to have left the guy wondering, but that wasn't right.

The hard line of Scott's jaw softened. "Do you know anyone who might've wanted to do harm to Arty Max?"

"You're going to need more paper. He wasn't the most tactful guy around."

"See any of those people there last night?"

"I really was only focused on giving him a piece of my mind. I couldn't even tell you who was there."

"But Kasey was there."

"I knew she was going to be, but I didn't see her."

"Did you leave anything behind?"

Cody nodded. "Not that I know of. I wasn't there that long."

"A bandanna?" Scott asked.

"No. I wear those mostly on stage. Why?"

"There was one in the room."

"I'm sure Arty has a bunch of those things lying around. We order them by the pallet. They're one of our best-selling items."

"That probably won't prove much then. Anything else you can tell me?"

Cody wasn't sure whether he could trust Scott or not, but he knew he hadn't done anything wrong. "Look. I don't know if you're doing all this to help me or not, but I'll tell you straight up. Arty did me wrong. I was mad, but I didn't do anything to him. Once I left that party, I was heading this way. I hope you believe that."

"If I didn't, I'd find something, anything, to lock you up and keep you away from Kasey and Jake, but yeah . . . for now. I believe you. I'll get one of my guys to take you back."

"Can you tell me what happened to him?"

"They're keeping that quiet right now." Scott pushed his pen into his shirt pocket. "I'll tell you what I can when I can."

"Thanks, Scott." Cody reached over and shook his hand.

An hour later, one of Scott's deputies dropped Cody back off at Kasey's house.

Cody went straight to his bus and called Annette. "Hey, girl. I'm surprised you haven't already called me."

"Not my job anymore. Arty fired me yesterday for helping you hook back up with someone from your past."

"What? That was none of his damn business." *Jesus, can I catch a break? Is this guy going to screw up every single part of my life or what?* "I'm sorry he did that. I didn't know about it."

"He was mad and he had the right to fire me since he was paying my fee. So, I'm out of the picture."

"I need you, so you can just consider yourself rehired. Don't worry about payment. You know I'm good for it."

"It's not that, Cody. I have a pretty ironclad contract with Arty and it includes a very clear noncompete clause, and that includes not working in any capacity for any of his acts for two years if we part ways."

"Yeah. Well, he's dead so I don't think that he's going to be giving you any trouble over that now."

Annette's voice went up two octaves. "Dead? You mean like really dead?"

"I can't believe you haven't heard. You always know everything before anyone else. I need you on your A-game, girl. They just hauled me in for questioning."

"Are you a suspect? You can't be. No one would ever think you'd do something like that."

"Hell, I don't know. A person of interest at the least after the way I showed my ass last night. Or haven't you heard about that either?"

"Sorry. I'm a little out of the loop today."

"They asked more questions than gave answers but I learned a few things. I need you, Annette. The press is going wild with this and since Arty and I had a big public blowup last night, I'm looking like a raging lunatic. I'm sure that I'm more than just a person of interest in their minds right now."

"Suspect? He had a heart attack, right? I mean, you know how high-strung he was."

"Yeah. That would have been my first assumption too. But no. Arty was murdered."

"How? When?"

"Last night. Sometime after the party, I guess. They aren't giving any details. At least not to me. I'm hoping some of your contacts with the press can do a little digging that will help us get to the bottom of it and at least get the heat off me. I was probably pissed off enough to beat the hell out of the guy, but I never would have killed him."

"I'm on it, Cody. I don't know how much my contacts can learn about something like this. They're more suited to tracking down gossip. Arty had a lot of enemies. I'm sure they'll move on to someone else quickly."

"He slept with someone else's girlfriend and had a secret child? I doubt it."

"We're talking about Lou?"

"Yeah."

"I'm sorry, Cody."

"Me too. Not as sorry as I would have been before I found out Arty screwed me over. Literally. I'll admit I was mad, wished him dead for sure, but I didn't kill him."

"Where are you?"

"We're all in Adams Grove right now, but we're pulling out to head to Texas in the morning."

"The truck commercial?"

"Yeah, and then I'll be heading back to Hillcrest for a break and to get the final mix done on the record."

"Okay. I'll be in touch."

"Thanks, Annette." When he looked up Kasey was standing there on the bus. "Hey. Sorry, I didn't hear you come in."

"Hope you don't mind." She walked over and gave him a hug. "I couldn't just sit in there waiting."

"Are you kidding me? If I hadn't come here last night, I'd probably be the number one suspect after that scene at Arty's."

"Well, thank goodness you called when you did."

"Thank goodness you saw that text." He shook his head. "I'm not so sure your buddy Scott was too happy I had an alibi, especially when it turned out to be you. I made it clear that I was in the guest room. He looked skeptical."

"Don't worry about it."

"I'm sorry if me being here is putting a strain on your friendship with him. I'd never want to make things hard for you."

"Stop. It's fine. We're adults. And friends. It's all good."

"Did Von and Riley leave?"

"Yeah, they headed home about an hour ago."

"Sorry I screwed up your day. I might need Von's investigative help if this doesn't smooth out pretty quickly."

"I hope you won't need his help." Kasey nodded. "But I know he'll help us."

Cody's phone rang. "It's my booking agent. I've got to catch this."

He turned and paced as he talked on the phone. "We were planning some downtime. We don't have anything else scheduled for the next few weeks, right? . . . Just those? . . . Okay, don't book anything else until you hear back from me . . . No . . . Yeah, I'll keep you posted."

Cody hung up the phone and tossed it on the table as he sat down.

"What's the matter?" Kasey rescued the phone and set it on the counter.

"They put the commercial on hold."

"I'm so sorry. You're welcome to hang here as long as you'd like."

There was nothing he'd like more, but once folks figured out he was here it would be a circus, and he didn't think Scott would be much help keeping things quiet. "I think we're going to go ahead and head home tonight. It's the best place to be until all this gets settled." *Was that a flash of disappointment in her face, or my own wishful thinking?* "The guys need to be with their families. We've been on the road a while, and although Arty could be a jerk, it's a loss for us."

"I'm sure you have a lot of mixed emotions about this."

"You're right. He's been good to me over the years. He got me some breaks that I don't know if I'd have ever gotten on my own. I'm still so mad at him, and her, but with him gone that part doesn't seem important right now." *I really don't want to leave you.* "Why don't you and Jake come out to the ranch?"

"Jake just started school. I can't just pull him out. Maybe I can get a rain check."

"Or come on the weekend. I can send the plane."

"Or I could drive out."

"Nashville is a long drive. Let me know when you can come and we'll work it out."

"We'll see."

"I'll be back down this way for Arty's funeral, I guess. I don't know what or who is even handling all that. Probably his attorney. He didn't have any family, at least not that I knew of." *Now there was Amy. She'd be his only family.* "I'd better go tell the guys about the change in plans."

❖ Chapter Fifteen ❖

In less than an hour the two buses were packed and backing out of her driveway. Kasey watched from the window with Jake and Shutterbug on each side of her. Kasey waved even though they couldn't see the guys.

"Can they see us, Mom?"

"They sure can. The windows are tinted, but they can see us just fine."

Jake waved with a little more enthusiasm, and Kasey could picture Cody sitting by the window like she'd seen him do so often when she'd traveled with them last year.

As the heavy rumble of the diesel engines faded into the distance, the absence of the bus generators felt almost too quiet.

She'd never really given much thought to Cody's life off the road before. On the road, in concert, was really the only way she'd ever known him.

Jake and Shutterbug went into the living room and lay in front of the television watching an animal show. Out of curiosity, Kasey got her laptop and googled to see if there was anything about Cody's house in Nashville. She'd been to the ranch for the Christmas celebration, but never to his house. She'd heard he had a bigger ranch there.

One article mentioned the whopping price tag, and another link showed him riding a horse on his property, but that was about all she could find aside from an aerial view that didn't look to be from a very reliable source. Annette had always done such a diligent job of keeping private things private for him. She shut the laptop down and scooched from the couch to the floor next to Jake, who had sprawled out on his tummy with his chin propped in his hands watching television.

"Love you, buddy."

"I love you too, Mom."

She brushed her fingers through his hair and wished she could quit thinking about Cody's invitation. It's not like that relationship could go anywhere, but her heart didn't seem to be paying attention. *He just left. Do I really miss him already?* She glanced down at Jake and smiled. "You're all I need."

Her cell phone rang and she jumped up to go get it.

Riley didn't even bother with a hello. "Oh, my goodness, Kasey, have you seen it on TV? It's all over the news that Arty Max was killed. They're saying that Arty and Cody had a huge fight and the pictures of Cody don't even look like him. He was smoking mad. I haven't seen you in any of the pictures yet. It's the top gossip on the entertainment shows tonight."

Kasey's stomach swirled in a sickening way.

"I haven't seen it, but I can just imagine," she said. "Cody and the guys just left. The commercial in Texas got put on hold because of all of this."

"I'm not surprised."

"They're heading back to Cody's ranch until it blows over. He did mention he might need Von's help if this doesn't smooth out quickly."

"We were just talking about that. You know Von would be happy to."

"That's what I told him. Besides, he has an alibi. He was here all night."

"Then it shouldn't be a problem, but you never know. Kasey, I know you and Scott are friends, but Von was saying he wasn't sure how Scott got in on the questioning of Cody so quick unless he was the one who made the call to the team in control of the case."

"I had the same thought," Kasey admitted.

"Scott could have just kept his mouth shut until things started sorting themselves out. That would have been a lot easier than giving the press even more ammo with the fact that they've questioned him."

"Cody said Scott told him that when it came across the wire he informed them he knew Cody's whereabouts."

Riley relayed information back and forth to Von while they talked. "The fact that Cody was questioned at all got to the news pretty quick too.

According to Von someone had to be giving that information to the press, because usually the police are kind of tight-lipped when these things happen with celebrities."

"I was hoping Scott would help clear things up. There are at least two other precincts involved with all this mess. It could have been anyone," Kasey said, but even she didn't really believe it.

"If you say so." Riley sounded doubtful.

Kasey sucked in a breath. "Okay, and Scott is a little jealous. Maybe you're right, but I can't even think about that right now."

"I think all Scott has on his mind is getting closer to you. Removing Cody from the equation would do that."

"No, it wouldn't. That's just crazy," Kasey snapped.

"Don't shoot the messenger. I'm just saying I think he believes that."

"He couldn't possibly think railroading Cody on something that isn't even true is going to bring him and me closer," Kasey said. "He'd get way more points if he helped."

"Scott wants more, and in his mind I think he thinks if he's not getting somewhere then some-one else is. We've talked about this."

"There's no spark between us. It's not like with Nick."

"For you, but for him, maybe it's total fire-works."

"I shouldn't have let him become such a big part of our lives. I've known for a long time now that this isn't that kind of relationship."

"The guy was smitten from the word go."

"I know, and Scott's mom is so daggone sweet. It's been so nice to have them in our lives, like the family we really don't have. If I break things off with him it will make it pretty awkward for me to spend so much time with her."

"I'd hate to be you trying to ratchet all that down a notch. I have a feeling he's kind of an all-or-nothing guy."

"I'd be sad to lose his friendship." She heard the horn honk out front. "Shoot. I've got to go, Riley. That's Scott. He just pulled into the driveway."

"What's he doing stopping by so late?"

"It's only eight o'clock. He does this all the time. Give me a call in the morning."

Kasey hung up the phone. "Jake, I'll be right out front." She headed for the front door.

"Okay, Mom."

Scott had already gotten out of his car and halfway to the porch. "I see your squatters have left."

That comment hit Kasey wrong. "They were not squatters. They were invited. By me."

Scott's mouth formed a tight line.

Did you seriously just roll your eyes? She bit the inside of her lip. "What brings you back?"

He hesitated, then visibly swallowed. "Can we sit?"

"Sure." She led him to the front porch.

He sat on the porch swing where there was room enough for two, but she took a seat in the chair next to it.

Scott cleared his throat and leaned forward with his fingers tented, avoiding eye contact with her. "When I was talking to Cody about where he was last night, he said he was with you." He looked up and held her gaze.

He's hurt. She nodded. "Yeah. That's true." *What did he hope she was going to say? That it wasn't true? That Cody lied?* His probing gaze made her nervous.

He sucked in a long breath, and then lifted his chin. "I mean what he said exactly was that he spent the night in your house."

"Right."

"Do you expect me to believe that?" he asked in a strained voice. His eyes narrowed and he watched her like he was looking for a sign that she was lying. She didn't appreciate feeling like she was suddenly the one being questioned.

"What are you getting at, Scott?"

"If you're giving him an alibi, lying to keep him out of trouble, that's a crime."

"I can't believe you just said that to me." Her hands locked into fists.

"Kasey, we've been close for over a year and

I've never spent the night in your house. Not for lack of trying either."

So?

Scott's jaw pulsed. "It's just a little hard for me to swallow . . . if it's true . . . that he slept here last night."

"I am not lying for him," she said, but his face twisted. "And, it's not like you're thinking either. We talked and then he crashed in the guest room. I'd have done the same thing for any friend in his situation."

"I bet," he mumbled. "His bus was in front of the house. He couldn't make it to the driveway?"

She sputtered a laugh. *This is not the way I want things to end between us, Scott.* "I don't have to explain this to you, but I will because we're good friends and I'd really like to keep it that way. Cody went through something traumatic—"

"Like murdering his agent?"

"Not like that at all." She blew out a breath. "Scott, don't do this. Cody needed some time before answering questions about Lou that the guys in the band were certain to have. We all knew that's where he'd been headed and we sure didn't expect to see him back that night." *Why am I bothering to tell you all this? Are you even listening?* "Cody and I talked. Then he slept in the guest room. End of story." *That kiss was in the moment, and it's not relevant. Quit making me feel so damn guilty for it.*

"Really?" Scott's gaze was challenging.

"Yes. Really. He slept in the guest room. I should not have to explain myself to you."

"If he was in your guest room, then technically you don't *know* that he was really in that room all night, do you?"

"You have no right to act like this. It isn't about Arty Max at all. This is about you and me. You're making me so mad that I'd like to tell you that I had hot, wild sex with Cody Tuggle just to get even right now, but that is not what happened."

She wished she could take the hissy fit back. She steadied her breathing, and chose her words carefully. "Yes, Scott. I am quite certain that he was in that room all night long. If he'd opened that window the alarm would have gone off, and if he left any other way, I'd have heard him. If I didn't, surely Shutterbug would have. Why are you turning this into a witch hunt?"

He didn't even flinch.

Jake swung open the door. "Hi, Mr. Scott."

"Jake, we're talking." She tried to calm her voice. "I'll be inside in a minute, okay?"

"Yes, ma'am." Jake shut the door and Kasey swung her focus back on Scott. She spoke slower, trying to control her tone. "Cody was mad. He had an argument with Arty. I left the party after Cody did and Arty was quite alive when I left."

"It feels very convenient."

"It's the truth, and I really don't appreciate your

tone. I was helping a friend, and I'm glad I did. And for the record, since this seems to be on it, I'd invite him into my home again." She could almost see him gasp at her words.

"And yet you make sure I'm out of the house by ten o'clock. If we're putting all the cards on the table, it seems awfully convenient that Jake was with Riley and Von last night. I mean, he's hardly ever out of your sight. Are you sure you didn't plan this evening with Cody all along?"

Don't. You. Dare. "Maybe I don't know you as well as I thought."

Scott stood so fast the swing rebounded against the back of his legs. "Believe me. I'm feeling the same way. All I can say is his timeline better check out, because you might have his back, but I don't. No celebrity will get off scot-free on my watch. Just because he's a rich superstar does not mean he can play by his own rules."

"He's not like that at all, and when did a case in Rappahannock County suddenly become 'your watch' anyway?"

Scott started to move then stopped. "He was here in my town. That makes it my business."

"Well, he's gone now. So you're off the hook."

He looked away. "This is a homicide investigation. I have a responsibility to the people who elected me sheriff in this county. It's not that simple."

Yes it is. "Look, if you're unhappy that I have a

friendship with Cody Tuggle, get over it. He was as much a friend after Nick's death and during our search for Jake as you were and I treasure every single one of those friendships that got me through that nightmare. All of them. You, Cody, everyone involved. Don't turn this into something personal."

He sat back down on the swing like he couldn't hold his weight up any longer. "I love you, Kasey. I've been trying to take this relationship somewhere and you keep dodging me like a rodeo clown. You keep me at an arm's length. Then, this man who can have any woman in the world strolls right in and sleeps over? I'm sorry, but I can't help but wonder. Am I not rich enough, interesting enough? Maybe a small-town guy is just too small-time for you."

You can't possibly believe I'm that shallow. She knew he'd had one relationship that ended because his fiancée didn't want to live in a small town, but this was different. "If you think so little of me, then I think you should probably leave."

He lowered his gaze and stood. His tone became chilly. "I was just asking."

"Don't. I'm not having this conversation right now. There's nowhere positive it can go from here."

"Fine." He got up from the swing.

She stared at the chains swinging back and forth, unable to even stomach looking at him. She sat there trying not to let the emotion overwhelm her until she heard the engine of his car turn over and his car pull out of the driveway. Her hands shook. She took in a couple deep breaths and then went back inside.

Jake was still on the floor playing with Shutterbug, so she went into the kitchen to call Riley.

"Hi, it's me," Kasey said.

"You okay?"

"I don't know." Kasey replayed Scott's visit for Riley in full detail.

"I told you he was up to no good. I just had a feeling, and you know how it is when I get a feeling."

"Yes, I know about you and your intuition."

"I hope he doesn't manipulate the situation to make things worse for Cody. Even if Cody's innocent you know how bad press can get out of control quick."

"I do know. And there's no if. Cody *is* innocent."

"You know Von only trusts a cop as far as he needs him, so he's probably not a fair judge of character, but he said to be careful."

"I tried to be careful about what I said. I mean, there's nothing to hide. Cody was here, so he's innocent."

"Von said you should go ahead and start time-lining everything you did from the morning of the party until now. And have Cody do the exact same thing. You need to account for every minute. Every fact you can think of no matter how small. It'll be much easier to remember it now than it will be later."

"I can do that," Kasey said.

"If you want to help Cody, then we need to get in front of this problem, and you know Von is the guy to do it."

"I appreciate this so much. Cody is a good man. He doesn't deserve all of this on top of the bad news about Lou and Arty."

"If anyone can put the pieces together, Von can. Keep us in the loop."

"I will." Kasey pulled a notepad out of the kitchen junk drawer and sat at the table. At least she was doing something to help. She had one page filled and was starting on the next when she heard Jake's giggle. It carried through the house and warmed her heart, but then she saw the time and realized he was up way past his bedtime.

She walked back into the living room. "Ready for bed, Jake?"

He rolled over and nodded. His eyes were half-closed already.

"Do I have to take a bath before I go to bed? I'm tired."

"We can skip it tonight. Let's brush those teeth though. We don't want any cavities."

"Okay." He ran into the bathroom and by the time she turned down his bed, he was minty fresh and grinning big so she could see how pretty and white his teeth looked.

"Perfect, my little model."

He changed into his pajamas, then knelt by his bed to say his prayers.

Kasey tucked him in. "Sweet dreams," she said as she closed his door halfway shut.

She fixed a cup of tea and took the notepad into the living room. She pulled her feet up on the couch and reviewed what she had so far, inserting details as they occurred to her. She flipped to a clean page and picked up where she'd left off with what Cody had been wearing before he left to go to Raleigh.

❖ Chapter Sixteen ❖

Transcribing the pages of notes into a spreadsheet in chronological order was tedious, but at least it made her feel useful. Kasey was dying to call Cody after the sleepless night. His crew had probably been home a couple hours now. *Just send this to him in an e-mail and let him know I'm here if he needs me. He knows that, but I'd really like to hear his voice right now. Maybe he'll call.*

She proofread the list, and corrected a couple of typos. Cody would just have to fill in his activities along the timeline, and then Von would have a pretty good visual on where the gaps were and what alibis needed to be verified. She saved the file and started an e-mail.

That was easier said than done because it kept turning into a letter instead of a note. She backspaced over more thoughts than remained in the final version.

Short and sweet. That's better.

Not five minutes after she hit Send on the message to Cody, her phone rang.

"I was just thinking of you when I got your e-mail," he said. "You must have been typing all morning."

"No, but it probably would have saved time if I'd typed it in the first place. It was Von's idea. He said it would help. I wrote it on paper last night, but then I figured it would be quicker to e-mail it to you so you could fill in the blanks. Are you home?"

"Yeah, we're back. Thanks for this, and tell Von I said thanks too."

"Have you heard anything about the funeral yet?"

"No. Annette's looking into it, but she said she's not sure if under the circumstances I should even go to Arty's service. I have mixed feelings about it myself. A week ago, I'd have been a pallbearer, and honored to do it. I would have even offered to stand up and share all of the things he'd done for me. Right now, all I can think about is how he deceived me, and this mess he's left me in."

"You're hurt, and you haven't had time to even really process everything, but Arty did a lot of good things too. Does that one thing cancel all of the good?"

"I don't know—maybe. I mean, I don't know if I'll ever forgive Arty, and he sure as hell wasn't a good man, but he was good at what he did."

"You sound tired." She could picture him lying across the couch on the bus with his foot up on the back bolster, but she couldn't even imagine where he'd be or what he'd be doing at home.

"I am tired. I don't think I've been this tired after a world tour."

"You're reliving one of the most painful memories you have. Only now it's with a whole new twist. Everything you thought you knew—"

"Is out the window."

"And really Lou was the one who betrayed you more than Arty."

"Yeah. I didn't even know Arty all that well back then. I'll sleep on it. Maybe things will be clearer after I've had a little more time. I'm sure if Arty planned his own funeral, it'll be one heckuva throwdown. You know how he was. He liked a lot of attention, a lot of pizzazz."

"Don't be surprised if you're in the lineup as some type of entertainment then." She could identify with the feeling of betrayal. "Cody, I'm sorry for your loss."

"Talking to you makes me feel better," he said.

She heard him take in a deep breath, and her heart hurt for what he was dealing with.

Cody cleared his throat. "I don't mind admitting that I'm struggling with this. I really appreciate you being here for me."

It was hard to imagine someone with his bigger-than-life persona having a bad day or struggling with anything. He'd kept her up when she was close to the edge of despair. She wanted to be there for him. "Do you need me to come there?" *I hope I'm doing this for the right reasons.*

"No, that's okay. I know Jake has school, and you're dealing with your own stuff. I'll be okay."

"I know you'll be okay, but that's not what I asked." She waited for a response but he hesitated. Maybe she'd imagined the connection before.

"It would be really nice to have you here. I'd love for you to see Hillcrest. I'm not sure *need* is the right word, but I sure would love to have you here."

"Done. It's a short week, and it's kindergarten. We'll head your way. I'll just call his school from there tomorrow."

"Whoa. Wait a second. I don't want you driving ten hours. I'll send my plane."

"Don't be silly. You sure don't need to be spending a small fortune sending your private jet to pick me up."

"It's just sitting there. And what I spend on gas will save me on worry, plus it will cut that ten-hour drive into a quick hop. Trust me, Jake will appreciate it and then you can even bring Shutterbug along."

"On the plane?"

"Sure. I have kennels I put on the plane for my dogs. I'll have the guys strap one in before they leave Nashville."

"That *would* make things easier." She sure as heck couldn't ask Scott to take care of Shutterbug so she could go see Cody. "Are you sure about all this? You know, having a five-year-old around is not what I'd call relaxing, and you've been on the road. I'm sure you need the downtime. I probably should have thought about that before I offered to begin with!"

"Don't worry. It couldn't be more perfect, and if I need time to myself there are plenty of places here on the ranch for me to seek refuge. Can you be ready this afternoon?"

"Yes, sure."

"Okay, I'll give you a call back shortly with a departure time from Adams Grove."

"Sounds good." She pressed End on the phone, laid it down, and then just stared at it.

She burst into a nervous laugh. *I can't believe I just did that.* She covered her mouth and nose with her hands and breathed in to keep from hyperventilating. *Riley is going to die. I hope Jake's not going to be upset about missing school. Oh Lord, what am I doing?*

Kasey couldn't even wipe the grin off her face. She went into the living room and sat down on the floor next to Jake.

"Hey, Jake. Would you be upset if you didn't go back to school this week?"

"Why?"

"I was thinking we might go visit Cody at his ranch."

"Do I get to go back to school when we come home?"

"Yes."

"Cool!" Then his delight turned to worry. "Will Shutterbug stay with Mr. Scott?"

"No. We're going to take her with us."

His grin told her he was going to be just fine with the decision.

"Why don't you pack up what toys you want to bring and I'm going to call your Aunt Riley and let her know about our trip. We'll be leaving later this afternoon."

Jake jumped to his feet and Shutterbug ran behind him to his room.

She bit down on her lip and dialed Riley's number.

Riley answered the phone with an "Everything all right?"

"Yep. I just got off the phone with Cody."

"He's working on his list?"

"Yeah, and I'll probably help him with it while I'm there."

"While you're . . . what?"

"Jake and I are heading to Nashville. He's sending his plane to pick me up."

"Kasey Phillips. You lucky duck."

"I'm just being a good friend."

"Whatever."

"His PR gal told him that he needs to lay low for a little while and he's not all that good at sitting still. Plus, he still sounds so sad."

"Hey, I think it's great. I can't wait to hear all about it. In detail."

She knew that tone. "Don't get your hopes up for anything like that. I'm not even sure what I'm hoping for yet."

"Says you. Do you need me to come watch Shutterbug?"

"No. Cody said to bring Shutterbug with us."

"You're taking the whole family. This is serious."

"I'm just being a good friend to him like he was for me. I know how he feels about this Arty mess. It's like what I went through when Jake was missing."

"I hadn't even really thought about it, but you're right. Someone you knew for years turns around and does something unspeakable."

"Yeah. It sucks."

"But you like him. I bet you never come back."

"Don't be ridiculous. I could never leave this house behind. I love this place."

"I know you do, but I have this feeling."

"Don't go all crazy with those feelings of yours." *Lord, that's all I need.* "You can reach me on my cell phone if you need me. Would you mind dropping in to see Grem for me sometime this week? I'll call her, but I like someone to lay an eyeball on her. You know how sneaky she can be."

"I have a bunch of those entertainment magazines she likes that I was going to drop by for her. I'll make a point of getting over there this week."

"That would be so helpful. Thank you for that."

"No worries. So, when are you leaving?"

"Not sure. Cody's supposed to call me back with a time. It'll be sometime this afternoon."

"Have you looked this up online? Goodness gracious, his ranch is huge! You better take pictures. I just did a search while we were talking. It's called Hillcrest. That's a pretty name. I wonder if it's on a hill."

"I have no idea. I looked to see if I could find anything online, but I didn't really see much."

"See. You do like him. Why else would you be googling his house? I must be a better searcher than you, because I found some pictures and it's amazing."

"Stop. You're making me nervous. Besides, we know he's successful."

"I know, but there's famous and then there's *famous* and this house is rock-star-legend stuff. Get online. I'll message you the link."

"No. I'm not going to go stalking him. I'll be there soon enough. I'll see it then."

"Kasey, it says right here in this article that it's rare that he ever entertains at Hillcrest. He says it's his safe haven."

"He's not entertaining me. I'm there to comfort him."

"That's even better," Riley said, and there was no mistaking the sexy vibe in her voice.

"You're such a hopeless romantic."

"Say what you want, but seriously, it's kind of special."

She was afraid to even say the words aloud, like saying that she wished for a romance with Cody might make it not happen, or make it so. *What do I want out of this? Am I really just trying to be a friend? Or am I hoping for more?* "We've been through a lot together."

"You can't tell me you don't fantasize about him. Half the women in the world, maybe more, have fantasized about him at least once. I have. I'll admit it."

"Oh, I'd be lying if I said I'd never thought about it, but stop. This is not happening."

"Why not?"

"Because he's a star, and I'm a photographer—"

"Who has quite a following of her own and some pretty awesome awards to prove it."

"That's nowhere near the same playing field as Cody Tuggle."

"You're beautiful. What's not to love about you?"

"I've got baggage. No man is going to sign up for that."

"Don't sell yourself short. You're way more than that and I think he knows it."

"If I outlived another man in my life, it might kill me. If it wasn't for Jake, I'm not sure I'd have made it through this time." *The bad thing is, I can see it with Cody, and it scares the heck out of me.*

"I could see you on his arm at a big Hollywood party, or at the CMA awards. You could be sitting right next to Carrie Underwood or Brad Paisley. Oh, I bet his wife is so sweet. She's adorable."

"Stop it."

"You and Mrs. Paisley could do lunch."

"Stop it, I said."

"Well, if you won't dream, I'll do it for you. I tell you what, I'll let it go, but only for now. If this goes anywhere, I reserve the right to a big fat I-told-you-so."

"Fine," she said. "Oh, that's my other line. It's probably Cody, let me get it. I'll call you and let you know when I know how long I'm staying."

"Love you. Have fun."

She hung up and answered the other line.

Cody sounded excited about the visit. "The pilot is getting the plane ready to head out to Adams Grove. It's only about an hour flight."

"Wow. That's fast."

"Yeah. Told you it was better than driving ten hours. I'm glad you're coming."

"Jake is ecstatic. He didn't want y'all to leave."

"You'll be here in time for dinner. What's Jake like to eat?"

"Don't go to special lengths for us."

"What's he like? Are hot dogs his favorite? I think I heard him say that."

He picked up on so many little details. "Yes. He loves hot dogs."

"Cool. We'll cook out. It'll be great."

He sounded like his old self, and she was getting caught up in his excitement.

❖ Chapter Seventeen ❖

Kasey sat in the lobby of the county airport. Now that she was here and waiting, she couldn't shake her apprehension. Maybe it wasn't the fact that she was getting ready to go to Cody's house that was causing her anxiety. Maybe it was this place. She hadn't been in this building since the night Cody's jet landed with Jake on board. The memory of that night was clear. The lights on the plane as it teetered slightly on the approach. The image of Cody walking down the narrow stairs with Jake on his hip. Jake's face. His sweet, smiling face.

Her heart raced, and her hands shook slightly at the memory. She'd prayed so hard for that moment, and yet when it finally came she'd been afraid to believe it until Jake was in her arms.

She swallowed back the nerves. *Think about the positive side of that night. Her whole life had changed, for the better, once Jake was back home.*

Jake stood at the window fascinated by a colorful wind sock flapping and snapping in the breeze.

Shutterbug lay at Kasey's feet unimpressed. Kasey hoped the yellow Lab wouldn't freak out on the flight. At least she'd be right there in the cabin and not in cargo. Shutterbug was such a laid-back dog she'd probably be fine as long as she had Jake in her sights. Kasey's mind fluttered like that wind sock, hopping from one thing to the next looking for something to worry about.

She flipped her wrist to glance at her watch. She'd gotten ready so quickly that even though she'd stopped in town to get bear claws as a host gift, she'd still arrived here before the plane.

Boing. She dug her phone from the front pocket of her handbag to retrieve the text.

PLANE SHOULD BE THERE ANY TIME NOW.

She texted back. WE'RE HERE AND READY.

COOL. SEE YOU SOON.

OKAY.

"Mom! Mom! It's landing. Look!"

She got up and walked to the window. "I think that's our plane."

"Is it the same plane I rode in last time?"

"It is. Are you okay with that?"

"Yeah. It was fun." His eyes lit up. "Can we go out there?"

Same situation. Two completely different memories for us. It's all in the perspective. "Not yet. The pilot has to come in and file his flight plan and stuff. He'll let us know when he's ready."

Jake knelt and wrapped an arm around Shutterbug's neck as the plane taxied down the runway and came to a stop just a little ways from the small terminal building.

A few minutes later the pilot walked into the building. "You must be Kasey and Jake." He extended his hand. "I'm Captain Rogers and I'll be taking y'all to Nashville." He leaned over and petted Shutterbug on the head. "We've got a special seat for this girl too. She'll have to be belted in for takeoff and landing, but I'll go over all that with you when we get on the plane."

"Thanks. I think we're ready then," Kasey said.

He bent down to talk to Jake. "I brought you some pilot wings since you didn't get any last time we flew together."

"Thank you." Jake looked a little puzzled but when the pilot pinned the wings on his shirt he beamed. "Look, Mom." He puffed out his chest. "Can I drive the airplane too?"

The pilot gave him a wink. “I’ll bring you up to see everything.”

Kasey flashed an apologetic look toward the pilot. “Sorry. He loves anything with a motor.”

The pilot laughed. “I was the very same way, and both my boys were too. Of course they’ve grown up to have their own toys, so this will be fun for me. I’ve just got to take care of a couple things and then we’ll be on our way.”

When the pilot came back he motioned toward them. “Ready?”

“We are.” Jake carried his backpack of toys. She balanced her camera case on top of the rolling bag, and then took Jake’s hand with the other. “Here we go.”

Just a few minutes later they were all climbing the stairs into the airplane. A large crate was rigged to D rings against the front wall. Kasey took the dog’s favorite toy from the overnight bag and put it inside the kennel. Shutterbug went right in and lay down.

“That was easy,” the pilot said.

“Surprised me too.” She buckled Jake into the seat, strapped herself in, then said to Jake, “Once we get in the air you can get up, but we have to stay in our seats until the pilot tells us, okay?”

“Okay.”

She took out her phone and texted Cody. WE’RE GETTING READY TO TAKE OFF.

He texted right back. I'LL BE WAITING FOR YOU. SEE YOU IN AN HOUR.

Sweaty fingerprints dotted her phone. She wiped it on her shirt, and prayed like heck she was doing the right thing for the right reasons.

Midway through the flight the pilot let Jake come up to the cockpit. Jake asked questions rapid-fire, but Captain Rogers seemed to be enjoying it.

Kasey enjoyed being an observer for a change.

"See that over there? That's where we're going to land," Captain Rogers said.

Kasey leaned forward and looked out the window, but it didn't look like Nashville. A pang of panic swept through her. "But that's not BNA. I've flown into that airport enough times to know this isn't it. That looks like a field."

He must have noticed the panic in her voice because he turned and gave her a smile. "It's the landing strip at Hillcrest. It's just outside of Nashville."

"Cody's ranch?"

"Yep. Time to get your seat belt back on, sport. We'll be there in just a few minutes."

"Come on, Jake." He ran back to her and sat in his seat. Kasey buckled him in.

His own airstrip? Just how rich is he?

She looked out the window. There weren't many houses nearby. She wondered how many acres you'd need to even have enough space to land a jet.

She listened to the sound of the engines' transition as they got ready to land.

What do you say to someone when you land in their yard, in their private jet?

I'm in over my head.

The lush green grass swept by in a blur. The plane slowed and the pilot made a landing so perfect they didn't even bobble in their seats.

The plane did a quick half turn then finally came to a stop.

She laid her hand on Jake's lap, becoming more and more nervous.

The engines started powering down.

The pilot came forward. "We're here. You ready?"

Jake unbuckled himself and crawled down to unlatch the crate where Shutterbug had lain quietly the whole flight. "You were so quiet. Were you scared?"

Shutterbug gave him two big licks, wagging her tail as she stepped gingerly out of the kennel.

The pilot pushed open the door and lowered the stairs.

Kasey took the leash and walked toward the door. She went first and led Shutterbug down, then turned and put her arms out for Jake.

Cody stood leaning against an antique cherry-red pickup truck with his legs stretched long and crossed in front of him. She could barely breathe. He'd probably done this a million times. How many times had he flown someone in to stay for a visit?

Emotion swept over her and she wondered if she might cry. But why?

Cody walked up behind her. "Let me get him for you."

"Hey, you." She tried to sound nonchalant as she stepped aside.

"Hey." He opened his arms and Jake jumped from the top step straight into them, laughing.

"Hi, Cody!"

"Hi, yourself." He put Jake down and Jake grabbed Shutterbug's leash and let her lead him around the grass, both of them running off the extra energy pent up during the plane ride.

He turned to Kasey. "Good flight?"

"Perfect and fast." She looked around. There wasn't anything in sight except a hangar and a little outbuilding. "How far are we from your house?"

"We're here. The house is just on the other side of the property. Jump in the truck. I'll get your stuff for you."

"Sure."

He loaded their luggage into the truck, then walked over and shook the pilot's hand. Cody rounded up Shutterbug and coaxed her into the back of the truck with the luggage. He slammed the tailgate and then helped Jake into the front seat between him and Kasey.

She couldn't help it. The first thing that came out of her mouth when Cody walked back up was, "You have a landing strip at your house."

"I do."

Shutterbug stuck her head through the open sliding-glass window.

"I've always liked the rounded fenders of these older-model trucks," Kasey said, then felt stupid for even trying to fill the quiet with small talk.

"Me too." Cody put his hand on her leg and squeezed it. "I'm glad you're here. Relax."

Easy for you to say. That little squeeze sent a zing all the way up to—well, there and to her heart. *Just who the heck do I think I am dropping everything to come stay with Cody Tuggle at his house on a moment's notice?*

Shutterbug stretched through the window and nuzzled Cody's neck. Right at that moment she couldn't help but be a little jealous of Shutterbug's position.

"I see you have that effect on all the girls."

Cody put both hands on top of the steering wheel and shrugged. "That's just a rumor."

"Says you," she said. "I've seen it in action, remember?" As they turned a corner an adorable white house with a long Southern porch came into view. "It's beautiful." Crape myrtles graced both sides of the driveway that led to it. "I love the tree-lined driveway. It feels so cozy."

Cody turned to Kasey. “Oh, that’s not my house.”

“Looks like a house to me.”

“My mom lives there.”

“Your mom?” She wasn’t doing a good job of hiding her surprise.

“Yeah. My mom. Don’t look at me like that. It’s not like I still live at home or in her basement or something weird. She just lives on my property.”

Jake’s face grew serious. “I’m going to live with my mom forever. I’m going to take care of her when she’s real old like a grandma too.”

“You’re a good boy,” Cody said.

With her own parents always at a distance, and Riley’s gone, she just never really thought about how parents played into the day-to-day of the lives of other people her age. She didn’t even have any in-laws to compare since Nick had been raised by his grandparents and they were long gone too. *Cody had said he was close with his mom. It probably shouldn’t surprise me that he’d have a house on his property for her.*

Kasey looked at the grassy pastures. “The horses. They’re beautiful.”

“Yeah. That’s all Mom too. She loves horses, especially racehorses. She’s been around them her whole life. It’s been fun for her to be able to live the life she’d always dreamed, plus when I’m not around, she kind of keeps things going at my house too. Waters the plants and stuff that the staff can’t seem to do right, according to her.”

Cody turned right at a fork in the lane and they drove down a long, wide driveway. "Sorry, no tree-lined driveway. I have to have room for the bus to get down here."

Huge oak trees that had to be hundreds of years old grew strong and straight. A black boarded fence flanked the far side of the extrawide lane—like Arty Max's ranch. She wondered who had theirs first.

Cody turned off into a narrower driveway. This one was fashioned of fancy reddish-colored pavers of some sort, and then his house came into full view. It stretched for what looked like a whole city block. A separate four-bay garage in the same architecture of light brick and stacked stone sat catty-corner off the far left wing.

Kasey stared at the behemoth of a home. "I love the blue tiled roof. It's got fabulous old-world charm." *How tacky would it be for me to dig out my camera right now?*

"Yeah, but it has pretty fabulous technology. Those tiles have solar panels in them."

"Get out."

"Seriously." Then he pulled up closer to a beautiful entryway.

"Wow. Cody?" She couldn't even finish the thought. The huge arched doors rose like a sculpture in the center of the stacked rock facade. A heavy wrought-iron lamp hung like something from long ago.

Jake sucked in a loud breath. “It’s a castle!”

Cody laughed. “It’s not a castle. It’s my house.”

With his brows pulled tight Jake asked, “Could we fit your airplane in that house?”

“Ya know, if we took down a few walls, it probably would fit. I’d never considered that.” Then he leaned down and whispered to Jake, “But I *have* ridden my motorcycle inside the house.”

“No way! I would be in so much trouble. That s so cool.”

Kasey rolled her eyes. “Oh, great. You know what he’s going to want to do now, don’t you?”

“I’ll hook you up, man.” He reached across Kasey and fist-bumped Jake.

Cody turned off the truck and left the key in the ignition. “Come on, y’all.”

He jogged around to the passenger side of the truck, opened the door, and held his hand out for Kasey.

How sweet. Chivalry ain’t dead after all. She slid out and walked to the bed of the truck. The juxtaposition of the old red pickup sitting in front of this amazing house made her giggle.

Cody lifted her overnighter out of the bed, and Shutterbug stood at the end of the truck bed wagging her tail.

Kasey started to follow Cody then stopped. “Do you want to leave Shutterbug out here? I don’t think she’d go anywhere.”

“Don’t be silly. She’s a house dog. *Mi casa es*

su casa and Shutterbug's too." He dropped the tailgate and Shutterbug jumped to the ground, then Cody led the way to the porch and opened the front door.

"You'll realize soon enough that my dogs actually own this place. Not me."

"I know how that is." Kasey followed Cody inside then stopped midstep. The coffered ceiling and warm wood tones somehow made the foyer feel cozy even though the space was big enough for a party of a couple hundred people easy. "Cody. I don't know what to say."

A woman probably about her age came into view. "Welcome!" she said with a Southern twang. "Hi, Jake. Cody told me all about you and your girl Shutterbug here. I'm Victoria, but everyone calls me Tori."

"Say hello to Tori," he said to Kasey.

A big lump stuck in Kasey's throat.

Jake put his hand out to shake Tori's. "Oh honey, I'm not a hand-shaker, I'm a hugger. Mind giving me a hug?"

I'm a hugger. *Sweet Jesus, what have I walked into? Is she an employee or one of the family?*

Jake reached up and gave Tori a hug and then Tori leaned down and patted Shutterbug on the head.

Shutterbug lifted her paw. "You are just about the prettiest thing." Tori shook her paw, then turned her attention back to Jake. "You hungry?"

"Yes, ma'am."

"Come on. I'll fix you a sandwich. It's going to be a while before dinner and you've got to be hungry. Flyin' always makes me hungry."

"Is it okay, Mom?"

"Sure, honey, go on. Thank you, Tori."

"My pleasure. Come on, Shutterbug. You come with us."

Kasey stood there next to Cody as Shutterbug's nails clicked off a tempo until they disappeared around a corner at the end of the hall.

Cody smiled. "I'm so glad you're here. Let me show you around."

Kasey stood there taking in the grand surroundings, almost unable to move. *How many others had passed through this hallway?*

"Come on." He took her by the hand.

She relaxed a little as they worked their way through the downstairs. It was huge—there was no getting around that—but the rooms were comfortable. Oversize furniture and lots of personal memorabilia made the grand surroundings somehow still feel homey. Just about every extravagance you could imagine was tucked away somewhere in what was more of a country star's indoor playground than a house: an indoor lap pool, a full gym, even one whole section set up with a pool table, foosball, and old-style pinball machines. It was like an arcade the size of her house and the whole back wall of that room was sliding doors that opened out to the big pool.

"And I was worried about you being able to sit still while you were here laying low."

He smiled sheepishly. "It'll be way better with you here."

"I think you would have found something to do."

"Let me show you upstairs." When they walked back into the foyer he picked up the suitcase and toted it up with them.

When they reached the landing there was a platform probably all of forty feet wide, and a balcony that looked over the property. The sun streamed through the windows and doors.

Kasey was drawn to the balcony. Cody followed along.

"The view is beautiful from here. What's that?" She pointed to an apparatus at the far right of the balcony.

"Oh that?" Cody's face developed a slight tinge of pink. "It's a zip line."

"A zip line?"

He gave her a crisp nod. "Yep. It goes all the way down to the pool."

"Now I've heard it all. I bet you've had some wild parties here."

"I'm not going to lie to you. Rock stars aren't the only ones who know how to have a good time, but it's all in good fun. My days are a bit tamer now than they used to be."

A bit *tamer? Good Lord, just how wild were things around here?* "I sure hope so, because I don't think you're going to get me on that thing."

"You've never zip-lined?"

"No." Kasey leaned over the railing and took in just how far the drop was. "And I think I'm okay with that."

"Don't knock it until you've tried it." He laughed and said, "Come on. Let me show you Jake's room."

She followed him to the far end of the hall, pausing as he slid her suitcase into what she assumed would be her room.

The bright green and yellow when he opened the next door was almost a shock to the eyes, but Cody was right. Jake was going to be in heaven.

"He's never going to want to leave," she said. "Where did you find that bed? It's got to be one of a kind."

"My dad was a farmer. He made that bed for me."

"Are those tractor tires for the headboard and footboard?"

"Yep. My dad was pretty creative. And obviously a huge John Deere fan."

"Obviously."

"My dad made that dresser too. He was handy. No way could I ever get rid of the things he'd made, so my Mom kind of helped me re-create a room here with some of my old stuff. I guess it probably sounds kind of corny, but I like having a bit of my childhood around. It'll be cool to see it through Jake's eyes."

"How old were you when your dad died?"

"Ten, but we made a lifetime of memories while he was alive. I'll never forget him. For a long time I kept this stuff thinking I'd have a kid of my own—then when I got this place with all these rooms I figured I'd just get it out of storage. That's my old bike. I chipped my tooth as Dad was teaching me to ride that thing. I rode it right into a tree."

"Ouch. I've never noticed a chipped tooth."

"Arty had me get that fixed for my first album cover."

"Ahhh. You do have a nice Hollywood smile."

"Thank you. You make me smile." He paused for just a moment. "The real kind of smile."

She remembered Jake coaching Cody on the real smile technique.

"And this," Cody continued. "This room always makes me smile."

"I hope Jake will never forget Nick."

"He won't." Cody placed his hand over his heart and patted it. "It's in our hearts. Even when the pictures fade a little, the smiles inside don't. To tell you the truth the guy in my head may not look a thing like Dad looked back then, but it's my image. My memory."

She blinked back tears.

He moved in and pulled her into his arms. "Trust me, he'll remember his dad without your help. You don't have to do a thing to make that happen. Those memories Nick made with Jake are imprinted in his mind and in his heart."

He pulled her hand to his lips and kissed her palm.

She felt his warmth all the way to her core, and before she could even swallow, he'd pulled her closer. In his arms her whole body tensed, then relaxed into the allure of his touch. Eager, but tender.

His mouth closed over hers. In no hurry, he pulled in a breath and every ounce of resistance she had fell away with it.

Her heart pounded so hard she wondered if he might even hear it as he cupped her face and his tongue teased her into responding in ways she hadn't prepared herself for.

His lips caught hers again, and then he tipped his forehead to hers. "Don't worry. My promises are good."

She blinked, wishing he hadn't pulled away. Her mouth felt clumsy as she tried to form the words. "Thank you." She scooched away, needing a little distance between him and the feelings heating up. *It's no time to lose control now. Get your wits about you, Kasey.* "You don't know what a relief it is to hear you talk about your dad like that. I worry all the time that he'll forget and if he does, that it would be my fault." *And what's scarier is the way you make me feel. Not only the kisses, but I feel safe with you.*

"Don't worry. It'll work out."

"I guess what we ought to be worrying about is this thing with Arty. Any more details?"

"No, but I suspect we'll hear something soon," he said. "Until we get sucked into that, let's go get Jake and I'll show you around outside and then take you down to the studio."

"You do your studio work here on the property too?"

"Now with everything digital, it's way overkill, but when I bought the place it was already here. We all do our pieces one at a time. The technology is so different now, but it was pretty state-of-the-art stuff when it was originally designed."

"The guys don't stay up here in the house?"

"No, they stay down at the studio. I need my downtime, quiet time. We spend more time together on the road than some couples do in a regular year."

"Are you turning into an old fuddy-duddy?"

"Life on the road is fun, you know that, but it can be hard too. And not just mentally." He rolled his shoulders as if reliving some of that physical pain. "Sometimes I do feel like an old man, like I'd better think about the things I haven't done yet in my life before it's too late. Things that'll make a difference."

"We all want to make a difference in our own way. Sometimes it's the little things that end up making the biggest difference." *Maybe that's the answer to my changing career needs too. Maybe I'm looking at this from the wrong perspective.*

❖ Chapter Eighteen ❖

Cody led Kasey downstairs. Even before they got to the kitchen the mouthwatering smells made her stomach growl.

"It smells good in here," Kasey said.

"Tori is an awesome cook. She's making macaroni and cheese and her famous baked beans. They're my favorite and I figured it would be a good combination with the hot dogs later. Tori makes the best macaroni and cheese ever."

As they walked into the kitchen, Tori flung a dish towel over her shoulder. "Only 'cause your momma taught me all of her secrets."

"Don't tell her, but you've improved that recipe." Cody ducked playfully behind Tori like he was making sure his momma wasn't in shouting distance.

Tori's mouth dropped wide. "Oh, I wouldn't dare tell her that."

"I'm good at secrets too," Jake said.

"We're going to take a little ride down to

the studio," Cody said. "Tori, will you take Shutterbug down and let her visit with Gibson and Rose?"

"Your dogs?" Kasey asked.

"Yeah. They're well socialized with other dogs. They'll be pooped out before it's time to go to bed."

"Perfect." Kasey turned to Tori. "Shutterbug knows all her commands, so don't let her play dumb on you."

"No worries. She and I have already become BFFs."

Tori called Shutterbug and walked out the back door. Cody, Jake, and Kasey went out the front. But instead of taking the red truck, Cody pushed a button on a panel and door number two of the garage slid up to reveal a John Deere Gator Utility Vehicle.

"Mom! It's a John Deere truck!"

"I had the same expression on my face the first time I saw it," Cody said.

Kasey shook her head. "Somehow that doesn't surprise me."

Cody turned to Jake. "More like a souped-up golf cart than a truck, but it sure is fun and goes fast too."

She helped Jake into the seat and slid in next to him.

"Ready?"

"Yes!" Jake leaned back in the seat and Kasey

put her arm across him from her side and Cody did the same. Their eyes locked as they realized their arms had landed, one on top of the other, in the unplanned gesture. She felt a swirl of anticipation at his touch.

I must look like a better playmate for her son than for her at this point. All I've done is show her my toys.

He wanted to gun it and he knew Jake would have fun if he did, but caution crept into his mind. He didn't want to scare her off completely by acting like another kid, so he puttered along at a leisurely pace.

"There's a fishing pond down at the bottom of the property. Do you like to fish, Jake?"

"Yes, sir. I know how to put a live worm on my hook too." His face grew serious. "You have to be careful because if you hook your finger you sometimes have to get stitches and a shot. That hurts."

"Voice of experience?" Cody asked.

"Little incident," Kasey said. "Probably won't happen again, though."

"Not on my watch. I promise I'm more responsible than I look."

"I'm not worried."

He sure hoped she meant that.

"We'll stop here before we go down to the pond." Cody got out and they followed behind him. "This is the studio." He opened the door and let them in. A wide soundproof glass window looked into the recording studio from the huge living room.

Jake ran toward the glass and lifted up on tippy-toes to look. “It’s like at the zoo, Mom.”

Kasey laughed. “Yes. I guess it kind of is like that. Only there aren’t animals on the other side of that one.”

“Here you go, buddy.” Cody walked over and lifted him up. “That’s where I make music that goes on the radio.”

“You sing in there?”

“Sure do.”

“And play guitar?” Jake asked.

“Yes. Sometimes piano too.”

“You play piano?” Kasey looked surprised.

“I played piano before I ever played a guitar.”

“I had no idea.”

“I’m full of surprises.”

“Where are the guys?” Kasey poked her head down the hall.

“They’re probably out back on the basketball court. I was hoping they’d be in here laying down some tracks so you could see, but I guess they’re chilling. They need some downtime too. I’ll show you that later.”

They followed Cody back out to the Gator and he drove down a path through a treed area to the pond.

“This is my favorite spot on the property.” Cody

surveyed the terrain. The only thing that would be better would be sharing it with her. "When I need time alone, I come here."

They walked out on the floating dock shaped like a guitar.

"I saw a big one jump." Jake grabbed his mom's hand. "Did you see it, Mom?"

"I didn't, but I heard it splash."

Jake looked up at Cody. "Can we go fishing?"

"Sure, but if we catch him are we going to release him, or cook him up?"

Jake put his hands on his hips. "We're going to fry him up."

"My kind of guy," Cody said. "We'd better head back up so you two have some time to settle in before dinnertime." They got back in the Gator and Cody drove back the same way they'd come. "My mom invited us down to her house for dessert after dinner if you're up to it."

"I'm never too tired for dessert," Jake said.

"He gets that from me," she said. "That sounds nice. I can't wait to meet her."

Cody stopped in the kitchen on the way back. Tori had already left for the day but she had everything ready to go on a wheeled cart for him to take to the outdoor kitchen by the pool. Just as he finished unloading the cart, the guys came cruising up on golf carts.

"Now you show up. I just finished toting everything out."

Pete bailed out of the cart. "We're known for our good timing."

"Right," Cody said. "I think you're known for good times, not timing."

"Yeah, yeah. That's it," Pete said.

Kasey helped Cody put everything out on the table, then took it upon herself to start setting up a little assembly line for everyone to make their plates.

Cody carried the pot with the hot dogs and a handful of long wooden-handled skewers so they could roast the dogs over the fire pit. "I think we make a pretty good team at this."

"Me too," she said.

"Come here, Jake. Let me help you get your hot dog going." Cody helped Jake get a good skew on the dog. "See there?"

"It's like putting a worm on a hook," Jake said. "Except they aren't wiggly."

"Never thought of it that way, my man." Cody looked up at Kasey. "After that thought, I might need extra chili on mine."

"Yeah, me too." Her mouth puckered like she'd just eaten a handful of worms.

After a casual poolside dinner with the whole band, Cody loaded Kasey and Jake up in the truck and they rode down to his mom's house.

The street lights had already come on and even in the shadow of the cab, Kasey looked nervous. He felt a little excited about it himself.

He pulled up in front of his mom's house and jumped out of the truck. "Hope y'all like homemade peach ice cream, because it's one of Mom's specialties."

"I love ice cream," Jake said.

Cody knocked twice as he opened the door and hollered, "We're here." He led them to the kitchen.

"Hi, Mom." He walked over and gave her a hug. "Good to be home." He turned and stepped back. "Mom. This is my dear friend, Kasey Phillips, and her little boy, Jake. Kasey and Jake, this is my mom, Denise."

She tipped her head and smiled wide. "Oh, you two. I feel like I already know you from everything Cody told me about you."

"Thanks for having us. It's really nice to meet you."

"The pleasure is mine. Jake, do you like horses?"

Jake nodded. "Yes, ma'am."

"I've got the best barn full of horses in the state. I'd love for you to come help me while you're here. I mean, if you want to."

"Okay. I can do that. Right, Mom?"

"Sure. It sounds like fun."

"Do you ride, either of you?"

Kasey nodded. "I do, but Jake hasn't really been on a horse in a couple of years now. Not since my husband passed. It would be good for him to get back on again."

"Then it's settled. We'll definitely do that this week. How long are you going to be with us?"

"I'll be heading back before next weekend so Jake doesn't miss too much kindergarten."

His mom smiled. "If we don't do it this time, I promise we will the next time. Who'd like some ice cream?"

"Me," Jake chimed in.

"Ice cream all the way around." Cody walked to the other side of the kitchen and got down bowls from a cupboard. "I'll help you, Mom."

Kasey watched as Cody helped his mother serve up the ice cream. "What can I do to help?"

His mom gave her shoulder a pat as she walked by and reached around Cody. "Not a thing. I hope you enjoy it though. The peaches are fresh from the trees right here in my backyard." Cody's mom snuck a spoonful out of the bowl. "I just love this stuff. It's Cody's favorite too."

He and his mother performed the task of scooping with ease. They barely needed to talk to get the job done. As he scooped ice cream, she set a small bowl of water next to him. Without a word between them, he dunked his scooper into it and tamped the excess water before making the next scoop.

The technique yielded a perfect sphere in a peach color so soft that Kasey wished she had a nightgown that color. *Where did that thought come from? I'm not even the silky nightgown kind of girl.*

Cody looked up and smiled at her like he'd read her mind. It was easy to see now where he got his good looks. His mother was a beautiful woman. *He has her smile and eyes.*

Cody's mom pushed a spoon into the ice cream and handed Jake the first bowl. "Here you go, sweetie."

"Thank you, ma'am," Jake said.

Once everyone was served they went out on the patio and sat under the huge umbrella with twinkle lights by the pool that sparkled with flickers of turquoise and orange from the tile along the side.

"What's that light over there?" Jake asked, pointing down the hill.

"That's my barn," Cody's mom answered.

"Do you have goats?"

"Just one old nanny goat. Mostly we have horses."

"My dad was a goat farmer, but I like horses too."

Cody took another bite of his ice cream. "When you finish I'll take you down there if you want."

"I'm almost done." Jake seemed to speed up in anticipation of the field trip.

"Don't eat it too fast," Cody warned. "You'll get a brain freeze. Those hurt."

Jake nodded. "I did that once."

"Me too."

Cody's mom put her spoon down. "Cody, I almost forgot to tell you." She leaned toward Kasey. "I swear I'd forget my way home if my car didn't know the way." She waved a hand in the air. "Anyway, I was down at the pharmacy and I ran into Julie Murphy. Of course, she'd heard all about that mess with Arty Max, and she said that they probably broke some laws talking to you like they did without your lawyer. That'll probably ruin any case they may try to build against you. Of course, I told her you were innocent so it didn't matter. Besides, as much as you pay those lawyers of yours they probably know to check all that stuff."

Kasey felt awkward listening to her talk like this community of people thought money could fix anything. Maybe it could, but that wasn't comforting. It was kind of a rude awakening, too, not to mention a cruel reminder of the awful circumstances that had brought her here to support Cody. Someone had died, after all. Even Arty Max didn't deserve to die at the hand of another.

Cody looked embarrassed by his mother's comments. "The police will figure out what happened, then we can all move on."

"Well, I just hope it's soon."

Cody's mom turned her attention to Kasey. "I'll be going into town tomorrow afternoon, so take a look around the kitchen in the morning and see if there's anything y'all'd like and I'll pick it up for you."

"Oh, I'm sure whatever Cody has is fine. We're pretty flexible."

"Don't be all polite. You'll have more fun if you just go ahead and act like you belong."

Cody licked the last of his ice cream from the spoon. "I guess maybe I ought to have mentioned that Momma kind of spits out whatever is on her mind without thinking about how it sounds. She's got no filter. She means well, but . . ." He leaned across the table and whispered loud enough for them all to hear him. "It's from limiting her audience to horses."

"Oh you, stop that." Denise smacked him with her napkin. "I'm just trying to make her feel welcome."

"He's doing a pretty good job of that already," Kasey said.

"See." Cody sat straight, and smiled his perfect smile. "You raised me right."

"Good to know it stuck." Cody's mom gave Jake a wink. "What do you think of this guy?"

Jake pointed at Cody. "Him?"

"Yes."

"Is he your little boy? Like I'm Mom's?"

"Yes, he is."

Jake looked as if he was sizing Cody up. "I thought you were a grandma."

Kasey cringed, and mouthed *sorry.*

"Not yet, but someday I hope I will be lucky enough to have a grandson or granddaughter."

"Me and Mom like Cody. He makes Mom smile. I like that."

Kasey wanted to crawl right under the table. It was true, but still.

Cody must have seen the look on her face because he came to the rescue. "Come on, Jake. Let me take you down to the barn."

Jake leaped from his chair and they jogged down the slope.

Kasey felt her heart skip a beat, and then do one more flip when Jake reached up and took Cody's hand and they moved out of sight.

Denise leaned forward and put her hand on Kasey's. "I know all about what happened. Cody kept me in the loop on all of that. You've had quite a time the last year or so, young lady."

"Yes, ma'am, I have, but it's okay. We're doing well."

"I'm so glad to hear that."

"So, Mrs. Tuggle, what—"

The woman laughed a loud, raucous laugh. "There is no Mrs. Tuggle. Just call me Denise. Tuggle is his stage name."

"His? Oh. I never knew. I'm sorry. I just assumed—"

"No worries. Our last name is Hill. I'm Denise Hill."

Now she felt like an idiot. Not only had she

taken a famous singer up on his offer to drop everything and fly on his jet to stay in his mansion on a whim, but she didn't even know his name? "Please tell me his first name is at least Cody."

"Yes. His name is Cody."

Thank God. "How did he come up with the name Cody Tuggle?"

"That's actually a pretty funny story," Denise said. "His full name is Cody Allan Hill. I named him after Cody and Buffalo Bill's Wild West show. I've always had a love for that stuff since I was a little girl. His middle name, Allan, was after my favorite singer, David Allan Coe. Who knew he'd end up even more famous than the guy I named him after?"

"Cody Allan Hill." *Kasey Hill. Stop that.* "So, when did the Cody Tuggle stuff come in?"

"It was early in his career and he'd gotten some pretty good attention but when Arty Max signed him, he thought Cody needed an image. A brand. A lot of the big singers have just used their first and middle names as their stage name, but Arty didn't like the sound of Cody Allan any better than Cody Hill, although *Hill* hasn't seemed to hold ol' Faith Hill back any."

There's that filter-free talk. I'm going to like this lady.

"Arty thought Cody needed something more rugged. So Cody was trying to come up with something and we were brainstorming. We were sitting at my kitchen table, in fact. I remember it clear as day. We'd gone through a bunch of names and he'd scratched out most of them, or Arty had said they weren't country enough. So Cody says to me, 'Mom, I need a real country last name.' And I tried to think of really country names. First I thought Hatfields, McCoys, and then I thought of the character on the soaps that was more redneck than country and threw out the name Tuggle."

"Arty liked it?"

"He loved it. He'd have died if he knew where I came up with it. I didn't tell Cody for years. He knows now, of course."

"What's the scoop?"

"The most country, rough-around-the-edges guy I'd ever seen at that point in my life was Billy Clyde Tuggle from *All My Children*. He was this no-good hick of a man who had a way of making pond scum look pleasant. A true villain. Somehow that name, Tuggle, had the right ring to it. People sure don't forget it."

"That's a funny story. I love it."

"I bet no one else even knows that story. I've never told anyone else . . . until now."

"Thanks for sharing it with me. I'll keep it to myself." She liked the instant connection she felt with Denise. She was good people. "So Hillcrest, the name of the estate, it's a play on the family name."

"Yes. Cody said he felt like when he bought this place it proved he'd reached heights he'd never even dreamed of. Hill. Crest."

The pride showed in his mother's face. "My boy has had his troubles, but he's paid his dues. I'm proud of him."

"I have to ask: How do you handle all the gossip? As a mother, if people spread those kinds of stories about my son I would come unglued."

"It was harder in the beginning. I used to get madder than an old wet hen. Mostly because I knew it bothered him too, but you know, at the end of the day both of us had to learn that it doesn't matter what people think. Besides, me getting all bent out of shape wasn't hurting anyone but me. I swear I was driving myself crazy trying to buy up all the local copies just to keep my friends from reading them, and that didn't work, by the way."

Kasey could picture Denise running from store to store in a trench coat with a scarf over her head carrying stacks of the rags, and burning them in a barrel out back.

"The people who matter know the truth. Like you. You knew what was true and not true pretty quickly, didn't you?"

"Well, yeah. I did. By the second day of the photo shoot I had a pretty good feel for who Cody Tuggle was, and it wasn't the promiscuous, wild-party guy they'd portrayed."

"Don't put a halo on the boy's head. He's had his moments, trust me. I'm sure he's not proud of all of them, but he's been in the spotlight for a long time. I've gotten used to it, and he's learned to manage it pretty well too. Anything that's important I'll hear from Cody directly."

She nodded. "I guess it comes with the territory."

"A price to pay for fame. It's not enough he gives his whole life to music and his fans, but he has to give up his privacy too. It's not always easy."

"He seems to have adapted well." *I'm not sure I could live in that fish bowl.*

"You might be surprised what concessions you could make. To do what you love, or be with the one you love—it's all the same. I'm a little worried about all this mess with Arty, though. I never did trust that man. I'm not even surprised somebody offed him. I'm sure he was asking for it."

Cody wasn't kidding about no filter. Denise sure hadn't lost any sleep over Arty's murder. Kasey didn't know if Cody had confided in his mother what all had happened with Lou and Arty so she made careful conversation. "I guess it takes all kinds."

Kasey heard the sound of Jake's laughter getting closer. Cody came galloping up the sidewalk with Jake on his back. "We're back."

"We're baaaa-aaaack." Jake's face was red and his laughter a bouncing gulp with each of Cody's bouncing steps.

"Someone has a case of the giggles," Kasey said.

"Put me down," Jake said.

Cody pivoted and lined up with a chair. "Let go."

Jake dropped to the chair. "That was fun. Thanks."

"It was fun for me too. Not a bad workout either."

"Good thing you came back with my son," Kasey said, trying to sound a little miffed. "You are not the man I thought you were."

Cody flashed a look over at his mom. "What?"

"Cody *Allan Hill?*"

"Oh, that," Cody said. "I don't even think about it anymore."

"Yeah, that. I didn't even know your name."

He dropped into the chair next to her. "You can just call me darlin'. Then it won't matter."

"You're supposed to call *me* darlin'," she said.

"I think I will." He stood up. "Darlin', are you two ready to go back up to the house and call it a night?"

"Yes," Jake said.

"I guess that's my cue." Kasey stood up. "Denise, thank you so much for having us. It was a real delight getting to know you. I hope we'll get some more time together while I'm here."

“Count on it. I’d like that a lot. If I’m not here in the house, then I’m down at the barn.” She reached over and held Kasey’s hand. “I really enjoyed getting to know you too.”

Denise gave Cody a wink and a nod, and Kasey wondered what the silent conversation meant between them.

It seemed like the ride back was so short they could’ve walked it, but Jake was already drowsy-eyed. It had been a busy day for her boy.

“Come on, Jake. You need to take a swim in the tub before bed. Run along upstairs. I’ll be there in a minute.”

“Yes, ma’am.” The words slurred out like he was already half-asleep but he didn’t argue.

Cody locked the front door behind them. “I’ll let Shutterbug in and then I’m going to be down here in my office. If you want company, come join me.”

“I might after I tuck this little guy in.”

“I had a fun day. Thanks for being here. For taking my mind off of . . . everything.” He placed his hand on her hip.

“It was a good day.” It was a positive step forward for her. “Jake had a great time too.”

He ran his hand up her arm. “I like having you around.”

Nervous energy flooded her airway. Jake called out for her. “I’ve got to get him in the tub.”

He kissed her lightly on the neck.

She pulled her shoulder against his cheek with a shiver.

"I'll be up for a while."

She glanced up the stairs. "I'd better . . . go." She felt his eyes on her all the way up the stairs. When she turned at the top of the landing he was still watching, and smiling. She waved and then headed for the bathroom. Her sleepy little angel had gotten a second wind when he saw the size of the jetted tub. She got him set and then let him splash and play while she read in the adjoining room.

"I'm pruney," Jake called from the bathroom.

"Hi, Pruney. I'm Mom. May I help you?" Kasey grabbed a giant towel and wrapped Jake up in it as he got out of the tub. "You smell yummy." She kissed his neck until he giggled. "I love you."

"I love you ten and five."

"Good. I like that in a guy." She pulled the plug on the tub and Jake streaked back to his bedroom and put on his pajamas. She'd just finished wiping everything down in the bathroom when Jake came back in the room with Shutterbug at his heels.

"I think I'm more tired than bedtime sleepy tonight." He reached his arms up for a hug.

"I'm pretty pooped out too. It's been a busy day. Come on, I'll tuck you in."

Even with all the lights turned off, the room was easy to navigate. Not only were there night-lights at every receptacle and switch, but there was also a band of glowing LED that ran along the top and bottom of each wall, kind of like theater lighting.

Jake knelt beside the bed and said his prayers and tonight he included Tori, Gibson, Rose, and Cody's mom too.

"You're a good and thoughtful boy," she said as she tucked him in for the night. "I'm going to leave the door open in case you need me."

"I won't. I'm a big boy."

"Alrighty, then. Sleep tight."

She walked out onto the balcony and leaned over the rail. The night sky was filled with stars. Part of her wanted to go down and see what Cody was up to. They'd barely been alone all day, but it had been a good day. The reminder of the tingle that his touch sent up her arm when they were downstairs made her smile. He was probably still awake, but she was afraid to risk ruining the perfect day.

She changed into her pajamas and slipped between the slippery, high-thread-count sheets.

Cody Allan Hill. What else don't I know about you?

❖ Chapter Nineteen ❖

The sun was just beginning to break the skyline when Cody opened his eyes. Alone. Not exactly the way he'd hoped. He swept his hand across the vacant pillow next to him. He'd hoped Kasey would come downstairs last night, and he'd even wondered if she might end up lying next to him right in this bed. *Maybe I was wrong about our connection.* But then Kasey wasn't like the other women he knew. He shouldn't expect she'd fall into his bed so easily. *And that connection . . . it's there. It can't be my imagination. I just need to take this slow. Let it ride the course.*

He imagined what she'd look like sleeping next to him with her hair splayed across the pillow.

Yesterday had been busy and that had been a good way to keep his mind off Lou's betrayal, and Arty's murder.

Hard to believe he's dead.

He rolled over on his back and pushed the covers off. Since he hadn't heard anything from Annette he had to assume she hadn't heard anything new about Arty's death. It hadn't been that long, but each day felt like too much time to let pass. Thank goodness there hadn't been much about his argument with Arty once the press had leaked that he'd been questioned and allowed to come back home. *I have Scott Calvin to thank for that. Even if he didn't start out with the best of intentions, he really did his job.* Cody was thankful for that. Under the same circumstances, he wasn't sure if he'd have been as noble.

Cody got out of bed, slipped into a pair of shorts, and did a few stretches. Normally he'd head straight out for a run, but he kind of hated to miss Kasey when she got up. He walked out on the balcony and glanced toward the other end. The drapes were pulled closed. She was probably still asleep. *Taking it slow . . . something I've never been good at.*

It was a perfect morning for fishing. Jake was sure to reel something in since the pond was stocked with plenty of largemouth bass, and he couldn't wait to see his face when that happened.

He'd meant to talk to Kasey last night about taking Jake out fishing this morning so he could get Jake up early and head out, but since she hadn't come downstairs he'd just have to wait until they woke up.

Restless, he went downstairs. He could already smell the warm scent of fresh coffee as he walked into the kitchen.

I'll take coffee upstairs for Kasey. We can have it on the balcony. That'll be a nice way to start the day.

Tori had left pastries out next to the coffee. Cody grabbed two mugs and the whole pot of coffee. Just as he started to head upstairs, he turned back and looked in the refrigerator to see what he could take up for Jake. There was a small mixer-size can of orange juice. It wouldn't go too well with a pastry, but Jake probably wouldn't even notice. *That'll work.* He tucked the cold can under his naked arm, balanced a couple pastries on top of the mugs, then unloaded all of it on a tray to take upstairs. As he reached the top of the stairs he heard soft sounds coming from Jake's room.

He walked over to the door of the bedroom. Jake sat on the floor with toy trucks and cars, cruising them over ramps made out of pillows and books. Shutterbug lifted her head from her paws.

"Can I come in?" Cody whispered.

"Hi! I think Mom's still sleeping." He held his finger to his lips.

"We'll be quiet then."

" 'Kay."

Shutterbug got up and shoved her cold nose under the leg of Cody's shorts, insisting on attention.

"Here." Cody handed Jake the juice. "Hold this."

He gave Shutterbug a head pat, then set the tray with the mugs and coffee on the dresser.

Cody heard a voice out on the terrace. He moved closer to the door. Kasey was sitting in one of the chairs talking on the phone.

"The house is gorgeous. We've had a lot of fun already, and he's a wonderful host."

He smiled at that, and leaned closer, listening while Jake pushed his car along the carpet highway.

"No, that will never happen. Oh my gosh, he has a housekeeper and people, and a cook who can make anything. No way. I couldn't. I'm like a fish out of water here. You should see this place. It's more than amazing. I'm nowhere near his caliber."

His heart sank. He'd hoped she'd feel at home here, but it seemed instead she was overwhelmed by it. Disappointed, and not sure there was a way to remedy that, he got down on the floor and pushed a car along the carpet next to Jake. *How will I ever fit in anywhere? I'm either not enough, or too much, and frankly I'm getting a little tired of being lonely.*

A moment later the door between the rooms opened and Kasey poked her head in.

"Good morning, Mom."

"You were so quiet I thought you were still sleeping."

"Nope." Cody raised his truck in the air. "We're racing. I brought coffee up. It should still be hot."

"Super." She poured a cup, sat on the edge of the bed, and watched them navigate the carpet and boy-made ramps. "Did you sleep good last night, Jake?"

"Yes, ma'am. I love this bed. Can we live here, Cody?" He shoved a pastry in his mouth and kept touring his cars around.

"You and your momma can stay as long as you like, Jake." Cody made squealing noises and spun his truck and then parked it next to the dictionary.

"What's on the agenda today aside from car racing?" Kasey asked.

"I thought I'd take Jake fishing down at the pond this morning." He looked to Jake.

"Yeah! Just boys?"

"Sure."

Kasey faked a pout.

"You can come if you really want to," Cody said.

"No. No. I'll just stay here with Shutterbug. We girls will find something to do."

"Let's get ready, buddy." Cody winked at Jake. "Those fish are probably ready for breakfast. I'll go down and get things ready while you pick up your cars and get dressed. I'll meet you downstairs," Cody said as he got up.

"Cool!" Jake said, and started sweeping his toys into his backpack.

Kasey's smile broadened in approval. "He's going to love it. Don't worry about me. I'll read, relax, and repeat until you come back."

Normally he'd have told her to ask Tori for anything she needed, but under the circumstances that didn't seem like a great idea. He'd given Tori the rest of the day off. "Make yourself at home. I gave Tori the day off so you're the lady of the house today, and I'll leave a golf cart out front in case you want to tool around the property and take some pictures."

Her jaw went slack, and then she smiled. "Cool."

Yeah, go ahead and think I'm a mind reader. I'll ask for forgiveness later. Cody got up to leave and then stopped in the doorway. "It's Labor Day. We'll have a cookout tonight. Hopefully a fish fry, but if we don't catch anything . . . hamburgers. Sound good?"

"I'm catching a whopper!" Jake said. "Big enough to feed everyone."

"Too bad he has no confidence," Cody teased Kasey.

"Yeah. Don't know where he gets that from." She tried to look innocent.

He loved her confidence, and if Jake wasn't there he'd be fishing for a whole other something-something right this minute. He pushed away the thought before his shorts gave it away and turned to go downstairs. "Meet you downstairs when you're ready, Jake."

❖ Chapter Twenty ❖

Kasey sat at the edge of the pool with her feet in the water. She'd been crying for over ten minutes and she didn't know how to shake the feeling that was nearly paralyzing her.

Pete rounded the corner with a smile.

She swept at the tears, pasted a smile on her face, and tugged the ball cap down on her head to hide her eyes.

"Nice out here, isn't it?" Pete said, but as he got closer he rushed to her side. "What's the matter?"

"Nothing. I'm sorry. Nothing."

"You're crying. That's not nothing. What's going on? Did Cody do something to upset you?"

"No. Of course not. It's just me." She trusted Cody—at least she thought she did—but the overwhelming fear came out of nowhere sometimes and the anxiety swept away all of her good sense. "I'm sorry you're seeing me like this. I'm just feeling worried about Jake."

"Why? Did something happen? What's wrong?"

"No. He's probably having a blast. He and Cody went off." She rubbed her hands together and balled up her fists. "I know it doesn't make sense, but ever since the kidnapping I've had a hard time letting Jake out of my sight."

"That's understandable."

"I was fine when he left with Cody; then all of a sudden I was sitting out here by myself and I got this avalanche of emotion out of nowhere." She looked up at Pete who was still standing next to her at poolside. "I'm sorry. You must think I'm crazy."

Pete stepped out of his shoes and sat down next to her, dipping his feet into the water too. "We all go a little haywire now and then. Don't worry about it. Cody's really great with kids. That guy has one of the biggest hearts. Jake's in good hands."

"It's not Cody. I think it's just being somewhere I've never been, and the murder, and . . ." Kasey shook her head, and sniffled back the tears. "This is so embarrassing."

"Arty's murder has us all shook up."

Kasey swished her feet in the water. "I wish they knew what happened, and who did it."

"You're safe here. In fact, this is the safest place you could probably be. The entrance is gated, and there's a security guard up there. There are cameras almost everywhere on this property. Major corporations would be lucky to have the system Cody has here."

"They're just fishing down at the pond. I'm being silly. I'll be fine."

"Oh, why didn't you say so?" Pete leaped to his feet and extended his hand to help her up. "Come on. Follow me."

She hesitated, but he took her by the hand and tugged her up.

"Where are we going?"

"You'll see." Pete led Kasey around the outer edge of the house to a smaller separate building with no windows. He put his hand across the pad next to the door and it slid open.

"What is this?" Kasey asked.

"Security. Come on in." Pete walked over to a bank of knobs and buttons that didn't look so much different from the cockpit of the plane. He pressed buttons and slid a lever, then all of a sudden, she could see Cody and Jake fishing from the man-made beach along the pond.

Jake's smile was broad.

She reached for Pete's arm. "Thank you."

He nodded. "Looks like they're having fun. I'm sure they wouldn't mind if you joined them. Want me to give you a lift on the golf cart? I'll take you down there."

"No." She shook her head. "No. I need to start working through this." She looked at Pete. "Don't tell him I freaked out, okay?"

"No worries." He gave her a quick, friendly squeeze. "You going to be okay?"

"Yeah." She looked back at the monitor. "Oh my gosh. Look!" Jake lifted his rod and Cody jumped into action alongside him to help him reel it in.

The tip of the rod arched way over and Jake's eyes got bigger than the bobber as they reeled in the line and the fish took a jump into the air. Jake's face was red and he was panting.

Cody ran to get the net, then jogged back to the water's edge to scoop up the twisting fish.

"It's huge!" Kasey clapped. "I bet Jake is dying!"

Pete pushed a button and the camera zoomed in on them. "Cody's having fun too. The pond is stocked with largemouth bass."

"I think this is Jake's first catch." She watched Cody slide the stringer through the big fish's gill and let it drift in the water, then walk over to the tackle box.

Jake ran to the water's edge and dragged the fish up to the sand. Cody hung the fish from the scale, but the bass didn't seem too happy about it, flapping his tail and splashing water on both of them.

Pete pointed. "Cool. He's taking a picture of it." He let out a hearty laugh. "He's showing him our fishing-picture trick. I bet he's going to have him . . . yep, stretch his arm way out." Pete turned and looked to Kasey. "They look bigger that way."

"Y'all are tricky."

"Man cave stuff."

Kasey's phone chirped. The text simply read, SUPPER. Then the picture came across. She flipped the phone around to show Pete. Every tear she'd shed this morning had been a big waste and she was so glad her little boy had spread his wings a little today.

"Looks like we'll be having a fish fry tonight," Pete said.

"Hope you know how to do that, because I can barely cook a fish stick."

"We're a pretty self-sufficient bunch."

Her phone chirped again. Cody had texted Kasey, YOU READY FOR US TO COME BACK? JAKE WANTS TO TRY TO CATCH ANOTHER. YOUR CALL.

HAVE FUN, she texted back, then showed Pete.

"Cool." He motioned her out of the building and checked the door to be sure it was secure.

"What do you think about all this stuff with Arty?" Kasey asked.

He shrugged. "I don't know. A long time ago Cody had one heck of a temper and I'd have been a little worried, but he's mellowed. He told me what happened. Cody and I go back a long ways. I know the kid thing really hurt him."

"Yeah. I know, and Arty really betrayed him. That was sad."

"Didn't surprise me as much as it did Cody. Arty was sketchy. I don't have the allegiance to Arty that Cody does. Sadder part about the whole thing is I don't think anyone will even miss Arty."

Those words seemed harsh.

Boing. Pete took the phone from his pocket. "It's from Cody. It's the funeral details that Annette forwarded to him." He thumbed through the message then read it aloud. " 'A service at the estate, with a celebration of life to follow.' Sounds like Arty. I need to let the guys know and arrange the plane. You okay here?"

"I'm okay now. Thanks."

"Give me your phone."

She handed it to him and he thumbed in something and handed it back to her. "I put my number in there. You need me, let me know."

She watched him lift the phone to his ear as he walked back to the golf cart and took off down the lane.

Kasey walked back over to the pool and put her tennis shoes back on, then gathered her camera and strolled down the garden path. It was a nice walk and she had no idea where she'd end up until she wound up right in front of the house.

The sound of her phone made her smile. *What did y'all do now?* She pressed the button. "Hey there."

"Kasey. It's Scott."

His voice surprised her. She winced. *I should have checked the caller ID.* She tried to hide her disappointment and be polite, even though she was still not happy about the controlling way he'd been acting. "Hey."

"I'm sorry about how things went the other day."

"Me too." She hadn't meant to be ugly, but he'd pushed her buttons.

"I want to make it up to you," he said.

“That’s not necessary.”

“How’s your grandmother?” he asked.

He wasn’t listening to her. What’s new?

She couldn’t lie to him, but this was going to get awkward fast. “She’s doing fine.” True, only she hadn’t visited, which was what he was thinking.

“What time are you going to be home?”

There it was. No wiggling out of that. “Not sure.”

“Late?”

“Later in the week probably.”

“Jake’s got school.”

I’m his mother. I’m fully aware of that. “We’re not in Virginia Beach, or home.”

“Where are you?” His voice rose at the end of the question and then he continued with a dull “Oh . . .”

“I’m in Nashville,” she said.

“Is that where Cody Tuggle ran off to?”

“He didn’t *run off*. He went home.”

“Yeah, okay.”

“Scott, why do you insist on making everything so ugly when it comes to him? He didn’t do anything. He has a rock-solid alibi.”

“Has he shared any of his problems with the law with you?” His words were short and clipped. “He’s not your type.”

I have a type?

“I take it he sent his private jet for you.”

You knew before you ever called. "Don't do this."

"Well, you could have at least told me you were going to be gone."

"Why, so you could judge me before *and* after?"

"I'm sorry I called," he said.

He'd hung up without even saying good-bye, and it was just as well. "Ridiculous." She stopped and sat on one of the benches along the garden path. "Why'd you have to go and ruin my day?"

She flipped the phone to the pictures Cody had sent. There was another one now. The two of them grinning into the phone's eye. "At least *y'all* are having fun."

The sun was bright and the few clouds that had been in the sky earlier had floated away. But now she felt lonely wandering around the huge estate by herself.

The golf cart was parked right where Cody had told her it would be. She sat down behind the wheel and turned the key to start it although she'd never driven one before. *How hard can it be?* She pressed the accelerator and it lurched forward.

She squealed louder than slick tires on wet asphalt. She glanced around to see if anyone had heard her. Thankfully it seemed she was alone. *Let's try this again.* She held her breath and gave the twitchy gas pedal a more gentle press, and the cart rolled forward.

"That's better."

She motored around the large circular driveway

in front of Cody's house, then tried to remember which way they'd come in when she first got here. A last-minute decision sent her left on the main road. The road curved and the long black-boarded fence that bordered the pastures curved right along with it.

Kasey recognized the horse barn down the hill. Its metal roof glistened in the sun. She turned down the gravel pathway sending dirt up like a rooster tail behind her. She slowed down to minimize the dust. Someone was riding a horse near the barn. Several other horses were turned out too. She parked the cart and walked inside.

Cody's mom was in the barn hosing down a huge black horse that seemed to be used to the routine.

"Good morning," Kasey said as she got closer. "I hope you don't mind me dropping by."

"Not at all. Just giving my boy a rinse-down after his workout. There are always a lot of chores to do on a horse farm."

"Looks like you're both enjoying it."

Kasey patted the big horse on its side. "Animals are a labor of love. That's for sure."

Denise nodded, and the horse seemed to do the same. "He likes you."

"He's pretty."

"I meant Cody."

"Oh." *What do I say to that? He's pretty too?*

Denise swept the water from the horse, then handed Kasey the brush. "Here, can you hold this? He's done. I'm going to turn him back out."

Kasey walked alongside Denise as she led the horse to the gate.

"What's his name?"

"Hillcrest Sparxx."

The horse took off in a gallop, snorting as he ran and tossing his mane. The sun shone on his coat, and the water droplets created the look of glitter as the strong horse pranced and shook them from his body.

"He's a runner, that one," Denise said. "Anyway, what was I saying? Oh yeah. He likes you. Cody rarely brings anyone up here anymore. Women, I mean. He's kind of shied away because of all the games they've played with him over the years. My boy has had his share of heartbreaks."

Bet he's broken a few of his own. Kasey felt a twinge in her gut.

"Oh dear," Denise shook her head. "Don't tell him I said that. I see it in your eyes. I'm scaring you."

"No. It's okay. Of course, it would be scary. And I'm a mom. I haven't even really thought about getting into a relationship since . . . well, you know. Besides, I don't know how anyone could live under the microscope that he does."

Denise leaned against the gate that led out to the pastures. "I don't know. Maybe it is and we've just gotten used to it. All I know is that I pray that one of these days God will reward him with the right partner." She looked to heaven. "I hope I'm around to see it."

"It's what all mothers want. Happiness, health, and a good life for our children."

"Yep. You'll want the same thing for your little Jake. A mother's wish."

Cody had named that song he'd written for her and Jake "A Mother's Love." A bond like no other. "I don't want to hold you up. I was bored. The guys went fishing this morning so I took the cart out for a little spin. When I saw the barn I couldn't resist stopping to say hello."

"I'm glad you stopped. If you're looking for something to do, take the path on down that way. There's a beauty of a waterfall. It's my favorite place to do some good thinking." She turned and pointed back in the direction of the house. "Or if you go back past the house on the main road it'll sweep around to the beach part of the pond. The path is clearly marked. You'll likely find the guys there fishing from the shore if they're not out in the pedal boat."

"Thanks, Denise. I think I'll let the boys be boys and take the waterfall route." She turned to leave.

Denise called out. "Kasey."

"Yes, ma'am?"

"Don't break my boy's heart."

Kasey felt a warm glow flow through her. "I won't. I wouldn't. Ever." She crossed her heart. "I promise you that."

"Good." Denise turned and walked back into the barn, and Kasey walked away wondering how not breaking a heart just landed in her lap. *Were her growing feelings for Cody that transparent?*

She took the path that Denise had recommended. It was only a short ride before the sound of the water got louder. *I must be getting close.* She took her foot off the gas pedal and let the cart slow to a stop at the base of the waterfall. The water dropped from a tall ledge of rocks, crashing against the pool below. The air was cooler here.

Kasey carefully navigated the rocky path out across the water. She took her shoes off and sat down on a huge rock that rose next to the churning stream. She dipped her feet in the icy current, then pulled her knees up to rest her chin on them.

A couple tiny fish darted in and out of the rocks. She wondered how they swam in the choppy water. It had to be like trying to swim in a Jacuzzi. *Kind of like I've felt the last year.* She took her phone from her pocket and took a picture of the waterfall and texted it to Riley.

She leaned back and tipped her chin to the sun until her feet dried and then she put her socks and shoes back on. She hated to leave this peaceful spot, but she figured the guys would be heading back soon. She started the golf cart and turned around in the narrow path to go back to the house. She turned back out onto the main road, feeling good about getting the lay of the land so quickly.

The hum of something behind her startled her, but there was no rearview mirror so she twisted to see what the noise was. Blue lights flashed and a line of three cars zoomed by so fast that she pulled off to the side of the road in a panic.

Sheer black fright swept over her. *Jake!*

She pushed Cody's number in the phone and then pressed her foot full force on the gas, causing a lurch that nearly lifted her out of the seat, but she didn't slow down. The electric cart whined as she pushed it to its limit. At one point she wondered if it would be faster just to get out and run.

"Pick up the phone, Cody!" *Please. Please. Please.*

"Are you missing us, Mommy?"

She let out a gasp. Jake's voice was an instant relief. She took her foot off the gas and gulped air, trying not to scare the bejeebers out of him. "Hey, sweetie. You having fun? Everything okay?"

"Yes. We are having so much fun."

Thank God. "Let me talk to Cody."

" 'Kay." She could hear him yelling to Cody.

"Hey there," he said.

"Thank goodness, y'all are okay." She pressed

her hand to her chest. "Something's wrong. I was just driving, and then—"

"Slow down. What's the matter?"

She turned off the golf cart. "I don't know. I'm on the golf cart. I was just coming back from down near your mom's house and three police cars just zoomed past me with their blue lights on."

"We're fine, so calm down."

"Yeah."

"I'll drop Jake off at the studio with the guys, and meet you there at the house. It'll take me all of three minutes, tops. I don't want Jake to be in the middle of whatever's going on. It could just be the alarms or something, but . . . calm down."

"I'll see you at the house." She tucked the phone between her legs, restarted the golf cart, and headed back to the estate. What a crazy day of hot and cold. A nice wake-up, a minor meltdown, a rescue, a cruddy call with Scott, then a spectacular waterfall, and now this.

What if Cody was right and it was the alarm system? She hadn't even considered there might be alarms as she made herself at home in the huge house this morning. Maybe she'd been the one to set something off.

The feeling in the pit of her stomach told her it wasn't something as simple as that though. *Scott, I sure hope you haven't tossed Cody under the bus again.*

The sharp tone of Scott's words earlier bothered

her. She almost wished she'd lied to him about where she was now.

The Gator was already parked in front of the house when she drove up, but as she cleared the corner she wasn't ready for what was in front of her.

❖ Chapter Twenty-One ❖

Cody looked up and saw Kasey standing there with her mouth open. The look on her face, seeing him being arrested, was worse than the procedure itself. Three policemen surrounded him, while another pulled his arms behind his back and read him his rights.

"For our protection," the cop said. "Sorry, man."

"It's fine. Do what you got to do." Cody shrugged. "I'm not going to resist. I didn't do anything." He didn't want to show that he was worried, but he was. He'd answered all of their questions, been cooperative, so why was he being arrested?

Kasey raced to his side, but one of the officers nearly clotheslined her midway.

"What's going on?" Her voice raised an octave.

A female officer stepped in front of her, and escorted her to the side.

Cody arched back to make eye contact with Kasey. "Call my mom. She'll call the attorney and get Tori back up to help. Call Annette, and then call Von." The glazed look of despair on her face twisted his gut. "Don't be upset. I'll probably be home before you finish calling everyone."

Kasey didn't say a word.

"Pete's got Jake playing at the back of the house. He's fine and can't see us outside." He wanted to reassure her. He wanted to hold her and tell her it would be okay, that it would always be okay.

She nodded.

The officer led Cody to the back of his car and Cody ducked his head to get in.

As they drove by, Cody saw the tears staining her cheeks. She had her arms wrapped around herself, and it killed him to see her that way.

I shouldn't have had her come. It was selfish. He should have waited until it had all blown over. *I sure hope I haven't screwed this up too.*

The cops put him in a holding room. Cody refused to answer any questions until his lawyer showed up. They tried the old "you look guilty if you don't talk to us" crap on him, but one thing his lawyer had beat into his head early on was to never say anything to anyone . . . no matter what and especially no matter how innocent you are. And he'd been downright pissed off when he'd heard that Cody had spoken with Scott in Adams Grove.

Finally, his lawyer showed up and came into

the room. “Hey, man. At least you listened to my advice this time. They said you haven’t spoken to anyone here yet.”

“Sometimes I listen to you.” Cody fidgeted in the seat. “Sorry, I guess I thought it was okay since I hadn’t done anything and the sheriff in Adams Grove is a friend of a friend.”

“That’s behind us now, but this doesn’t look good. They must have found something. You need to tell me everything, then we’ll talk to them.”

“I didn’t do anything. I have an alibi. I don’t know what all this is about. I still don’t even know any of the details of what happened to Arty. I’m hoping you can help me get to the bottom of it.”

“Let’s go through it one more time for my benefit.”

Cody went through the chain of events. It sounded even more stupid every time he had to tell the story.

“It’s motive, and they can charge you with the assault, if for no other reason than just to hold you. Well, let’s see what they’ve got,” his lawyer said. “I’m betting they don’t have anything they can hold you on. I’ll have you out of here shortly. We’ll answer their questions and get on with it.”

Three hours later Cody’s lawyer dropped him off at Hillcrest, but at least he had more information now than he’d started with.

Denise, Kasey, Jake, Pete, and Tori all looked up when he walked into the room.

"I've been so worried," Denise said. "Son, what the heck has gotten into these people? They can't possibly think you had anything to do with Arty's death."

He hugged her. "It's okay, Mom. Can't blame them for trying to get to the truth."

Cody tried to swallow the concern that he felt when he looked at Kasey. Yesterday she'd looked so relaxed and alive. Today she looked like the Kasey going through hell a year ago. Still beautiful, but the pain in her eyes was there again and it just about killed him that he was the reason for it.

"Anything I can do?" Pete asked.

"Be sure the guys know everything's cool and keep the album on schedule. And when y'all go to Arty's funeral, don't talk to anyone about the incident."

"You're not going to the funeral?" Pete asked.

"No. My attorney advised against it."

Pete pushed his long hair over his shoulder. "You got it. I can take care of that. Kasey, I can take Jake back down to the studio to hang out with us for a while. Give you some time if you want."

Kasey put her arm around Jake. "Do you want to go with Pete?"

"We'll shoot some hoops or something. Sound good?" Pete said to Jake.

Jake raced over to Pete, and as they turned to go out the back door Tori yelled after them, "I made fried chicken for dinner. Bring the gang back up around six thirty."

"Wouldn't miss that." Pete pulled the front door closed behind them.

"I'm going to be in the kitchen if y'all need anything," Tori said.

Cody walked over to Kasey and wrapped his arms around her. "I'm so sorry I'm putting you through all of this."

"It's not your fault," she said. "You're the one going through it all. I wish there was more I could do to help."

"I can see the worry on your face. I'm so sorry for that." He interlaced his fingers with hers. "Thanks for hanging with me."

He'd been so afraid she'd be gone when he got back. That thought had been more frightening than being falsely accused for the murder of Arty. If there was one true love for everyone, he knew now more than ever that she was his. He just didn't know how he'd convince her of that.

Kasey sighed. "I hope this whole thing today isn't my fault."

"Your fault? How could it be your fault?"

"Scott called me earlier. I told him I was here. He wasn't happy about it. He may have had something to do with them picking you up again."

He shook his head. "I really don't think so, and

even if he did, it doesn't matter. I'm easy to find, and I don't have anything to hide. They are just putting more pieces of the puzzle together. And they're likely to find a lot more connections to me as they continue the investigation. Arty and I have years of history."

He sat down on the couch next to his mom and guided Kasey next to him by the hand.

Kasey kept hold of his hand. "When I talked to Von, he said he's getting statements and revalidating every single piece of your timeline. I ran into one of my photographer friends at Arty's party so I contacted him while you were gone. He's sending me his pictures just in case there's anything in them that can help or jog a memory. He's e-mailing them to me tonight."

"That's good." Weariness enveloped him. "What an emotional ride. I want to feel bad for Arty, even though part of me is still so mad at him."

"Do they know how he died yet? They're being so evasive on television," Denise said.

Cody nodded. "Someone shot him. They wouldn't say much more than that, or even if it was the cause of death. I guess it's confidential until they get more answers." He took his mom's hand in his other and squeezed both of their hands. "Y'all need to know that it was my gun that they found at the scene," Cody said. "That's why they picked me up."

The color drained from Kasey's face.

"What?" Denise looked concerned. "You didn't take a gun with you that night, did you?"

"No. Hell, no. It's my old Beretta nine millimeter. Mom, you remember it. I used it in that music video. Pretty gun, but I didn't have a use for it. It was really more of a collector's gun. I sold it to Arty a couple years ago. It's still registered to me."

"That's the one with all the engraving on it. The real fancy one?" Denise asked. "I don't think I knew you'd sold that one. I remember Arty salivating over it."

"That's the one," he said.

Kasey pulled her arms across her chest and then ran her hands up and down her arms. "Guns always freak me out a little."

"Don't you worry," Cody said. "I made sure every gun I own is locked up in the gun safe before you and Jake got here. You're safe here."

"No one heard the gunshot?" Denise asked. "Cody, that just doesn't make sense. There are always people hanging around that estate."

"I guess not," Cody said. "They think the time of death was between midnight and one in the morning. Maybe everyone was gone for the night."

Kasey scooched forward on the couch. "That's good news though, right? I mean you were at my house by one and I'm a couple hours from Arty's so there's no way you could have been there during that time."

Cody realized she was reconvincing herself of

his innocence. *Ouch*. "My alibi still stands. My accountant will have a receipt from the gun transaction too. Can't blame them for bringing me in. Between the gun and one of my bandannas being there they wouldn't have had much choice.

"There's more. The safe was open, so they're looking at robbery as a motive, but there were so many valuables around, they don't think that's likely."

"Maybe Arty had it open when someone surprised him." Kasey shrugged. "Or maybe he caught them in the middle of breaking into it and they panicked."

"Possibly, but the kicker is that part of what they found in the safe has to do with me too. Arty *was* skimming money off all of my merchandising. Had been for years, I guess."

"Oh my goodness gracious." Denise shook her head.

"Guess he couldn't get enough," Cody said.

Denise frowned. "Well, I'm glad you're not going to that good-for-nothing's funeral. I'm sure not going either."

"Von and I talked about it earlier. He's going to meet me there. Pete said I can fly down with them." Kasey's phone signaled she had a message. She lifted the phone and flipped through the contents. "Can I use the printer in your office? Andy just sent me his pictures from the party and I have a few that I took too. We may as well see if there is anything we can add to solve this mystery and get it out of our lives." She leapt from the chair.

"Yeah, sure. I'll show you where everything is."

"I'm going to go upstairs and get my laptop. I'll be ready in one sec."

She ran up the stairs, and Denise turned to her son. "Honey, I'm going to go back to the house and get some chores done. Let me know what I can do."

He hugged her. "Thanks, Mom. For always believing in me. I think they're getting closer to figuring things out. At least I hope so. I have that private event scheduled for day after tomorrow. So far they still want me to play. I'm hoping Kasey will come with me."

Denise started to leave and then walked back over to Cody. "She's really special. I had a good chat with her earlier today, before things went nuts around here. I can see why you're so drawn to her. I like her."

"I like her too." He didn't need his mother's approval, but he sure did like the validation. "I just hope this whole mess doesn't ruin our chance for something together."

She left just as Kasey came back downstairs with her camera and laptop in hand.

Cody led Kasey to his office, and turned on his printer. "Anything else you need?"

"No. I think I can handle it from here. I'll print

them all out, but we might even see them better right here on your screen since it's gigantic." She did her best Vanna White impression in front of the twenty-four-inch monitor.

"You think that's big?" He hit a toggle on the desk and a seven-foot screen slowly lifted from the floor to the ceiling, and on it, the computer image projected.

"That'll teach me to be impressed." She shouldered him out of the way to take the chair and start downloading pictures.

"Maybe you can give me another chance to impress you." He stepped behind her and rubbed her shoulders.

"I'm already significantly impressed with you." She leaned her head back against his belly and looked up at him.

He leaned over and kissed her, his hands working their way from her shoulders down her arms.

She wriggled from him, sat up, and put her attention back on the computer screen. "I'm not going to get anything done with you doing that."

"And that's a bad thing?"

"This is important." She reached for the mouse and began clicking and moving stuff around the screen.

"Okay, I can see I'm not going to be much help for a while. I'm going to go down to the studio and I'll see you at dinner."

"Okay. I'll see you in a little bit." She stopped

him before he got out the door. "Can you bring me what you had on the timeline? I told Von I'd send the updated list to him. He's going to give me a call later so we can compare notes."

"Yep. I'll bring them down."

He went upstairs and changed into running clothes and then peeked into his office as he headed back out. Kasey had her hair pushed behind one ear and was leaning in toward her laptop screen working. She was a girl-next-door knockout, and right this minute she looked more beautiful to him than any of the *Playboy* models he'd dated.

He put the list on her desk. "See you shortly."

Kasey watched Cody from the office window as he stretched and then jogged through the garden toward the studio path. She couldn't pull her attention away until he was out of sight. Her stomach cramped. *What will I find in these pictures? Will it even help?*

By the time dinner was ready, she had eight-and-a-half-by-eleven color photos strewn across his desk and a few propped up on the bookshelf behind her. She paper-clipped and shuffled things around like a secretary on speed.

Cody walked in and stopped in the middle of the room. "What is all this?"

"Every single thing I can think of," she said.

"You've been busy. Come eat. This can wait a

little while." He reached for her hand but she just kept right on flipping through papers.

How can he possibly eat? My stomach feels like a volcano erupted in it. We've got to find something. "I just want to get all these marked with the time stamps from the files." She stopped and asked, "Would you mind making sure Jake eats?"

"Mind? I'd be happy to. I got this."

He left and it felt good to be able to ask for help. It sure wasn't something she was used to, but it seemed to just be part of the routine around here—to help one another. *I could get used to that.*

She wasn't even sure how much time had passed when she heard the rustle of multiple footsteps stomping down the hallway. When she looked up Cody, Jake, and Shutterbug were in the doorway.

"Hi, Mom. We brought you dinner," Jake said.

"Thank you."

Jake marched over to the desk and put the plate down in front of her. "I put all the best stuff on there for you all by myself."

Kasey glanced at the selection. All Jake's favorites.

Cody coughed and muttered. "I tried to work in some salad or something healthy, but Jake wanted to handle it."

"It's perfect," she said.

Cody walked over to the desk. "Everything going okay here?"

"I've got everything labeled and I sent copies of it all to Von. He and I talked earlier and went through the timeline again. I gave him the details about the time of death. He's closing any gaps with follow-ups from our list."

"Thanks so much for all of this," he said.

"Don't be silly. It's why I came." *And to spend time with you.* "I had hoped that I'd find something in these pictures that would set everything right again, but then I guess that was high hopes. I mean, there's no bringing back Arty."

"No. There's not," Cody said.

The silence was awkward and even Jake looked a little uncomfortable, his eyes darting between the two of them.

Cody said, "Are you almost done here?"

"Just about. Not too much longer." She looked down at Jake, who had laid his head down on the desk. "You've had a long day, Jake. You ready for bed?"

Jake nodded without argument.

"I'll take you upstairs." Cody stooped down in front of Jake. "Climb on, buddy."

Jake flung himself on Cody's back like one of those guys in a Velcro suit against a wall. Cody lifted him up and wrapped his arms under the hook of Jake's knees. "Say goodnight to your mom."

Cody turned and dipped down so Jake could hug her from there.

"Night, sweetheart. I'll come up and tuck you into bed in just a little while," she said.

"I'm a big boy. Cody can do it."

"Well, if you're such a big boy you can walk," Cody teased, but Jake jumped down and Cody gave her a cocky grin and walked over to the door.

Jake gave her a kiss and then raced over to his side.

Cody waved and said, "We're off." Shutterbug led them out of the room and Kasey felt a peace come over her as she watched her little man march up to Cody and lift his hand waiting for Cody to take it. She swallowed hard wishing the tickle in her nose would quit before a tear fell. At least it was the good kind of tears.

❖ Chapter Twenty-Two ❖

Cody took Jake through his prayers and tucked him into bed.

"I love you," Jake said and wrapped his arms around Cody's neck. Then the little boy dropped down to the pillow and squeezed his eyes tight.

Cody stood there for a moment watching Jake, then quietly stepped into the hallway and listened to be sure he was okay. He wasn't sure he'd ever felt more important in his whole life. It was almost a little overwhelming. He listened to Shutterbug's tags jingle as she settled in to protect her master.

I could get used to this.

He walked down the stairs wondering if it would have been the same fifteen, hell, seventeen, years ago if he'd had children. Probably not. He was a different person back then.

When he walked into his office, Kasey was leaning back in his leather chair talking on the phone. She had one foot propped on the edge of the desk, bobbing back in the chair as she talked. "Yeah, I know. That'll be perfect. He said he'd have his pilot fly me down, so I'll just meet you at the airport at noon if that'll work. Then we can ride to the service together, and the band will go separately. Yeah. I got it. No. I know Pete will help."

She looked so at home sitting at his desk like that. She seemed to wear his environment like a favorite T-shirt. *Do you feel it too?* The conversation he'd overheard her having with Riley replayed in his mind. *How can you say you feel so out of place here when it seems to me like you're what's been missing all along?* Cody felt like he was eavesdropping. He cleared his throat so she'd know he'd walked in.

When she turned and saw him she dropped her foot like a guilty schoolgirl getting caught with her feet on the furniture. *Sorry,* she mouthed.

He threw a hand in the air. It wasn't anything he hadn't done himself. He sat in the chair across from her while she talked.

"I know. I don't know what to expect, but at least with you there I know we won't miss any important details. If there are even any to be found," she said and shrugged. "Yep. Thanks. I'll see you then." She hung up the phone. "That was Von again."

"I gathered."

"I think we're in good shape here. Can you look through these pictures with me?" She got out of the chair and pushed it back from the desk.

Cody stepped around and put an arm around her hips. "Okay, what do we have?"

"I've put them in time order; there's a mix of the ones I took, and the ones my friend Andy sent me."

He glanced across all of them and then came back to one in particular. "This can't be from the night of the party."

"No, why?"

He tapped the picture and tugged it forward. "It's Annette."

"Yeah. So?"

"So, she told me that Arty had fired her earlier that afternoon before the party, so she wouldn't have been there that night. Could it have been from earlier in the day?"

Kasey frowned. "I'm not sure if I saw her there myself, but . . . no, Andy definitely said all these pictures are from that night. And look, that's the chocolate fountain in the background. It's from that night for sure."

"What else you got here?" He scanned the next few pictures pointing out the people he knew.

Kasey wrote the names on sticky notes and tabbed them.

Cody paused. "That's Amy."

"Lou's daughter?"

He nodded. "And Arty's daughter."

"She's pretty," Kasey commented. "She's really talented. I heard her sing that night."

The next picture was of the big lighted marquee that was in the front tent. She'd taken that picture.

"Amy Foxx?" Cody snickered. "Sounds like something Arty would come up with. Yeah, that's her on stage. That must've been where she was heading when she stopped in at her house and I met her." *If she hadn't stopped, I may never have known.* A blessing or a curse, he wasn't sure.

"I guess he was representing her too," Kasey said.

"He'd hardly let her go to another agent." Cody scanned the other pictures.

"Well, then I guess tomorrow at the funeral should be interesting," Kasey said.

"I'm sure she and Lou will be there."

Kasey put a star next to each of the people he remembered seeing at the door of Arty's office that night. That could be important.

"Von said he got a list of all the license plates from the valet service too. Your fan, Jace, put the

T-bird in the database even though you skipped the check-in line."

"Good for him. So he's got me coming and going?"

"Yep."

He sat in the chair and faced her. "Thanks for doing all of this." He spread his legs and pulled her between them with his hands clasped behind her rear end.

"It's better than sitting around waiting for another surprise."

"Some surprises are good," he said.

"Sometimes they're not."

"I don't want you to worry. Things are going to work out, and I like having you around." He pulled her onto his lap.

"I was thinking about taking Jake with me and going home from Arty's house. Von can give me a ride."

The chair tipped back a little. "Why?"

"I can't stay here forever. Jake's got school. I've got to figure out my employment situation, and you've got an album to put together. I don't want to put you behind on that."

Cody wrapped his arms around her. "I don't want you to leave, and the album is on schedule. Pete's been down there with his head in the earphones mixing every free moment he's had. I need to sit in and take a listen to what we've got so far, but he's the genius on that stuff. Besides, you don't want to take Jake to a funeral. Leave him here with me. You can go home this weekend. What's another day or two of kindergarten? I don't think that's going to ruin his education."

She didn't respond, but that made him even more nervous. "What's going through that pretty head of yours?"

Kasey slid off his lap and hiked herself up on the desk in front of him. "Cody, it's fun here, but I have a real life to go back to."

"Why can't I be part of your real life?" There, he'd said it. It was out there.

She pulled back. Then looked away. "You are part of my life. I wouldn't be here if I didn't consider you a very special friend."

"No." He shook his head. "No. You're not laying that friend crap on me. Scott can be your friend. Hell, Pete can be your friend, but I'm more than that. What you and I have . . . that's not just friends. There's something special here. Don't tell me you don't feel it."

"I . . ."

"Kasey, I felt it when you were with me a year ago. This is very real to me."

"I'm just a photographer."

"You're just about the best thing that's ever walked into my life, and I'm not letting you slip away."

She jumped down off the desk. "I have a say in this."

"I'm sorry. I didn't mean it like that." Desperation was showing and it wasn't an emotion he was familiar with. "Please just stay through the weekend. We need to talk about this."

She walked toward the window. With her back to him he wasn't sure what her thoughts were, but when she turned around her eyes were glassy.

"Don't cry. If there's one true love for me, Kasey . . . I believe it's you."

She sucked in a breath and walked over as he stood and took her into his arms.

She leaned forward and kissed him. "You scare the hell out of me, Cody." She laid the palms of her hands on each side of his face. "I do feel it. I won't lie to you, but this is huge. I have a son to think about. I have me to think about. I'm just finally getting through each day after losing Nick. I never thought I'd love again."

"But you can." He inhaled her scent, wanting it to last longer. "I wish I was going with you tomorrow," he said. "I could fly with you and wait in the plane."

"No. I'd rather you were here with Jake. Pete will be there, and Von. I'll be okay."

"I know you'll be fine. I just want to be with you."

"I'll be back tomorrow night."

"You will?"

She nodded. "I'll be back."

"Thank you." He kissed her full on the mouth.

His heart was pounding with such force that he hoped he hadn't kissed her too darned hard. "You're not going to regret this. I'll be waiting. Are you comfortable leaving Jake?"

"Yes. I trust you to take good care of him, and he'll be thrilled with the idea."

"It'll be fun."

"You might want to hold that opinion until after tomorrow. You're liable to be sacked out after playing with a five-year-old all day. Trust me. It's a job."

"Will you come to Kentucky with me for the show day after tomorrow? It's not that far. We'll take the buses. You can bring Jake or Mom can watch him."

She looked hesitant.

"Don't say no. I'm sorry. I'm not good at slow." He held his hand up. "Don't say anything. We can talk about it tomorrow when you get back. Come on. Let's get some rest."

He led her up the stairs and walked her to her bedroom door. "Is this where I kiss you good-night?"

She lifted her face to his and just as she began to answer, his lips brushed hers, and she kissed him back. *It's hard to kiss when your mouth wants to smile.*

His lips explored hers. He pulled her into an embrace, his fingers laced through hers as he buried his face into the crook of her neck, sucking in a breath and hoping for the strength to walk away. *Slow down.*

"I guess I better go." He nodded toward his room and took a step back, still holding her hand. *Follow me. Come on.*

She tugged him toward her room, and he followed her there.

He crawled alongside her on the comforter. The kisses came naturally, he felt her heartbeat against his chest. His hands explored her body, every curve he'd longed to touch.

Her breathing was as anxious as his.

"Mom?"

They froze, then Cody forced himself to roll away from her and stood by the bed. "I may have to use the zip line to burn off this adrenaline, but I guess since we don't want Jake to know about that either . . . I'll just go swim some laps."

She giggled. He loved the sound of her laughter.

"I'm sorry," she whispered to Cody. "See, my life can be complicated." She jumped out of bed. "Coming, Jake." She straightened her top as she went to his room.

He heard her talking to him as he snuck by the open door. He went downstairs and then stripped down to his nothings and dove into the pool. When he came up for air, he shook his hair from his face and glanced toward the balcony. She stood there in the moonlight like an angel.

My angel.

❖ Chapter Twenty-Three ❖

Kasey dressed in her black slacks and borrowed a dress shirt from Denise to wear to Arty's funeral. She said good-bye to Jake and Cody and then walked outside where Denise was sitting in her car waiting to take her around to the airstrip.

Denise handed Kasey a newspaper and a manila envelope. "I don't like to subject myself to this junk, but I wanted you to be prepared for what's being said out there. Don't tell Cody. I like him to think I don't even bother, else he'd always be worried about my feelings."

A mother's love. Kasey knew exactly how Denise felt. "Thank you, Denise."

"We're Hills through and through. Folks can call him Tuggle all they want, but it's what's on the inside that counts and that boy is every bit the gentleman his daddy and grandpa Hill were. We both know he's innocent and hopefully this will all be behind us soon."

Denise slowed to turn off the main road. "Now, don't you worry about Jake. I know what you've been going through. Honey, I promise you that boy will be safe. I will not let anything happen to him. Cody and I are going to take Jake horse-back riding today. That'll take our minds off everything and there's nothing better than a horse to teach a boy responsibility."

"Thank you, Denise. I'm trying so hard to put that anxiety behind me, but it—"

"Don't say it, honey. I know. I'm a mother. I totally get it. Now, more importantly, don't put yourself in any harm's way trying to snoop around. Just let this thing ride its course."

They pulled in front of the hangar. "Thank you, Denise."

"By the way, Cody mentioned that he asked you to go to the benefit concert with him tomorrow. I don't want to try to tell you what to do . . . but I want you to know I'd be thrilled to take care of Jake if you want to go."

If she refused Denise's offer she'd take it personally. "Let's see how I do today, but thank you. Thank you so much."

"You're welcome, honey. You'd better run. Looks like everyone else is already on board."

She settled into the seat next to Pete and fastened her seat belt for takeoff.

As the plane took off she looked out the window. From here she recognized the buildings and landmarks of Hillcrest now. The barn, the pond, the studio, and Hillcrest rose above it all with its gleaming blue, solar-tiled roof. She wondered if Jake and Cody were watching the plane take off from where they were.

She lifted her hand to the glass.

Pete leaned in. "You okay?"

She turned and nodded. "Yeah. I'm good." She eased back in the fine leather seat. "How about you? You ready for today? I bet the press will have a hundred questions about Cody not coming."

He shrugged. "That's fine. I'm used to it."

"Cody said Annette told him she wasn't going to be there. I'm sure she usually diverts some of that for you."

"Not really," he said with a smirk. "The more she diverts from Cody, the more they come to me."

"Hadn't thought of that. Well, it should be interesting."

"It'll be fine. Don't worry about it. Arty wasn't all that well liked. I'll be curious to see how many people actually show up aside from those of us he's represented . . . out of duty."

She pulled a folder out of her tote bag. "I wanted you to take a look at these pictures with me."

"Sure. What do you have here?" Pete took the folder.

"It's pictures from the party at Arty's house. The night of the murder. Cody and I've been through them, but I thought you might take a look and see if there was anything you noticed that we didn't mark."

Pete flipped through the pictures, nodding. "This looks like . . . no . . ." He went through the stack and came back to that one picture. "I'm not sure, but that looks like this girl we call Georgia Peach." He squinted.

Kasey pulled her computer out of her tote bag. "I can pull it up on my laptop and maybe you can see it better."

"Yeah. Do that."

She hit the power button and waited for the machine to come to life. The picture was high-resolution so she was able to blow it up pretty big with good clarity. "Here you go," she said, passing him the computer.

He used the trackpad to scan across and over. "Yeah. It looks like her." He leaned over. "That girl right there. I swear it's her. I wish Cody was here to confirm it. He'd know for sure."

"I'll text him. He still has a copy of these there. What do you know about her?"

He filled her in on what little he knew. Kasey texted Cody, then sent the details to Von to see what he could track down between the guest list, car log, and other details he'd gathered.

Pete put his noise-canceling earphones on and closed his eyes.

It was just a short hop from Nashville to Virginia. It seemed like they were already descending. She could get used to this mode of transportation, especially into these tiny airports. No wait. No TSA pat-downs. No problem.

As the plane started to touch down Kasey noticed Von's truck parked next to a limousine.

Probably the one that had been hired to take the band over to the service. She felt a nervous energy about going to the funeral. She didn't really know Arty, but it hadn't hit her until just now that the last funeral she'd attended was Nick's, and suddenly that dull ache found its way back into her bones. She rolled her shoulders and let out a breath.

The whole band was already up and stretching before they came to a complete stop.

She was the last one off the plane. She walked over to Von and gave him a hug. "Good to see you."

"You too. Riley sends her love."

She could tell that he'd already thought about how the day might make her feel. He had that big-brother I'll-take-care-of-you look on his face.

"Y'all can ride with us," Pete said.

"That's okay. We're going to lay low. Y'all go on. We'll be right behind you," Kasey said. "You ready?" she asked Von.

They followed the limousine to the church where they were having the service because the original plan for an elaborate service at the estate had become impossible with the police still around.

Kasey took her camera out of her purse and put fresh batteries in it, then tucked it into her pocket. Then she put a pen and paper in the other pocket in case she needed to write anything down.

"I feel like I'm on an undercover mission," she said.

"We kind of are. Welcome to my world," Von teased.

"This'll have to be better than sitting around on surveillance. That part of your job sucks." She remembered from when they'd been trying to track down Jake. Hours of sitting in his SUV was no party.

"It's all a matter of perspective," Von said.

Pete couldn't have been more wrong about the attendance of Arty's service. The parking lot overflowed with folks and the press hung out in clusters trying to catch a shot of someone famous.

Kasey took advantage of the flood of people to take pictures of everyone as they started moving toward the church. It was grasping at straws, but she couldn't sit idly by with fingers pointed at Cody until they solved the case.

Pete walked over to Kasey. "I've seen some of Cody's superfans. I guess they were hoping he'd be here. Guess who else is here?"

"The peach? From the picture?" she guessed.

"See the girl standing by that silver Toyota truck? That's Georgia Peach. She's at every concert within driving distance."

Kasey snapped a couple pictures and zoomed in for another. "That does look like the girl from the party photo."

"Now that I see her again, I think so too."

"See any others?"

"Let me see," Pete craned his neck. "Yeah, yeah, yeah. Over there. The girl in the bright blue."

"That's easy to spot," Von said. "Don't think she's trying to blend into the crowd."

"And look. I guess Annette changed her mind. She's here, and that's Lou walking with her with that girl. Is that Amy?"

Kasey nodded. "Looks like her."

"That's just wrong. I can't believe Arty did that to Cody," Pete said.

Von locked his truck. "Let's go on in."

Pete went up to the front of the church and sat with the band in the area that had been reserved for them. Kasey and Von sat toward the back so Von could see everyone coming and going.

There was no body, simply a picture of Arty at the front of the church. Most people probably thought it was just the way the guy wanted it to be, but Kasey knew that they hadn't released the body yet.

It was a nice service, though there wasn't a tear in the place. Not even Amy, who looked sad, but didn't cry. It was the most unusual and unemotional service Kasey had ever been to.

Afterward, she and Von caught up with the guys in the parking lot.

"That was short and sweet," Pete said.

"I know. I think the flight was longer," Kasey said.

Von took pictures of the cars in the parking lot before everyone left. "Never know what will come in handy. Anyone say anything?"

Pete shrugged. "Nothing but sorry to hear about it. I guess word's getting out about Amy because even Georgia Peach told me to tell Cody how sorry she was that Arty had betrayed him like that." Pete shoved his hand in his pocket. "Oh, and here's her real name and address. I told her I had something for her from Cody and she gave it to me. Don't let me forget to actually send something."

"You're awesome." Kasey took the scrap of paper, but she wondered how Georgia Peach would have found out about the secret so soon. It wasn't totally unlikely that she could have heard Annette talking to Lou.

The limo pulled around and the guys piled in. "We'll meet you back at the plane," Pete said.

"We're right behind you." Von got in the truck and they followed the limo to the airstrip.

Kasey took a picture of the information Pete had given her before handing it over to Von and promised to e-mail him her files as soon as she got on the plane and connected. Von was planning to stay in town and do a little more digging.

She called Cody's number to check in on Jake while they got ready to take off. She could barely get a word in edgewise as Jake went on and on about his day riding horses and that Miss D had given him a cowboy hat that used to be Cody's when he was a little boy just like him.

"We're getting ready to come home. I'll see you in about an hour. I love you," she said.

I don't think he even missed me. She wasn't sure if that was good or bad, but she hadn't had that surge of panic that she usually got when she was apart from him, and that had to mean progress.

❖ Chapter Twenty-Four ❖

The next morning Kasey got up early to get Jake ready to go with Denise for the day. Jake was still on a high from the previous day of riding and was raring to get back down to the barn with his new best friend, whom he now just called Miss D, and his new favorite horse, Hillcrest Flashback.

Denise had come down on horseback to pick him up and he had thought that was just about the coolest thing ever. She'd had to call after him to have him come back and give her a kiss good-bye.

After struggling with what to do with Jake, it was Cody who had come up with the perfect solution. Well, probably not perfect for him—he wouldn't get what he wanted—but perfect because it would give Kasey the chance to let Jake out of her sight again for a little longer, but be nearby at the same time.

Cody stepped up behind her as she watched

Denise and Jake ride off toward her place. He dropped a kiss in the crook of her neck. "I wish you were coming with me, but we'll be back tonight. Can I ask you out on a date for when I get back?"

She cast him a sideways glance. "What did you have in mind? Because I'm not going zip-lining."

"I'll be too tired for zip-lining after the concert anyway. I was thinking you and me, on the rooftop balcony—"

She leaned back. "A rooftop balcony?"

"Yep. Only one access. From my room."

Her throat went a little dry at the thought. "That sounds dangerous." *And inviting.* "And like we're moving really fast."

"You gonna let me finish?"

She pressed her lips tight and nodded.

"You and me, on the rooftop balcony. A bottle of wine. Stargazing."

"Me gazing at you?"

He tossed his head back. "No. I'm trying to be romantic here. Work with me, would you?"

"Sorry."

"There's a new moon tonight. It's supposed to be the best night to see stars and galaxies because the sky will be inky black. I thought it would be nice. Quiet. And we'd be alone."

"That *is* romantic."

"If I promise to be a gentleman do we have a date?"

"I think we do."

He hugged her tight, then kissed her. Soft. Tender. And leaving her anxious inside.

"Then, I'm out of here." He lifted his duffel bag and walked toward the second driveway where the buses were parked. "You're going to be okay today. You know that, right?"

"Yes."

"I'm proud of you," he said. "I know it's not easy to face those kinds of fears. You call Mom if you start feeling anxious. Or me. We've got your back."

"I know." She was kind of proud of herself too. For letting Jake go. She was finally trusting her own judgment again, and that was a good step. Now if she could just trust her heart. It felt very right, perfect even, and that was what made it so frightening.

She walked back inside and grabbed her laptop and a cup of coffee. She sat by the pool and caught up on the news. There wasn't even a snippet or a Tweet about Arty Max or Cody relative to the murder. It seemed that was already yesterday's news. Only it wasn't, because until they figured out who had committed that deed, Cody wouldn't be entirely off the hook.

The last time she'd had a whole day to herself with no responsibilities was Jake's first day of school, and that hadn't gone so well. Today would be better.

She went upstairs and showered and changed but the time was creeping by. She wasn't anxious—that was good—but she didn't know what to do with herself. She remembered seeing the stack of DVDs from the reality show that had followed Cody's tour. It hadn't aired yet, but that would be fun to watch.

Kasey picked one out of the middle and pushed the button for the giant screen Cody had showed her the other day. It came right up and the footage played. It was just the raw footage, not the edited stuff.

She watched the replay as one of Cody's guys walked down a line of waiting fans handing out guitar picks and announcing, "Be ready with your camera if you want a picture and he'll sign one thing for you. No kissing on the mouth either. He's been sick. You don't want to get sick."

Her face scrunched like she'd just tasted something bad. *That's just gross to think that these women would want to go in there and suck face with someone they didn't even know. Really?*

The camera moved into the bus and captured a few of the meet and greets. They filed in for the few moments with him. He did seem to have a knack for making it seem like each fan was the only thing on his mind—in their moment during that short time. He signed hats, a woman's tote bag, and then two scantily dressed girls with way too much makeup draped themselves over him begging for a threesome. He graciously declined and signed their rear ends, and when they left, he asked one of his guys to be sure they'd actually made it off the property.

She looked for the remote to fast-forward. *I thought it was here on the desk.* She moved a couple things around on the top of the desk, and then opened the desk drawer to see if it was there. The center drawer wasn't that deep. She tugged on the right-hand drawer, it was locked. The left one wasn't though. She opened it and retrieved the remote, but something else caught her eye.

She lifted a photo out of the drawer.

It was the one that had Georgia Peach in it. The one Pete had helped her with. Only Cody must have recognized her all along because although he hadn't mentioned it to her or marked it on her copy, there was a sticky note right under her face. With her real name written on it in Cody's handwriting, and a phone number.

Why hadn't he mentioned it when they'd looked at the pictures together?

The picture shook in her hands.

She ran upstairs to compare it to the information Pete had gotten from the girl. She'd snapped a photo of that scrap of paper before handing it off to Von. It seemed like forever before her computer came up. She scrolled through the files looking for it.

With a double-click it opened. She glanced

down at the note Cody had written, and compared it to what Pete had given her. The phone number was different. He hadn't gotten this from Pete. Was he covering for her? Maybe she was more than a superfan. A superfling?

She could hear Pete's words. *He used to have a temper.*

His mom's words. *He's had his moments.*

Scott's words. *He's had trouble with the police before.*

There has to be an explanation. Chill out. But they'd found his gun. His bandanna. He'd threatened Arty and he had more than one motive. Unless the timeline they'd laid out was wrong, there was no way he could be guilty. Right? Or was he covering for someone? What other red flag did she need flapping in the wind to tell her something was wrong?

She sat down. *Denise will be heartbroken. I'm heartbroken.* A heavy feeling limited her ability to breathe. She only knew one person to turn to.

Von didn't answer his phone. She heaved in a breath and steadied herself as the call went to his voice mail. "Von, we might be looking in the wrong place. Call me as soon as you get this message."

She had been right on the edge of a huge mistake—what a fool she was.

❖ Chapter Twenty-Five ❖

Kasey checked her cell phone again. *Why haven't you called me back, Von?* If she couldn't trust Cody to tell her everything about the past, she certainly couldn't trust him with her future . . . or Jake's.

How can I face Cody? I can't tell him I found that picture in his desk. He'll think I was snooping, and accusing him of something with that girl wasn't going to sit much better. A part of her wanted to leave and take Jake home, but coordinating that from here wasn't easy and part of her prayed there'd be a good explanation.

Too many unanswered questions made her feel sick to her stomach.

She ripped a piece of paper from her notebook and scribbled a note for Cody. After reading it, she shoved it into her purse instead and left.

A little after four, her phone rang. She grappled for it, and looked at the display praying it would be Von and not Cody. It was. "Hello?"

"Sorry I didn't call you back sooner. It's been a crazy day."

Von sounded exhausted.

"What's going on? Where are you?"

"I only have a minute. So, listen up. We've got a problem. I'm at the criminal investigation office at the Virginia State Police. They're helping the Rappahannock County guys with the Arty Max case. I'll text the address to you when we get off the phone just in case, but I should be there at the airport to pick you up when you land."

"Land? I'm coming there? What's happening?"

"Annette is saying that picture you took of her at Arty's is Photoshopped and with your skills, that's not such a far-fetched claim."

"I did not Photoshop those pictures. I'd never lie about something like this. For anyone."

"Calm down, Kasey. You and I know that, but it's a murder investigation. They have to follow all leads."

She shook her hair back. "I hadn't even considered someone might think the pictures were tampered with."

"Do you have the original files?"

"Of course."

"Good. I need you to bring them with you. I don't have any other proof that Annette was at the estate, so that's probably the best we can do. Their forensics guy can confirm that the pictures are legit."

"I think there's more. I think that Georgia Peach girl has something to do with it," Kasey said.

"We'll talk about that when you get here. Cody's pilot is filing a flight plan right now. I need you to get down to the airstrip."

Jesus. What is happening? I can't leave Jake

here. I should never have come. "Jake is with Cody's mom. I should bring him with me."

She heard his frustrated sigh on the other end of the line. "Kasey, I know you don't like to leave him but this is no place for a kid. Let Cody's mom take care of him. He'll be okay. One of the security guards from Cody's estate will drive you over to the airstrip."

"You're scaring me," she said.

"Calm down. I promise you everything is going to work out. Captain Rogers is going to fly you here. I'll be at the airport to pick you up."

"But can't you tell me—" Her mind was reeling. "Does Cody know?"

"Yes. I'll explain everything when you get here."

She hung up the phone and called Denise. Cody must've called her while she was talking to Von because she already knew about the trip. "I'll take care of Jake. Don't you worry about a thing. Hang on," Denise said. Kasey heard Denise asking Jake if he wanted to do a sleepover and Jake's enthusiastic response. "Jake wants to ask you something."

"Hi, Mom. Can I sleep over with Miss D and the horses?" His little voice was so full of excitement. "Please?"

"Sure, baby. You have fun. Let me speak to her, okay?"

Denise got back on the phone. "We're fine. Get

on out of here. Take care of this business so we can get it behind us."

"Yes, ma'am," Kasey said, but she prayed that what she was doing was going to clear Cody and not make it worse. *One thing at a time.*

She ran into Cody's office and retrieved the picture with the phone number on it, then let Shutterbug outside.

When she opened the front door a white car with a security logo on the side was sitting with its engine idling just as Von had said. The driver stepped out and opened the door for her. "Thank you." She silently thanked Denise as well as they drove by her house. She knew Jake would be fine, and she could focus on whatever it was that was getting ready to play out in Virginia. *Please, God, let it be okay.*

The plane was lit up and ready to go. Captain Rogers sat in the cockpit, and the stairs were down. She ran to the plane and raced aboard.

A million thoughts tangoed through her head. Good news? Bad news? She pulled out her phone and checked for messages. Von had sent the address as he'd mentioned, but nothing from Cody. She stared out the window on the short flight. Things looked so small from up here, and yet so many complicated lives filled the vast spaces below.

The sound of the engines changed as they began their final descent. As the plane loomed closer to the ground her throat felt dry. When they landed, she climbed down from the plane. Von wasn't there, but a police car was. An officer met her planeside.

"Miss Phillips, Perry Von sent me to pick you up."

She nodded and got into the back of the cruiser without a word. She'd never sat in the back of a police car before. The partition between her and the officer felt ominous. She couldn't make out but a few words pumping out of the police radio with all the static.

The policeman pulled into a parking spot, and met her gaze in the rearview mirror. "We're here."

There was no handle on the inside of the back door, so she waited for the officer to open it. She got out and followed him into the precinct.

Von was standing just inside the door.

"Thank goodness. I've been so worried," she said. "And then when you weren't at the airport . . . What's going on?"

Von half hugged her. "Calm down. Do you have the original pictures?"

She handed them over. "But there's more."

"More pictures?"

Kasey shook her head. "No. There's this." She put the picture and phone number into his hands.

He studied them, then looked up with a smile. "Yeah. I know about this. Where'd you get it?"

"I found it in Cody's desk when I was looking

for the remote. I was trying to call you about it today. I'm not sure what it means, but . . ."

"Cody already told me about it."

She straightened. "He did? So, he wasn't keeping it a secret?"

"Well, I guess if he didn't tell you, you could think . . . No, it's just all been coming together very fast. I'm sure he didn't want to get you involved before we knew what we had."

She let out a breath. "Well, I'm here. I'm involved. Are you going to tell me what the heck is going on?"

"Are you okay? You sound mad. I thought you'd be relieved. This is finally coming together."

"Yeah. I'm good." *He hadn't kept anything from her?* She'd had herself so worked up over it all day, now that it wasn't true she was finding it hard to shake the anger she'd felt at him.

"What was going through that wild imagination of yours?"

She took the picture back, crumpled it into a ball, and shoved it into her purse. "I can't believe my brain sometimes."

"Everything is fine, Kasey. Didn't I tell you that?"

"Yes. You most certainly did. Sometimes I'm just not as good a listener as I thought." *And sometimes I'm my own worst enemy.*

❖ Chapter Twenty-Six ❖

Von led Kasey through the busy police precinct to another waiting area. As soon as they walked in, Cody jumped up from a chair and walked toward her.

Cody looked exhausted, and worried. She glanced at Von. "Are you sure everything is okay?"

"It's been a long day," Von whispered.

Cody came to her side. "Thanks for coming. I would have called you myself, but things have been crazy here today."

"You've been here all day?" Kasey looked at Cody then Von, who nodded in agreement.

"Just about. I caught a flight right after the benefit."

"Oh." Kasey realized that had to have been hours ago.

A detective walked up to them. "Everyone here?"

"Yes." Cody extended his hand. "Thanks, man."

Von walked over and gave the detective the drive with the original pictures on it. "I think everything your man needs is right here."

"Thanks for getting it here so fast," the detective said. "Follow me. We're going back through Annette's confession with her again."

"Annette's confession?" Kasey's mouth dropped. "Did you know all along?"

"No, I thought one of my fans had something to do with it," Cody said.

"Georgia Peach?"

"Yeah. But when they talked to her, it turned out she had another piece of information that helped." Cody shook his head. "I may be *her* biggest fan now."

"Just a couple things to clear up and I think we're done." The detective led them into a room with a long glass window.

Cody sat down next to Kasey and took her hand in his.

Annette sat at a table with her hands folded.

"She doesn't look so good," Cody said.

The detective read off the legal stuff. Annette's attorney sat next to her.

"Arty and I have been seeing each other for close to a year. I mean we've worked together longer, but over the past year we started realizing we could make a lot more money together rather than apart so we partnered on things."

"Good Lord, is there anyone you know that guy didn't sleep with?" Kasey said.

Cody squeezed her hand.

Annette's voice was low and steady. Kasey wondered if they'd given her a Xanax or something because she'd never seen Annette so subdued. "It was an accident. I didn't mean to kill him. I loved him, however much you can love a man like him."

Kasey's hand moved into a fist as a reflex to the words. *I can't believe this.*

"He and I had argued just before the party. He was mad about me helping Cody reconnect with an old girlfriend. I didn't think it was a big deal, but Arty liked being in control. That was his thing. So I didn't think much of it."

She looked down at her hands as she spoke. "I had no idea Arty had a daughter."

"How'd you find out?" the detective asked.

"I'd gone into the big tent to check on the acts he had singing. Most of those are new artists and they need some guidance. One of the young girls, Amy Foxx, had gotten there late. She signaled me over, but her set was starting so I just stood off to the side and watched. She's good. Really good. The guests seemed to be really enjoying her performance too."

She sat taller in her chair. "So, Amy comes offstage and I ask her if she wants to do an extra set later because everyone seemed to really like her but she wasn't interested. She shoved a white box at me and asked me to give it to Arty."

"Did you?"

"Not right then. I was curious, so I opened the box. It was a pie, for God's sake. Who brings their agent pie? But then she turns around and says to me, 'And tell him I got to meet Cody Tuggle today—no thanks to him.' "

Anger pushed the edges of her mouth. "It clicked for me. I knew that Cody had gone to see Lou. If this chick met Cody, she had something to do with Lou. Anyway, there was a card in the box, so I took it to the kitchen, and I opened the card."

"What did the card say?" the detective asked.

"It said, 'Dad, I hopc you enjoy this pie more than me singing on a stage. Baking is what I really want to do. Love, Amy.' "

"How'd that make you feel?"

"Like I'd been kicked. I didn't know he had a kid. I thought he and I were partners. Like fifty-fifty-everything partners. 'One of us dies the other gets it all' kind of partners. Him having a kid changed that." She wrung her hands. "After Cody blew up at Arty, I put two and two together. Or three or four in this case. That was just wrong. I was mad at Arty, but I didn't plan to kill him."

Her attorney nodded.

"He probably told her to say that," Kasey said to Cody. "I thought she said Arty fired her. She didn't mention that."

Cody shook his head. "Must have been a lie."

Annette stressed each word. "Really. I did *not* plan to kill him."

The detective didn't look impressed by her comment. He probably heard that from everyone he questioned. "What happened next?"

"Everyone pretty much cleared out after Cody left, and I went into Arty's office to talk to him. He was being such an ass. He said he'd thought I'd left."

She scoffed at the thought. "I wasn't leaving. It was my investment in there too. He said I didn't know what the fight was about and I plopped that stupid pie in the middle of his desk. He just looked at it. I threw a fork at him. It scratched his cheek. I'll admit that felt pretty good, then I told him it was from his daughter, and he knew the jig was up. I told him that we all knew what he'd done and no one would ever trust him again."

"Did that make him angry?" the detective asked.

"No. He just laughed." She closed her eyes for a second, then continued. "He told me I ought to leave and that he didn't think we could continue our relationship. Since Cody knew about Lou and Amy maybe he'd put his attention on them for a change. I couldn't believe he even said that to me."

"That's when you turned a gun on him?"

"I just wanted to get a rise out of him. Make him quit acting so smug." She gulped a glass of water and then set it back down with a shaking hand. "I took the gun out of his drawer. He always kept it there. I really didn't even know if he kept it loaded, but I pointed it at him. Ya know, just to get a rise out of him, like I said." She shrugged.

"Did it?"

She shook her head. "No. He just laughed again and asked me what I was going to do with it. Told me he knew I wouldn't shoot it so to just put it back where I'd found it. Then he started eating that damn pie and he acted like it was so good, and that just made me madder."

She took in a breath and stared off. "I took a step back and kind of waved the gun at him, and it went off. I don't even know how it went off."

"What'd you do?"

"I screamed. Then he fell forward gasping."

"And . . ."

Annette looked up. "And I put the gun in the drawer and ran out."

"But the gun wasn't found in the drawer."

"I know," she said. "That's because I went back in there to wipe off my fingerprints. I was in a panic. I grabbed a bandanna that was on the shelf where Arty keeps all of his awards and rubbed it clean."

"That's why the bandanna was on the desk?"

"Probably. I'm not even sure what I did with it." Annette's face contorted. "Arty was all blue, and like, gurgling." She shrugged. "I didn't mean to shoot him and I didn't know what to do." She wiped her nose with the back of her hand and her attorney handed her a tissue.

"Thanks. I was going to shoot him again to make him quit suffering, but I couldn't do it. So,

I opened the safe to make it look like a robbery and then I got scared and I left."

Cody's mouth hung open. "Shit. She didn't even call nine-one-one?"

"Nope. Pretty shallow, huh?" The detective turned his back on the glass. "We've gone through this with her a few times now. I think that's about it."

Von nudged Cody. "At least you're off the hook. But you haven't heard it all. Tell him, detective."

"Which part? First of all, you know that fan you gave us the information on had snuck into the party."

"Yeah, but she didn't have anything to do with it, did she?"

"No, she'd just gone trying to see you. When you had the fight and all the people gathered around Arty's office, she hid in a closet. She says she fell asleep in there and when she woke up she heard the argument between Arty and a woman, and the gunshot. She knew you were innocent. She was one of the anonymous calls we had."

"I bet she was scared to death," Kasey said.

The detective nodded. "More than she bargained for, that's for sure. She said she was too scared to call 911 from there. I don't think she'll be crashing too many parties in the future."

Von leaned forward. "It gets even better."

"Yeah," said the detective. "So this is the kicker, and we haven't told Annette this yet. When Annette shot Arty it was just a flesh wound.

He didn't die from that gunshot. Wouldn't have died from it either. He must have sucked a hunk of that pie into his windpipe when the bullet grazed him. If she'd just called for help there wouldn't have been a story to tell."

"Even after all he did, I don't wish that on him." Cody shook his head. "That's just . . . I don't get it. How do you leave someone to die?"

"Excuse me." Kasey needed some air. How does someone just let someone die? An officer let her out of the room and pointed her down the hall toward the ladies' room.

"Crimes of passion. They never make sense," Von said.

"He's right," the detective said to Cody. "Your buddy here helped us a lot. Thanks for working with us on this, Von."

"You're welcome. I knew Cody was innocent."

The detective turned back to Cody. "I know it put you in a bad situation with the press and all. We'll be making a statement in the morning. I hope that will cool things off for you."

"Thank you," Cody said.

The detective left the room. Cody and Von stood, and Cody shook his hand. "Thanks for helping me out. I appreciate it."

"You just take care of Kasey. She was my best friend's bride. I was their best man. If you break her heart you'll have me to answer to."

"I promise my intentions are honorable."

"Good. They deserve someone good in their lives." Von cuffed Cody on the shoulder.

I agree, and I want to be that someone. "I guess I should tell you that I'm planning to ask her to stay at Hillcrest with me."

"Oh, great. If she says yes, I'll never hear the end of this." Von laughed. "You don't know my wife too well yet, but Riley told me the day that Kasey left to go see you in Nashville that she bet Kasey wouldn't be coming back."

"How could she have known that? I didn't even know that's what I was hoping for until yesterday."

"You don't know my wife. She's got an intuition on her that's better than a bloodhound on a fresh scent."

"Well, let your little Magic Eight Ball know she was right. At least if I get my way." Cody smiled, feeling more confident about asking Kasey now, and he'd already thought it through so he'd have an answer to every argument she could throw in the way of a future with him.

"I'll tell Riley. Reluctantly. I hate admitting when she's right, and you'd better have a spare room with Riley's name on it too. She and Kasey can't be apart but for so long."

"I've got plenty of room and you just might find something to do on the ranch too. Y'all have an open invitation."

❖ Chapter Twenty-Seven ❖

Von drove Kasey and Cody back to the airport. Cody boarded the plane while Kasey said her good-byes to Von.

Von lifted his chin toward the plane. "When you found that picture, and that note. You thought he might have had something to do with Arty's murder, didn't you?" Von's eyes seemed to search her for answers.

"You know I can't lie to you. I thought he may have been covering for her, and that scared me to death. If he'd lied to me, I couldn't have forgiven that. I've really grown to . . . I trusted him. Even with Jake, and if that were the case . . ." She swallowed. "I was afraid I'd put Jake back in some kind of danger."

"He's a good guy, Kasey."

"Yeah. He is." She glanced over her shoulder at the plane. "You should see him and Jake together." She shrugged. "I never thought I'd feel this way again. I—"

"I know. You don't have to explain. I get it." He smiled. "I can see it."

Tears welled in her eyes. "You don't think I'm crazy? I keep telling myself that he's out of my league, but my stupid heart does backflips when he gets near me. And I keep thinking of Nick.

What would he think? Is it the right thing to do for Jake? What if I make a mistake?"

He leaned against the side of the SUV. "I've seen the way you look at him. I've only seen you look at one other man that way."

"Nick," she whispered.

"Yeah. And what you and Nick had, it was amazing." He took her hands. "Kasey, Nick wouldn't want you to be alone. I don't want you to be alone."

"You'd be okay if I decided to try something with him?"

He nodded. "I would. And in case you haven't figured it out, he feels the same way about you. The way he looks when he talks about you. There's something there."

She felt her body tense. "It's scary to let go."

"You and Nick were great together, and I never thought I'd be able to see you with someone, but I can see this."

"I can too. I can picture it so clearly. If I open myself up, I don't want to get hurt. What if instead of falling in love I just . . . fall?"

"If you fall, Riley and I will always be there for you, but he feels the same way about you. He told me so."

"He did?"

"He sure did. Riley is going to be so excited for you. She knew there was a special something between you two."

"I guess she was right. Again." Kasey cut her eyes to the side. "Do we have to tell her right away?"

"She'll know."

"That's true. That girl knows everything." The plane's engines whirred to a start. "I guess I'd better get going."

Von gave her a hug. "I love you, girl. You're going to be just fine and I can't wait to see where all this takes you. I think your life is in for a change . . . and it's going to be a really good one."

"Thank you for everything, Von. You are such a wonderful friend, and so amazing to be able to always put these puzzles together. Tell Riley I'll call her once I get some sleep." She turned and headed to the plane, only turning back once to wave.

"Stay out of trouble," Von called after her.

"I'll try."

Cody was talking to the pilot, so she took a seat on the couch in the back.

"You okay?" Cody said.

"Yeah. Tired, but okay," she said and there were those feelings again. The little zing in her belly, the almost swirling feeling in her heart when she watched Cody. *How could I be so lucky to find this twice in a lifetime?*

The plane took off, and once they hit cruising altitude Cody got up and sat next to Kasey. "You know there's probably going to be a lot of hubbub about this for a few days. Press. All that."

"And you don't have an Annette to keep it in the box for you anymore," she said.

"Exactly."

Cody slid next to her on the couch. She pulled her feet up and turned to rest her head in his lap. He stroked his fingers through her hair. "It's been a long day."

"I'm glad it's a short flight."

"Me too. Sorry about the date. I didn't mean to stand you up."

I'd forgotten about that date. It felt so long ago now. "You're forgiven."

"I'll make it up to you."

She relaxed into his lap and closed her eyes. "Good. I'll let you make it up to me." The sun had barely started to peek over the horizon by the time they landed at Hillcrest. Captain Rogers gave them a ride in his car around to the house. He waved as Cody and Kasey went inside.

She started up the stairs, but Cody didn't follow her. "Aren't you coming up?"

"Yeah. In a minute."

He didn't even give her a second to respond; instead he disappeared into the kitchen.

She went to her room and slipped out of her shoes, and when she turned around, Cody was standing in her doorway holding one of those recyclable handled grocery sacks.

"Come on." He nodded and reached his hand out to her.

"What?"

"We've got about fifteen minutes. We missed the stargazing last night, but there ought to be one hell of a sunrise."

She took his hand and let him lead her to the elevator in the corner of his bedroom. It had the feel of an old-timey lift with the metal grate door. He pulled it over and then pressed the button. They could have climbed a ladder faster, or maybe it was just the anticipation of being alone with him after all they'd been through.

When the doors opened he let go of her hand and preceded her onto the rooftop balcony, where he pulled out orange juice, two glasses, and a bottle of champagne and set them on the table next to a double chaise lounge.

She crawled up onto the chaise and laid back. "If I fall asleep here I may never wake up." She stretched out and sighed. "It's nice out here."

He poured a little orange juice into each glass, then popped open the champagne. He topped off both glasses and handed her one.

Cody eased into the chaise next to her. "Thank you, for being here with me."

She took the glass. "Cheers."

He put an arm around her and they eased back into the chaise and watched the sunrise.

"The view from here is amazing. I could get used to this," she said.

"Well, funny you should mention that." He rolled over on his side and took the glass out of her hand. He placed it on the table next to him, and took her hands into his own. "I know this is fast, but I warned you I wasn't good at slow."

"I believe you," she said.

"Well, remember when you told me that when I'd met my soul mate I'd know it."

"Yes."

"You were right. Kasey, I think the reason we were brought together that day for the photo shoot and the connection we made wasn't just a job. It was for something bigger. It was for this. I want you to stay. You and Jake. You're my soul mate. I think I knew it back then, but I damn sure know it now. I want you in my life."

It's what she wanted. Exactly what she'd wanted to hear, but now that he'd said it icy fear rushed her. "I need someone who will be here for me forever. Not a here-for-now guy. I'm a girl with baggage. Jake's my priority."

"And he should be. I want to have all of your baggage in my life." Cody's voice softened. "I know this will work. I feel it."

"I don't know if I can live in your world. It's way bigger than me."

"Fine. We'll live in Adams Grove—in yours. I'll ratchet back. Hell, I'll give it up. Maybe I'll just kick back and enjoy what I've already achieved."

"No, you can't give up music. You love this life. The energy you get from the fans . . . it's what makes you tick. I can't take that from you. I'd make you unhappy. You'd have regrets."

"Don't put words in my mouth. These are the only words you need to worry about." He tipped her face to his and gazed into her eyes. "I love you."

She tensed at the words. Fear. Hope. Joy. Panic. She closed her eyes, trying to be sure what all she was hearing was true. Was she asleep, dreaming, or was this really happening for her? "Look at me." He tipped her chin back and looked her in the eyes. "I promise you, Kasey, I am not just saying the words. This is me. I love you, Kasey. I think I might have fallen in love with you a long time ago, but you had just gone through losing Nick. I wanted to take care of you then. I love you and I want you in my life and this . . . This. All of this. I'll give it up right now if you'll just give me a chance. I've never been a dad, but I will do a good job and I will make you proud. Please, please—"

"I love you too, but . . ."

"No. No buts. And don't squawk about having to figure out a new career. I have that all figured out too. We're going to get to work on that other book. We'll get a tutor for Jake and we'll just play the whole school thing by ear as we move forward. We can do some research on our options and figure it out as we go along. Together."

"Are you sure?"

Cody pulled her close. "It won't matter if I don't have you. Please trust me. It's right. If you love me, then let's do this. We'll take it a step at a time and we'll compromise and we'll collaborate and we'll make it work."

She didn't say a word. Was afraid to because the struggle inside her was swirling so fast that, like a roulette wheel, she really had no idea where it would finally settle. With her heart. Or with her mind.

"I love you." He leaned in and kissed her. "Could you fall in love with me too?"

"I already did."

He took her hands in his. "Kasey Phillips, when I look at you I know that I'd do anything for you. What I feel . . . it's . . . What's bigger than fireworks?"

"I don't know," Kasey said. "Meteor showers?"

"I feel meteor showers when I see you." He pulled her against him. "Do you feel them?"

She smiled, but didn't answer.

He ran his hand along her thigh and leaned in to kiss her. He kissed her on the mouth and then trailed kisses to her neck and down her chest.

She sucked in a breath and arched to meet him. Her hands found their way to his hair and she pulled closer to him.

"Do you feel them now? One meteor? Two?"

"Shh." And she took the lead on the kiss until he was the one moaning.

He made a sweet noise as he pulled her tight to him. "See, meteor showers when you're in my arms. You see them too. Admit it."

Kasey tried not to laugh. "I don't think that's going to be your next hit song."

"Probably not." He laughed too. "I don't need another hit song if I can have a life with you." He kissed her neck, then her chin, then her lips. "I love you. Do you think I'm crazy?"

"Yes, but not for that. I feel like the luckiest girl that you want me."

"Maybe that's my next hit song." He hummed a little melody. "Something about this little girl of mine, makes me want to leave the bad boy behind. If being a good man is what it takes, I'll make her mine with no mistakes."

"You *are* a good man."

"Your man."

"I like the way that sounds," she said.

"I want you to stay here with me. Or I'll go home with you. I'll fly us back and forth. Whatever we want. I want you . . . any way you'll have me." Cody held both of her hands to his heart.

"I'm never going to leave your side," she said.

acknowledgments

I would like to express my gratitude to the many friends who saw me through this book; to all those who provided support, talked things over, read and reread versions along the way, and allowed me to drone on endlessly about how fabulous Cody Tuggle is even though he only exists in my head. Thanks too for understanding when deadlines got in the way of get-togethers, and for your flexibility to be sure we could still make it all happen.

In addition, a very special thank-you to Pete Evick, the lead guitarist for the Bret Michaels Band and his own amazing band, EVICK, who graciously gave me the gift of his time answering lots of questions and what-ifs about the music business. Pete, I'm grateful for the assistance and blessed by the new friendship. You're the real thing.

As always, the Montlake Romance team is amazing, and I love being a part of this family. Thanks to the whole team and especially Kelli Martin, Jessica Poore, and Krista Stroever. You make every step an exciting one, and I appreciate all you do.

To my family, you truly make me who I am, and you make me feel like the luckiest girl in the world.

Hugs and happy reading!

about the author

Nancy Naigle was born and raised in Virginia Beach. She balances her career in the financial industry with a lifelong passion for books and storytelling and is the author of *Sweet Tea and Secrets* and *Wedding Cake and Big Mistakes*. She is the coauthor of the novel *Inkblot* with Phyllis C. Johnson. When she isn't writing or wrangling goats on the family farm, she enjoys antiquing and cooking. She lives with her husband in Drewryville, Virginia.

Center Point Large Print
600 Brooks Road / PO Box 1
Thorndike, ME 04986-0001 USA

(207) 568-3717

US & Canada:
1 800 929-9108
www.centerpointlargeprint.com